FATE KN
ON A DO

Lorrin O'Lee sat entranced, gazing at the breathtaking, golden-skinned child-woman Kaiulani. As Admiral of the island emperor's navy, the rugged Yankee sea captain was sworn to protect Princess Kaiulani's virginity. As a man, powerful contrary impulses were rising within him.

His reverie was shattered by a knock on the door, and the voice of a seaman: "Begging pardon, sir, but there's a ship flying signals. She's requesting permission to send a boarding party."

Lorrin looked across at Kaiulani and let out a low chuckle.

"What is it?" she asked softly. "Why are you laughing?"

"Do you believe in fate, Kaiulani?"

"Yes, of course I do," she said, large eyes shining. "I believe that everything is ordered."

"Then your fate has just intervened, for if I were to stay in this room with you for a moment longer, I fear I would cease to be your protector."

He rose. "I leave you, Princess, with your virginity intact."

Lorrin started to leave and then, on an impulse, he walked over to her, swept her up in his arms and pressed upon her upturned, half-parted lips, a lover's kiss, a tongue which probed the senses and sent Kaiulani's head to spinning . . .

The Making of America Series

THE
FAR
ISLANDERS

Lee Davis Willoughby

A DELL/BRYANS BOOK

Published by
Dell Publishing Co., Inc.
1 Dag Hammarskjold Plaza
New York, New York 10017

Dell ® TM 681510, Dell Publishing Co., Inc.

ISBN: 0-440-02581-8

Printed in the United States of America

First printing—July 1981

THE
FAR
ISLANDERS

1

As THE SUN dipped into the Pacific, brilliant colors fanned across the western sky. Vibrant bands of glowing hues, from gold to orange, through red, lavender, and finally royal purple, spread forth, as if a celestial palette had been prepared for the use of a master painter.

The ocean itself was tinted by the sunset so that sweeping breakers rolled in from a magenta sea, boomed against the shore, then retreated, leaving a smear of irridescent bubbles shimmering on the sand. The white sand and the graceful arches of the palm trees were back-lighted by a blazing halo of gold, and they shined brightly as if making one final effort to hold onto the exquisite beauty of the moment, against the encroachment of nightfall.

As Lorrin O'Lee stood on the balcony of Colonel Ashford's home and watched the dazzling display of light before him, he considered it analogous to the Pacific Paradise of Hawaii, trying to hold onto the beauty of its moment against the encroachment of civilization. Its moment was right now, March 7, 1887, at 5:58 P.M.

Hawaii was an independent nation in the sunset of its Polynesian splendor. It was ruled by King David Kalakaua. Americans who had refused to sign loyalty oaths to the King did not have the right to vote, and thus governmental control was in the hands of the King and the native Hawaiians.

But economic control was in the hands of the American businessmen, most of whom were descendants of missionaries who had come to Hawaii half a century earlier to convert the heathens. The current generation conducted their business dealings with the same burning zeal which had driven their forebearers to their clerical pursuits. The saying was: "The missionaries had come to Hawaii to do good, and they had done very well indeed."

And yet, despite the economic influence of the *haoles*, as the whites were called, they had little official control, and only a minimum amount of influence over Kalakaua—a fact which didn't set well with them. There was a general unrest among the American Hawaiians; more and more frequently, clandestine meetings were being held to discuss the situation.

Lorrin was at such a meeting then, a meeting of the League of American Hawaiians. Lorrin O'Lee was a twenty-seven-year-old American; tall, blond, blue-eyed, with broad shoulders and a narrow waist. He cut an impressive figure in his white silk shirt and the brown trousers which he tucked into his well-polished, knee-length boots. He was clean-shaven and handsome and walked with the confident swagger of a seaman. He was, in fact, master of his own ship, the *Centurian*.

Behind him, Colonel Ashford and the others talked on, but Lorrin heard only bits and pieces of the conversation. He was looking out to the bay, where a group of native fishermen were driving fish through the reef-guarded surf. The water was being beaten in rhythmic strokes by well-muscled outrigger canoemen, whose vessels skimmed swiftly across the water. Several young native girls drew the nets into a large circle to trap the catch. It was a scene of unashamed golden-skin nudity, and the bare, wet breasts of the girls bounced and glistened in the golden glow of the sunset.

"I put it to you, gentlemen," one of the men behind Lorrin was saying. "How does our situation differ from Texas? Americans went to Texas to wrest control from the Mexicans, and then turned it over to the United States."

"I'll tell you how it differs," Sanford Dole said. Dole, the wealthiest American on the island, had recently introduced the pineapple to Hawaii, and it showed signs of being as profitable as sugar. Dole was a man of great influence. With his support, any plan conceived by the League of American Hawaiians had a good chance of success. Without his support, any plan was doomed to failure. All eyes were on him as he paused, flicking the ashes of his cigar into an ashtray. "The ones who took Texas away from Mexico were Americans, born and raised in America."

"By God, *we* are Americans," one of the men said indignantly.

"Oh?" Dole said. "Tell me, for whom did you vote in the last Presidential election? And to which

Congressman will you write to, to protest the tariff
the United States has placed on our sugar imports?"

"Well, of course I can't do that," the speaker
sputtered.

"No, you cannot," Dole said. He put the cigar
back in his mouth. "Let us face facts, gentlemen.
We are not Americans, we are Hawaiians. Our personal destinies will be always linked with the destiny of this country."

"Are you trying to say that we should place our
lives in the hands of that . . . that clown who calls
himself a king?" Ashford said, angrily. "Over my
bloody grave!"

"At this moment, I cannot see that we have a
choice," Dole replied calmly. "In fact, I strongly
recommend that we give more of our support to
Kalakaua or we may face the possibility of finding
ourselves subjects of another crown—the British
Crown."

There was a moment of stunned silence, as the
men tried to digest Dole's words.

"Surely you haven't forgotten the English support for Queen Emma to succeed to the throne?"
Dole continued. "Had they been able to get that
Anglophile in over Kalakaua, Hawaii would now
belong to England. Queen Victoria would never
risk a military confrontation to take Hawaii, but if
she offered the protection of the British Lion to a
weak and beleaguered country, Kalakaua might be
coerced into accepting. Unless . . ." Dole let the
word hang.

"Unless what?" Ashford asked, voicing the question of all.

"Unless we can convince Kalakaua that it is his
destiny to found the Empire of Greater Polynesia."

"What do you mean?" Ashford asked suspiciously.

Dole smiled. "Lorrin, perhaps you should come back in here. I believe this will be of concern to you."

Reluctantly, Lorrin turned from the tranquillity of the sunset and rejoined the financial barons of Hawaii in their smoke-filled parlor.

"Here is my proposal, gentlemen." Dole put out his cigar and surveyed the group. "We outfit the *Centurian* as a naval vessel, have Kalakaua appoint Lorrin to the rank of Admiral, and investigate the possibility of bringing in more of the outlying islands under Kalakaua's control."

"But why would you want to do that?" Ashford asked. "Kalakaua is a pompous, over-inflated ass now. This would only appeal to his vanity."

"That is exactly why we will do it. Kalakaua's ego is as big as his stomach. If we feed it, he will be dependent upon us. We will make him more and more dependent, until at last, he can do nothing without our support." Dole looked at Ashford, then continued. "If we control Kalakaua, we control the nation."

"I don't know," Ashford responded. "I would much prefer one swift, clean stroke." Ashford was a relatively small man, but he carried himself with such military bearing that he seemed larger than he really was. He was a man of action, considered a radical by some, a hero by others. His hair was closely cropped and he sported a neatly trimmed moustache. Now his brown eyes sparkled as he lowered his voice to Dole. "My regiment of Honolulu Rifles could take over the palace in one hour."

"I've no doubt but that it could," Dole replied

irritably. "And there may come a time, if all else fails, that I shall agree with such action. But for now, I strongly recommend a less aggressive approach. After all, gentlemen, we were instrumental in putting Kalakaua on the throne in the first place. Let us try and live with what we have done."

"Mr. Dole, what exactly do you have in mind for the *Centurian*?" Lorrin asked. He gave a little laugh. "After all, as it is my ship, I am more than a little interested."

"I suggest a voyage," Dole said, lighting a new cigar, and puffing between words, filling the room with the smell of expensive cigar smoke. "A voyage of no more than three months. You will visit as many unincorporated islands as possible in that time, and invite them into a coalition with Kalakaua. Your ship should be heavily armed and carry a troop of marines, also well-armed."

"Are you suggesting that I proceed militarily against the Islands?" Lorrin asked.

"I don't believe that will be necessary," Dole said. "After all, most of the Islands have populations of only a few hundred souls, and firearms are scarce among them. A simple demonstration of strength should be enough to convince them that their interests would be better served if they joined us."

"Have you spoken with Kalakaua about such a plan?" Ashford asked.

"Yes, I have," Dole replied. He took his pocket watch out, flipped open the gold case and squinted at it. "In fact, I am giving a rather well advertised party at eight o'clock tonight. Kalakaua will make the appointment then. Lorrin, I shall want you there. After all, if you are to be appointed to the exalted rank of admiral, you should be present for the ceremony."

"Wait just a minute," Lorrin retorted. "Not so fast. I haven't agreed to do this yet. The *Centurian* is a working vessel, not a tourist scow. And I am a merchant captain."

"You feel ill-equipped to handle a military command?" Dole asked.

"A *military* command? Yes, I could handle a *military* command," Lorrin answered slowly, aware of the web Dole was trying to weave. "But to dress up in an admiral's costume for such a folly as you propose?" Lorrin let out a hearty laugh. "I would do better on stage in a Gilbert and Sullivan operetta."

"Captain O'Lee, I do believe that I have an option on your next cruise, do I not?"

"Yes, sir, you do. I am to deliver a shipment of canned pineapples to New York."

"New York can wait for their canned pineapples." Dole glared at Lorrin. "It is my wish that you use the *Centurian* in the manner I have described. If you do this, I shall triple your fees and pay your crew's wages from my own pocket. In addition, I will allow you to bargain with King Kalakaua. Certainly you can get additional funds from him."

Lorrin's mouth spread into a wide, slow grin. "Mr. Dole, you realize that such a venture could make me a wealthy man?"

"Yes, I realize that," Dole said. "I am hoping that such enticements will persuade you to accept this assignment."

"I *am* persuaded," Lorrin said.

One of the members of the League scoffed. "I am glad you are a man whose soul can be bought," he said. "It is unfortunate that you are motivated by greed instead of patriotism."

"Patriotism, is it?" Lorrin replied, looking toward the one who spoke, and at the others who were present. "You are moved by patriotism, are you? Patriotism to what, may I ask? Patriotism to a democratic principle, or to an economic principle? Patriotism to King Kalakaua, or to King Sugar? No, gentlemen, we are all moved by the same patriotism. We are in it for what we stand to gain. At least I am not a hypocrite."

"Surely you have some principles?"

"Tell me," Lorrin replied. "Upon what better principle would you build your life?"

"The principle of moral behavior," his challenger answered. "The Hawaiians don't know the meaning of the word. We must make them moral!"

"I see," Lorrin said. "And so you would legislate the morality your fathers couldn't bring about with their preaching?" He shook his head. "If I really believed that moral fervor guided all of you, you would find me a most unwilling participant. No, sir, I believe in the principle of economic betterment. It is a pure, undiluted, realistic motive. It is greed, gentlemen, pure and simple. And one can place one's faith in greed—for in greed there are no surprises."

Sanford Dole threw his head back and laughed uproariously. He slapped his knees and guffawed loudly. "Well, there you have it, gentlemen, the guiding words of the new admiral of our nation," Dole said. "Perhaps not quite as inspiring or as noble as 'Don't give up the ship,' but certainly words we can live by. I would not be surprised if children someday read our words in their history books."

The meeting of the League broke up soon after, and as they were leaving, Dole called out to Lorrin.

"Would you like a ride, Captain? Or, should I call you Admiral?"

"I've always liked the sound of Captain." Lorrin smiled at Dole. "I think it a fitting title. I thank you for the offer of the ride, but I fear I am not going your way. I must visit the ships' chandlers to check on a few things."

"We don't mind going out of our way for a bit, do we, Uncle?" It was a girl's soft voice, and Lorrin glanced toward the carriage. There he saw Dole's niece. She was recently arrived from the States, having left, it was reported, because of a scandal, though none would venture to guess what the scandal might have been. She was about twenty, with long, auburn hair, high cheekbones, a sensuous, full mouth which seemed to smile in appreciation of some private joke, and cool, ice-green eyes. Lorrin had once heard one of the other women complain that the girl managed to look almost naked, even when fully clothed. It was a remark passed in private between two women, and certainly had the speaker known there was a possibility she would be overheard, she would never have said it. But Lorrin, who had overheard the remark, chuckled to himself, because it was amazingly accurate. The girl wore western-style dresses, with perhaps three times as much material as in the clothes worn by the Hawaiian women, and yet she gave up nothing to them in sensual appeal. A very low necked blouse revealed an ample bosom, and though she wasn't bare-bosomed as were many of the Hawaiian women, the effect of relative concealment managed to render her more seductive than any island lass in O'Lee's memory.

"You have met my niece, Andrea Dole, haven't you?" Sanford said. "Of course you have, she's been here now for over three months. I don't think there is anyone on the island who *hasn't* met her."

"Why, Uncle," Andrea said, teasingly. "You make it sound as if I were going door-to-door meeting people."

Sanford chuckled. "I doubt seriously, Andrea, whether you could meet any more people that way than you have already met. I know you are certainly the center of attraction at all my parties."

"But I won't be tonight," Andrea said. "Who could outshine King Kalakaua?" Andrea smiled broadly at Lorrin, and her smile was dazzling. "Oh, Captain, you are coming tonight, aren't you?"

"I dare say he is," Sanford said. "He shall be one of the guests of honor."

"Really?" Andrea said. "How marvelous. Oh, Uncle, do convince him that we shall be glad to drop him at the . . . chandeliers . . . or wherever it was he said he had to go."

"Ships' chandlers," Lorrin laughed. "It is a place where equipment for ships and crews can be bought. But I'm sure it would be out of your way," he added, his eyes on Sanford.

"Nonsense, it won't be out of the way at all," Sanford insisted. "Climb aboard."

Andrea moved over and patted the seat beside her, and Lorrin climbed in. As soon as he was settled, he felt Andrea's leg pressing against his. At first, he thought it was because the seat was too small, but he quickly saw that she had enough room to move away from him. Apparently she didn't want to move. In fact, he was sure that she was intentionally increasing the pressure against his leg, and even through the cloth of his pants and the material of her skirt, he could feel the heat of her leg.

The carriage moved on rubber-tired, well-sprung wheels, so that it glided as smoothly as if it were floating on a cloud. The air was soft, and carried on its gentle breath the sweet fragrance of blooming plumeria. The sun which had set so brilliantly was completely gone now, and night had fallen. The candles and lanterns of the native houses made bubbles of golden light in the blue-velvet darkness, while ahead, the streets of the city were bathed in the warm glow of the gas streetlamps, a visible sign of Honolulu's projection into the modern world.

"Why are you a guest of honor tonight?" Andrea asked. "If you don't mind my asking."

"I wonder the same thing," Lorrin admitted. "It's some fool notion of your Uncle's, and though I will go along with his plan, I don't mind saying that I'm not all that anxious to make a fool of myself by accepting mock honor."

"It's an important part of the plan, my boy, believe me," Sanford said. "And besides, who is to say that the honor is not real? Certainly you aren't the only sea-captain in Honolulu. To be chosen as our nation's first admiral is a great honor."

"Oh," Andrea bubbled. "An *admiral!* How wonderful! I've never known an admiral before."

"And you don't know one now, madam," Lorrin shook his head. "Because I feel myself undeserving of such a title."

"Nevertheless, it is a title which shall be bestowed upon you tonight," Sanford smiled in amusement, his eyes twinkling merrily. "And if I know Kalakaua, it will be bestowed upon you with great pomp and ceremony."

"That's what I'm afraid of," Lorrin said. "I dread coming for just that reason."

"Well *I* certainly don't dread it," Andrea smiled at him. "I am looking forward to it. It should be such a gay evening."

Lorrin leaned forward in the seat. "Driver, right up here are the chandlers. You can let me out at the corner and I'll walk the rest of the way. There is no need for you to turn down that way."

"Oh, we can take him all the way, can't we, Uncle?"

"Of course we can," Sanford answered.

"No," Lorrin put in quickly, "Please, Mr. Dole, you know yourself that the docks at this hour of the day are not the most desirable place to take someone as lovely as your niece. Please, I would feel better if you would just let me out at the corner."

"Perhaps you are right," Sanford said.

"I'm not afraid," Andrea pouted.

"Nor am I, my dear," Sanford assured her. "And certainly not with Lorrin here with us. But why invite trouble?"

As the carriage stopped, Lorrin felt an increase in the pressure on his leg. He looked over at Andrea, and saw that her face was slightly flushed, pinkened like the skin of women with whom he had made love. The thought was a terribly erotic one and he felt a blast of heat and a jolt of sexual energy, and he had to take a deep breath to maintain control of himself.

"I'll see you tonight, then?" Andrea said.

"What?" Lorrin replied, so flustered with the sexual excitation that for an instant all thought and reason fled. "Oh, oh, yes," he said. "Of course, I shall see you tonight."

Andrea was smiling as the carriage drove away, and Lorrin knew that it was a smile of victory. She was playing some sort of sexual game with him, and she had won the first round.

"We shall see, Miss Dole, who has the last smile," Lorrin said under his breath.

2

SANFORD DOLE had two residences on the island of
Oahu. One residence was the plantation home, a
beautiful white house surrounded by gardens, set
high on a hill overlooking thousands of unspoiled
acres. His other residence was in Honolulu, a pala-
tial estate which rivaled the King's palace in size
and grandeur. It was at the Honolulu estate that
the evening's celebration would take place.

Lorrin's hired carriage turned up the long curving
driveway and through the beautifully maintained
flower gardens to the house. Tiki lamps burned on
both sides of the driveway, swaying in the warm
night breeze like a strand of glowing, golden pearls.

Lorrin's hack queued up with all the elegant
carriages which were rolling through the coral-
paved driveway. Among the handsome victorias,
broughams, and landaulets, the rather plain-

looking surrey stood out like a cabbage among flowers.

In the line ahead Lorrin could see uniformed servants greeting the arriving guests, and escorting them into the house. One man, in a fancy dress uniform, was directing the activity. He was, Lorrin assumed, the head doorman.

"Here now! What are you doing bringing a delivery in through here?" the doorman challenged Lorrin's hired driver. "Can't you see there's a party going on here? Get out of line and go around to the back of the house."

"My fare happens to be attending this party," the driver answered indignantly.

The doorman looked back at Lorrin. "Excuse me, sir," he said. "Are *you* a guest here tonight?"

"Yes," Lorrin said.

"And who might you be, sir?"

"Lorrin O'Lee."

The doorman looked slightly stunned at the words, and he took a couple of paces back. "Kano, Mano," he called. "Come quickly, the Admiral is here."

The head doorman was American, but most of the other uniformed servants were Hawaiian, including the two he had just summoned. They both saluted Lorrin.

As he climbed out of the surrey, Lorrin sensed the eyes of other guests upon him, and felt the contempt they had for anyone who must travel in such a lowly fashion. Lorrin had never been one to put on airs. He was a sea captain, a man who, while at sea, was as close to being like a god as anyone could come on earth, for he had absolute power over his seamen. The fact that his men respected him, and signed on for voyage after voyage, was evidence of his ability to handle such power without abuse, but it didn't detract from the power he had. Because of that, and because he was a man with a clear image of his self-worth, he did not let the open contempt of the other guests disturb him. In fact, he knew that he was better able to deal with this than he would be with the false honors which were to be bestowed upon him tonight when he would be proclaimed Admiral. He went with the two escorts, with no sense of shame over his inglorious arrival.

Inside the house, the main ballroom of the Dole Mansion was brightly lit by a dozen suspended gas chandeliers. The crystal prisms of the chandeliers projected splashes of rainbow colors on the Algerian marble walls. The cornices of the room and the moulding of the ceiling were richly gilded. Most impressive was the luster of the guests themselves. The women were all in expensive gowns, with their hair up in elaborate, gravity-defying hairdos, which left their earlobes bare to display the dangling bobs which winked and flashed in gold or precious gemstones.

The party-goers moved about, providing an ever-changing pattern of color and design, like a slowly rotating kaleidoscope. Someone thrust a drink into Lorrin's hand, and he leaned against the marble wall and watched with bemused interest as the men clustered around Andrea like bees around a flower.

And in fact, Lorrin thought, no flower could rival the beauty of Andrea Dole this evening. She was wearing a pale gold gown with an extremely low-cut neckline. Around her slender neck was a golden chain, from which was suspended a large pearl. The pearl rested just in the cleavage of her bosom, calling attention there, as if such help was needed. Her hair was done in one long roll, and it fell forward over one shoulder, its auburn luster contrasting beautifully with her alabaster skin and the pale-gold of the gown.

As Lorrin lifted his glass to drink, he watched her over the rim, and he felt a strange tingling sensation in the palms of both hands. He realized that he had a very strong, compulsive desire to walk over to her, pull the top of her gown down, and fill both hands with those beautiful breasts.

"It's a wonderful party, isn't it?" someone asked casually as he walked by.

"Yes," Lorrin answered. "It's a wonderful party." He almost laughed aloud, as he wondered what the reaction of the guests would be if he actually were to give in to his wild impulse. In fact, what would Andrea's reaction be? He chuckled, silently, again. The reaction of the guests, he believed, would be shock. The reaction of Andrea? Perhaps pleasure.

"What do you find so amusing?" a voice asked.

Lorrin looked around to see Walter Wilson. He had not realized that he was smiling at his own thoughts, and the question surprised him.

"Oh, nothing," Lorrin grinned. "I was just amused that Miss Dole seems to attract so much attention . . . and, obviously, from men of all ages," he added, noticing an elderly man who seemed to be as eager for her attention as any of her younger admirers.

"Yes," Wilson said. He cleared his throat and looked around before he continued in a low, conspiratorial whisper. "Her problem has always been an inability to choose her suitors with wisdom and discretion. You heard, of course, what happened in San Francisco?"

"No," Lorrin said. "Nor do I wish to hear," he added quickly.

"Well, of course, I don't blame you," Wilson whispered "And I'm not one to go around spreading gossip, but—"

"Please, Reverend Wilson, spare me this," Lorrin said curtly. Although he didn't know the missionary very well, Walter Wilson had quite a reputation as a gossip and troublemaker. Lorrin had noticed that most gossip-spreaders prefaced their most malicious slanders with the words, "I'm not one to go around spreading gossip, but . . ."

"Very well, I shall," Wilson said. "After all, debauchery is not the most pleasant subject to bring up at a party, and they say the man who ruined her was married and had four children." Wilson clicked his tongue in an expression of disapproval.

"I said I didn't want to discuss it," Lorrin repeated hotly, now at the end of his patience.

"Oh, of course, of course," Wilson said. "Please forgive me for bringing it up. But in God's work, I find that I must often come in contact with the Devil and his filth. It is important that I recognize it, and not be attracted by its beauty, but repelled by its evil. Thus, I sometimes have what might seem to be a fixation on the shortcomings of others."

There was a sudden blare of trumpets and a buzz of excitement swelled from among the guests.

"The King has arrived," Wilson said. "If you will excuse me?"

"With pleasure," Lorrin said, smiling at Wilson. Wilson, he noticed, wasn't even aware of the cut.

Lorrin gratefully watched Wilson's departure. He couldn't help but notice that Wilson wore a pair of striped pants which seemed ill-fitting, a bit too short for his long legs, and too large for his small waist, though in fact, that was merely an illusion brought on by Wilson's skinny, six-foot frame.

Wilson was the son of a missionary. His father, John Wilson, was somewhat of a hero to the Hawaiians, for he had come with the early missionaries, and had worked long and hard to bring his religion to the islands. As his fellow preachers slipped more and more into the abandoned, materialistic lifestyle of Hawaii, acquiring land, starting businesses and amassing wealth, John Wilson lived off the meager sustenance provided by the Church. His unswerving dedication had at first surprised the others, but eventually brought him the respect of all who met him. John had fathered two sons, Walter and Matthew, both of whom had been urged to follow in their father's footsteps. Matthew had inherited his father's sense of dedication and compassion, and, having renounced material wealth, he carried on his ministry in a leper colony on the island of Molakai.

Walter, on the other hand, used his position as Minister to the King, an honor he had inherited from his father, to promote his self-interests. He had learned early on that the way to gain prestige and influence over Kalakaua was by acting the part of King's lackey; flattering his ego and by granting him religious dispensation for the excesses for which the King was well known.

"I am terribly put out with you, you know," a

woman's voice said. Lorrin turned to see Andrea standing there, her hands on her hips, her eyelids lowered, and her lips in a pout. It was, he supposed, a pout of consternation, but never had she looked more provocative than at this moment. "You haven't spoken to me all night," she complained.

Lorrin felt a dryness in his throat and he had to swallow before he could speak.

"You didn't seem to want for company," he finally said.

"They were boring, all of them," Andrea said, dismissing them with a wave of her hand. "And I wore my prettiest gown just to get your attention. It was all a waste."

"No," Lorrin said easily. "It wasn't a waste. You look lovely."

"Thank you very much." She smiled as she looked around the ball room, which had emptied rapidly. "The King does like to make a grand entrance, doesn't he? There's no one left in here but you, me, and the orchestra."

"You weren't interested in seeing him?" Lorrin asked.

"No," Andrea answered. She laughed. "I've only recently arrived from San Francisco. I guess I haven't gotten used to the idea of a King, yet."

At the mention of San Francisco, Lorrin felt a flash of inexplicable anger. It was but a momentary flash, and then it went away. Odd, why should he feel anger? Then he remembered; Wilson had tried to tell him a story, something about Andrea and debauchery and a husband and four children, and San Francisco.

Why should that concern him, he wondered.

"Is something wrong?" Andrea asked.

"Wrong? No, why do you ask?"

"I don't know," Andrea said. "It's just that for a second a most unusual expression came over your face . . . as if I had said something wrong. I'm sorry, maybe you have a high regard for the King and I have offended you. I didn't mean to."

"No, no," Lorrin said. He smiled. "You've said nothing to offend me. As a matter of fact, I think the King is a pompous windbag."

Andrea laughed, and her laughter sounded like the ring of fine crystal. She looked directly into his eyes. "If you really feel that way, why don't we leave before he arrives?"

"Leave?" Lorrin asked in surprise. "And go where?"

"We won't actually leave the house," Andrea said. "We'll just leave the ballroom. Have you ever toured Uncle Sanford's town home? It's beautiful. Let me show you around."

"All right," Lorrin agreed. "You've got yourself a deal."

Her tour moved up grand staircases, down long, elegant halls, and in and out of exquisite rooms. Lorrin finally found himself gazing through open French windows at the sea. He could see Diamond Head, looming large and black, as the moon painted the dark sea with luminous silver strokes. The light from the few houses he could see glowed like fireflies in the night. He could also make out the silhouette of his ship, the *Centurian,* at anchor in the bay, her red and green anchorage lights but dim glows from this distance.

"It is beautiful, is it not?" Lorrin heard Andrea whisper.

"Yes, it is certainly beautiful," Lorrin said. He laughed. "And I can see my ship from here."

"Wouldn't you much prefer being here, looking down at it, to being on it, looking up here?"

"At this exact moment, I would say yes," Lorrin admitted.

"Do you know where you are now?" Andrea asked. "You are in my bedroom."

During the entire conversation, Lorrin had stood looking through the window. Andrea's voice had come from the dark, behind him, somehow, strangely disassociated with the time and place. He felt, rather than heard, Andrea come up behind him. Her arm went around him, and she leaned into his back.

"Do you know what you are doing, girl?" Lorrin asked quietly. Then, suddenly, he felt a heat flashing through his body like wildfire. It felt as if the girl leaning against him were nude! He spun around in quick surprise, and though he had only the soft light of the moon with which to see her, it was enough to confirm his belief. She was totally naked.

Andrea smiled, then turned slightly, and her body was highlighted and made all the more mysterious and intriguing by the subtle shadows and lighting of the night.

"Make love to me, Lorrin," Andrea said. She put her arms around Lorrin's neck and pulled his lips down to hers.

Lorrin's mind was a battleground of conflicting feelings. On the one hand, the feel of the girl's naked body leaning against his, the rose-petal softness of her lips, and the eager darting of her tongue had filled him with intense desire. And yet, no woman, other than a few waterfront whores at some of his ports of call, had ever been so blatant about sex.

He found himself remembering the rumors of her dark past in San Francisco.

At the thought of this Lorrin felt the flash of anger returning, and he felt as if the girl was using him. He gripped Andrea's wrist to remove her arm from his shoulder. Then, as if controlled by a force outside of him, he found that instead of pushing her away, he was pulling her to him, kissing her hungrily, deeply, longingly.

Andrea opened her mouth on his and ran her tongue across his lips, then thrust it into his mouth. She took his hands and put them on her nude body, indicating that he should move them, guiding them to touch her in those places where she wanted to be touched.

Lorrin was propelled out of a sense of time and space. His breath came in short gasps, and his heart pounded so fiercely that he felt as if it were going to burst from his chest. Quickly he stripped out of his clothes, and stood there in the silver light of the window, burning flesh against burning flesh, holding her body molded against his.

It was a most unusual situation for Lorrin to find himself in, for in this sexual adventure, Andrea was quite clearly the aggressor. And, just as clearly, she was in charge. She directed his kisses and his hands, so that the fires in her own body were stoked to the existential edge of desire.

Finally, Lorrin swept her up and carried her over to her bed, laying her gently on the silk coverlet.

Andrea smiled and lay back on the bed, letting

her breasts rise and fall as she breathed, looking up
at him with a strange, smoldering look which Lorrin found maddening. Her smooth, alabaster body
beckoned him to her, and his manhood rose and
strained as his senses were charged with a sexual
stimulation which was greater than anything he
had ever known.

"Now, my Admiral," Andrea said, speaking in a
voice that was as seductive as the song of the
sirens, yet as bubbly as champagne. "Take me
now."

"I swear, woman, I've never met another quite
like you," Lorrin mumbled, coming down over her,
feeling himself lose all control, becoming now totally subservient to her slightest whim and desire.

"Yes," Andrea said, bubbling a short laugh of victory as he entered her. "Oh, yes, yes, yes, yes!"

Later, as they walked back into the crowded
ballroom, Lorrin looked at the girl under the bright
lights, examining her closely. She was as beautiful
as always, perhaps even prettier now, for her skin
literally glowed with the after-effects of their lovemaking. Other than that, he thought to himself,
there was not one tell-tale sign of what had so
recently transpired.

"Ah, there you are, with Andrea," Sanford said,
seeing Lorrin and Andrea come back into the ballroom. "Where have you been? We've been looking
all over for you."

"It's my fault, Uncle Sanford," Andrea said without the slightest evidence of fluster. "I knew that
after the ceremony made him an Admiral, I would
have little chance to talk to him, so I took him on
a tour of the house."

"You were gone that long, just to tour the house?" Sanford asked.

"It's a large house, Uncle, as you well know," Andrea answered easily.

What a cool liar you are, Lorrin thought, marveling again at the facets of personality this fascinating girl continued to show.

"I'm sorry if we caused any distress," Lorrin added. "I just needed a little time to relax before the ceremony. I hope you understand."

"Of course I understand," Sanford said. "You didn't want to go through with this in the first place. But, believe me, Lorrin, this is best for everyone. I hope *you* understand." He laughed. "Besides, think of the money you will be making."

"That thought does sustain me," Lorrin said. He took a deep breath, then let out a long sigh. "Where is His Majesty?" he asked.

"Knowing His Majesty, I would assume he is in one of three places," Sanford said. "Where there is food, drink, or beautiful women. Come, we'll find him."

"Oh, *there* you are, Andrea, you naughty girl. You ran away from us," a handsome though somewhat foppish young man accused. With him were three others who, it seemed to Lorrin, were all cast out of the same mold.

"Why, Victor, you mean you've been looking for me? How flattering," Andrea said, and she allowed herself to be led off by the entourage. She cast one last, penetrating look over her shoulder at Lorrin, and her eyes barely managed to suppress the laughter at the tremendous joke she and Lorrin had just played upon the entire crowd present.

"She is a very pretty girl," Sanford said with a

sigh, as Andrea left. "Perhaps a bit too pretty for her own good."

Sanford led Lorrin into the dining room where the large table was laid out with foods of all kinds and descriptions. True to Sanford's suggestion, King Kalakaua was behind the table, piling food upon his plate, flanked on both sides by beautiful women.

Kalakaua was a man in his mid-forties. He wore a white uniform, adorned with medals of every hue and size, and a cape of red and gold, which were the traditional Hawaiian colors. He was thick-shouldered and thick-waisted, with a slight belly rise. His hair was jet black, without the slightest hint of gray, and his olive-complexioned face was squarely framed by heavy sideburns. His dark eyes sparkled as he inspected the variety of food that was spread before him.

"Your majesty," Sanford said, approaching him. May I present Lorrin O'Lee?"

Kalakaua looked up at Lorrin. He had to look up, because at six feet, two inches, Lorrin stood nearly six inches taller than the King.

"So, you are to be Admiral of the Realm?" Kalakaua asked.

Lorrin glanced quickly at Sanford, then, when he saw Sanford urging him on, he cleared his throat and answered Kalakaua.

"Yes, your Majesty. At your sufferance."

Kalakaua took a bite from a chicken drumstick, then stepped back and looked at Lorrin. "Yes," he said. "Yes, I think you shall do nicely. Tell me, what did you have in mind for compensation?"

"Land, Your Majesty," Lorrin said, and out of

the corner of his eye he saw Sanford look at him,
first with surprise, and then with amusement.

"Land?"

"Yes, Your Majesty. I should like four thousand
acres of land."

"Four thousand acres? Aiee, you drive a most
difficult bargain. Why do you wish so much land?"

"I am going to raise pineapples, as does my
friend, Sanford Dole."

"No doubt, you shall soon be as wealthy as Mr.
Dole, too," Kalakaua said. He took another bite and
looked pensively at Lorrin for a long moment.
Finally he sighed. "Very well. I shall find four thousand acres and set it aside for you, after you have
completed the mission. Is it agreed?"

"Agreed," Lorrin said with a wide smile.

Kalakaua set his plate of food down and picked
up a napkin to wipe his fingers daintily. "And now,
for the ceremony," he said. He lifted his hand and
the band, which was in the midst of a dance piece,
stopped right in the middle of the song. Some of
the people who were dancing groaned in disapproval at the interruption of the song, but the
trumpets of the band played Kalakaua's fanfare,
which had been composed by the King himself,
and at the prospect of some royal pronouncement,
everyone forgot their disappointment over the
interruption, and turned their attention to the
King.

Kalakaua motioned to one of his assistants, who
brought a large box to the King. Kalakaua opened
the box and took out a long blue coat, with gold
epaulets and gold and silver braid across the front.
He also took out a tricorn hat and a sword with a
black, silver-worked handle.

"Put this coat on, please," Kalakaua said, holding the coat toward Lorrin.

Lorrin tried to keep the look of amusement off his face as he went along with King Kalakaua's ceremony. The whole thing seemed rather ridiculous to him, but he gave no hint of his feelings to Kalakaua because he didn't want to upset Sanford Dole, and also because the promise of four thousand acres was all the inducement he needed.

A silk pillow was put on the floor, and Kalakaua pointed to it. "We would ask you to kneel," he said, using the Royal 'We' he had heard Queen Victoria use when he visited England.

Lorrin cleared his throat, then got down on his knees, kneeling on the pillow provided for the purpose.

Kalakaua took the sword and lay the tip of the blade on Lorrin's shoulder.

"Attend to these ceremonies all who are here present," Kalakaua said. "And know that by Royal Commission, Lorrin O'Lee is made Viceroy of the Sea, and Lord High Admiral of the Realm. As Lord High Admiral of the Realm, he is also made a member of the House of Nobles. Princess Kaiulani, would you please?"

A young girl approached Kalakaua then, carrying a velvet box. She was about seventeen, as slender as a willow, with long, jet-black hair, and flashing black eyes which somehow managed to portray a look of innocence *and* fire.

"This is the flag of our country, Admiral," the girl said, removing a brightly colored red, white and blue cloth from the velvet box. "Fly it proudly, wherever you go, for it represents a proud people, and a proud nation."

The voice of the girl was like a song, melodic and moving. She handed the flag to Lorrin, and as he took it, her fingers touched his. They were hot and cool at the same time.

It had been but a short time since Lorrin had been with Andrea. He would certainly have thought all sexual desire would be satiated by now, but as he looked at this girl he felt a desire for her beyond all sense of perception. It was more than sexual desire, it was a desire for total possession. Never had the mere presence of a woman moved him so. He felt feverish and weak, yet his blood rushed so that he wanted to leap up and shout, to claim her as a mighty animal of the jungle claims his mate.

"Thank you, Princess Kaiulani," Kalakaua said. He looked at Lorrin and smiled. "You may rise, Admiral O'Lee."

The party guests cheered in unison, and all rushed forward to shake his hand.

Lorrin acknowledged their congratulations, but all the while his eyes were searching the crowd, trying to find the beautiful, mysterious Princes Kaiulani. Strangely, she had disappeared completely, and he was beginning to wonder if he had ever seen her at all. Perhaps she was but a trapping of the ceremony, as unreal as his titles, Viceroy of the Sea, and Lord High Admiral of the Realm.

3

THE *Centurian* had been built in 1873 by the A. Sewall & Company, Shipbuilders of Maine, to carry cargoes of grain, sugar, tea and spices across the Pacific. Though steam-powered ships were beginning to take over the Atlantic shipping lanes, the Pacific still belonged to the three- and four-masted sailing ships known as windjammers. This was because coaling stations were too few and too far between to make steam a viable source of power for the Pacific trade routes. Thus the windjammers, beating through a screaming Cape Horn storm, or running swiftly before the trade winds, continued to be the most dependable means of shipping on the world's largest ocean.

Lorrin O'Lee came naturally to his trade. He was, in fact, born at sea, as his father did what many sea captains on the long Pacific routes did, taking his wife to sea with him.

Lorrin's father was Patrick O'Lee, son of Jebediah and Zelda O'Lee of St. Louis, Missouri. Jebediah O'Lee had been an exceptionally harsh man, given to enforcing his discipline with the frequent use of a strap. Patrick left St. Louis when he was fourteen, travelled down the Mississippi River on a flatboat and shipped out of New Orleans to begin a lifetime at sea.

Patrick never returned to St. Louis. He heard once that two cousins, Dan and Burke O'Lee, had gone to St. Louis to live with his mother and father, after their own parents had been killed in an accident, and Jebediah's stern treatment soon drove both of them off as well. The Civil War came between Dan and Burke then, Dan fighting for the North, while Burke fought and died for the South. Patrick, because he was already engaged in the Pacific trade, felt a sense of total detachment from the war, even though the O'Lee family suffered such personal tragedy as to see brother turned against brother, and hearts divided against themselves.

Patrick married Sybal James, the daughter of another sea captain, and Sybal took up the life of a Captain's wife. Lorrin was born at sea, to be precise, at 33 degrees north and 162 degrees west, under the American Flag on board the *Distant Star*. He sailed with his parents until he was fifteen, at which time he went ashore in California for his formal schooling. He graduated from college the same week he learned that his mother and father had died of a fever in Hong Kong.

Lorrin's father had been a thrifty man, and he had left enough money for Lorrin to buy his own ship. Lorrin found the *Centurian*, a three-masted bark, and bought her outright. A lucrative trading

contract with Sanford Dole insured the survival of
his shipping enterprise.

But with Lorrin's appointment to Admiral, he
and the *Centurian* were embarking on a new adventure. The Royal Flag of Hawaii fluttered in the
breeze from the top of the main mast. The upper
left corner of the flag was blue, with a red on white
St. Andrew's Cross. The field of the flag was identi-
cal to the Union Jack of Great Britain. Alternating
stripes of white, red, and blue furled out from the
field.

In addition to the flag, there were other changes
being wrought on the ship. The nameplate *Centurian* was removed, to be replaced with a new
one—*Kahili Pahoa*. *Kahili Pahoa* was Hawaiian for
"Royal Dagger." King Kalakaua liked the symbo-
lism of the name. In his mind, the *Centurian*, or
Kahili Pahoa, was a royal dagger, held at the
throats of the outer islanders forcing them to sub-
mit to his will.

The ship was now armed. A total of sixteen guns
were brought on board and lashed to the deck. Firing ports were cut through the railing, and doors
were installed so that the ports could be opened
and the guns run forth.

Though King Kalakaua and his cohorts came
down to watch the guns being placed on board the
ship, and to compliment each other on their fine
'navy,' Lorrin knew it for the sham it was. Lorrin
had already seen some of the newer battle-ships-of-
the-line. He knew that they were powered by
steam, were protected by an eight-inch layer of
steel plate, and carried modern artillery which
could hurl explosive projectiles four thousand
yards and more with pinpoint accuracy.

The *Kahili Pahoa* might be considered a dagger at the throat of an unarmed group of native tribesmen, but to any navy in the civilized world, she would be little more than an oddity—a ship sailing out of time and place.

Lorrin stood on the quarterdeck of the *Kahili Pahoa* and watched with amusement as Lieutenant Manakaloa drilled his platoon of marines.

Carl West, a huge man at six-foot-seven and 265 pounds, ambled up to Lorrin. He spat a stream of tobacco over the rail, then ran his hand over his bald head and squinted at the drilling Marines.

"Ain't they cute?" he asked sarcastically. "I'll be damned if they don't look exactly like a bunch o' little toy soldiers I seen once."

"We're going to have to try and get along with them, Carl," Lorrin said. "After all, they are the backbone of our military force," he added, smiling at Carl.

"Yes, sir, you tole' me, sir," Carl said. He squirted another stream of tobacco over the rail. "Still, I can't understand for the life of me what we're 'a needin' with a bunch of toy soldiers. Iffen you just wanted to go out to the islands 'n skeer hell outta' a bunch o' the natives, why, hell, I could do that with my bare fists. I been doin' it for years, anyway."

Lorrin laughed. "That's not quite the same thing. I don't know if Kalakaua would accept having his empire founded by bare knuckles. He needs artillery and infantry. Besides, you know what they say, don't you? Artillery lends dignity to what would otherwise be considered little different from a barroom brawl."

"I've been in some dandy barroom brawls," Carl

grinned. "From California to New South Wales."

"I dare say you probably have," Lorrin said. He took his tricorn hat off. He didn't like being on deck without a hat, but the admiral's tricorn, with its ostentatious spread of feathers and frill, was heavy and uncomfortable. He wiped his forehead and wished he had his soft, unpretentious, comfortable felt hat. "But, for the time being, let's do things their way, shall we?"

Carl shook his head in disgust. "If they're ignernt enough to pay three times our wages, then I guess I'm willin' enough to go along with them." He looked at the guns. "I just hope we don't run into no real navy, that's all."

"Don't worry, Carl, I've got more sense than to get us involved in anything which might lead to a confrontation."

"Confrontation? Hell, I ain't worried about that as much as I am about some real navy seein' us, 'n laughin' their fool heads off."

"Cap'n O'Lee, the Royal Canoe is comin' across the bay," a lookout reported.

Lorrin looked over toward the great, twin-hulled canoe. It was skimming quickly across the waves, propelled by more than fifty oarsmen.

"Damn," Lorrin said under his breath. "He takes this navy business seriously, doesn't he? This is the third time today he's come out to check on the work."

"He's got 'im a new toy to play with," Carl said.

Lorrin laughed. "That's your king you are talking about," he said. He started toward the rail. "I guess I'd better see what His Majesty wants this time."

As the Royal Canoe drew closer, the sound of

the coxswains drum could be heard, pounding out a relentless rhythm to drive the rowers on. The men chanted as they rowed, and their chants and the beat, beat, beat of the drums made strangely beautiful and exotic music.

"Bo'sun," Lorrin called, as the Royal Canoe came alongside.

"Aye, sir."

"Prepare to pipe the King aboard. Sideboys, in place."

"Aye, sir," the bo'sun replied. He signaled to the required 'sideboys'—guards of honor who would stand at attention by the railing as the King stepped on board.

The railgate was opened, and a boarding ramp stretched from the deck of the *Kahili Pahoa* to the deck of the Royal Canoe. Kalakaua, wearing a red uniform trimmed in yellow, swept regally up the gangplank. The bo'sun's whistle made its shrill call, starting with a highpitched bleat and trailing off as the King stepped on board.

"Very nice, very nice," Kalakaua said, looking at the honors with a broad smile. "It is the way of all navies, yes?"

"Yes," Lorrin said. "What business brings you aboard this time, Your Majesty?"

"Oh, yes," Kalakaua said. "I do have business. But first, how is everything going? Are the cannons sufficient? They appear to be very nice cannons."

"Yes," Lorrin said. He didn't know what else to say. They were more than sufficient to do the job the King had in mind—that of coercing the natives. But they were woefully inadequate should they ever actually be needed.

"That is good, that is good," Kalakaua said, smiling broadly, as usual. "And the marines, they are good men, are they not?"

"Lt. Manakaloa is to be commended for his work with them," Lorrin answered.

"Good, good. I am proud of our Navy. With a Navy, Hawaii can take its place among the other nations of the world. How soon will you be ready to sail?"

"I'm ready now, Excellency," Lorrin said. "In fact, I grow impatient at standing idle in the bay."

"Good, good," Kalakaua said, smiling broadly. "It is good that you are anxious to serve your country, Admiral O'Lee. And now, I have your first mission."

"You have a mission for the *Centurian*? Excuse me, Your Majesty, I mean the *Kahili Pahoa*."

"Yes," Kalakaua said. "I wish for you to set sail immediately."

"What shall be my destination?"

"Lahaina."

"Lahaina? But that's in Maui. Maui is already part of your Kingdom."

Kalakaua chuckled. "Yes, of course it is. I merely want you to take a passenger to Lahaina, that's all. My niece wishes to return home. After you have delivered her, then you may sail to French Frigate Shoals, and bring any such peoples as you may find in any islands, under the flag of the Greater Polynesian Empire."

"Your Majesty, as the *Kahili Pahoa* is now a warship, I don't have the facilities to transport passengers. This is especially true if the passenger is a child. Would it not be more convenient for you to schedule transportation for your niece on some other vessel?"

"I prefer to send her on your ship, Admiral," Kalakaua said. He smiled. "I want my sister to see this ship, and to realize that I, Kalakaua, am consolidating my power. As you may know, Liliuokalani covets the throne for herself. Perhaps this will dissuade her."

Lorrin started to protest a second time, but he knew that such a protest would be useless. And after all, it was for just such political purposes that Dole had originated the idea of a Hawaiian Navy in the first place. Lorrin smiled.

"I shall be glad to transport your niece to Maui, Excellency. And to provide Liliuokalani with visual evidence of your strength."

"Good, good," Kalakaua said. He clapped his hands, and called down to the Royal Canoe, which rolled quietly alongside the *Kahili Pahoa*.

"Mr. West," Lorrin called. "Prepare your cabin for occupancy by a passenger. We're taking the King's niece to Maui."

"I don't wish to be any trouble, Admiral," a soft voice said. The voice was as melodious as the delicate tinkle of a windbell, and Lorrin turned to look at the speaker.

It was the girl who had given him the flag. He felt a catch in his breath, and a quick, building heat in his body. She was exquisitely beautiful.

"I . . ." Lorrin started, then, he paused several seconds before he was able to find words. "I want to apologize, Princess, for what shall be terribly crude quarters. Especially for someone like you."

"Please," the girl said. "Don't apologize to me, Admiral. It is I who should apologize. I am intruding on your domain, and for that I am sorry."

Kalakaua read the reaction to the girl in Lorrin's

face, and he chuckled. "So, you find Kaiulani beautiful, do you not?"

"Beyond words," Lorrin said reverently, and Kaiulani looked down in a blushing smile. Her long eyelashes, like palm fronds, dipped across her eyes . . . innocent, but smoldering with a barely subdued fire.

"You are most kind to pay me such a compliment," she said.

"Compliments are often but the idle words of politeness," Lorrin said. "But I speak God's truth, Princess." He cleared his throat and he pointed to the flag. "Look," he said. "Your flag waves from the top wand."

Kaiulani looked up toward the flag, then she smiled broadly. "Oh, how wonderful!" she said. "And how beautiful the flag is up there. See how the colors ripple as the flag furls and unfurls in the wind!"

"When will you be leaving, Admiral?" Kalakaua asked.

"I will leave with the evening tide," Lorrin said. He looked at Kaiulani and smiled. "The Princess will go to sleep in Oahu, and awaken in Maui. It is but a short distance across Lahaini Channel."

"Good, good. I am glad she is in your hands now." The King started back to the rail. "I must return now, I have pressing matters of State to attend to. Be happy, Admiral, that you were not born of royal blood. Reigning is no easy task."

"I am sure, Excellency, but Hawaii is the better for your dedication and rule."

"Yes, I know," Kalakaua said, matter of factly.

"Goodbye, Uncle," Kaiulani said.

"Goodbye, niece. Tell your mother my love is with her, as it is for all my people."

Kalakaua walked down the ramp to his canoe and took his place on the throne. The drums started anew, and the chanting began again. The twin hulled craft pulled away from the ship and started back toward the shore.

"Mr. West," Lorrin called.

"Aye, sir."

"Make ready to get underway with the evening tide."

"Aye, cap'n," West said. "If we can just get the bloomin' toy soldiers to stay the hell outta' the way."

"You're second in command, Mr. West," Lorrin said. "Issue whatever orders you feel are necessary."

"Aye, sir," West said, smiling broadly at his Captain's words.

"Princess, if you will come with me, I shall show you to your quarters," Lorrin said.

"Please, Admiral, I am uncomfortable with such formality and prefer that you call me Kaiulani." She smiled. "I hope you don't mind."

"No," Lorrin said. "Of course I don't mind." He felt slightly giddy, and he wondered why such a young, and apparently innocent, girl, affected him so.

Lorrin led the girl across the deck and down a ladder. It was dark below deck, but enough of the sun's golden beams streamed in through the vents and scuppers to allow one to see quite easily, once the eyes were adjusted to the dim light.

"This is the mate's cabin," Lorrin said. "But, for tonight, it shall be yours. It is small, but it is clean."

"It shall do very nicely," Kaiulani said. "But where will the poor mate sleep?"

"For tonight, there will be no sleep for either of us," Lorrin said, and when he saw the look of concern on the girl's face, he smiled. "Don't worry, neither of us ever sleep the first night out of port."

"Oh," Kaiulani said, her eyes shining brightly. "It must be truly wonderful to sail around the world, to see marvelous places. Have you been to England?"

"Yes."

"And China?"

"Yes."

"And to America too, of course. Were you born in America?" Kaiulani asked.

Lorrin smiled. "No, I was born at sea."

"You were born at sea? On a ship?"

"Yes," Lorrin said. "My father was a sea captain, and my mother went everywhere with him."

"Oh, women can do such things?"

"Yes."

"How wonderful that would be," Kaiulani said. She hugged herself and did a small dance. "I shall dream tonight. Do you know what I shall dream?"

"What shall you dream, Kaiulani?"

"I shall dream that a handsome captain, like you, comes to take me in his arms and marry me, and takes me to sea with him to see many wonderful places and do many wonderful things."

Lorrin cleared his throat. "If there were such a captain, Kaiulani, he would be a very lucky man."

"Cap'n, steam launch approaching," West called down.

"Aye, I'm coming on deck," Lorrin shouted back. He started out, but turned to look back into the small cabin. "Just make yourself at home," he said. "If you need anything, just let me know."

"Thank you," Kaiulani said.

Lorrin climbed the ladderway, and stepped onto the deck just as a boat was approaching. It was a small, steam-powered craft, with an engine and stack amidships, and a small paddle at the stern. Lorrin recognized it as belonging to Sanford Dole.

The chugging of the engine and the slapping of the paddle ceased, and the boat drifted the last few feet until it was along side the *Kahili Pahoa*. The boarding ramp was lowered and Sanford Dole, V. V. Ashford, and Andrea came aboard.

"And how is our Admiral?" Dole asked, laughing, as he set foot on deck.

"The Admiral is fine," Lorrin said. He reached his hand out to help Andrea make the last step onto the deck, and she squeezed his hand more than necessary. She looked at him with cool, appraising eyes, and in that gaze, managed to convey to Lorrin all the fire and passion of their shared moment of rapture of a few days earlier.

"I am very angry with you," Andrea said, though the words weren't spoken in an angry voice.

"Oh?" Lorrin said. "Have I offended you in some way? If so, I'm terribly sorry, and I ask that you please forgive me."

"Your offense has been in not coming to see me," Andrea said, her lips in a pout. "I've waited and waited for you, but all in vain."

"I'm sorry," Lorrin said. He gave a helpless shrug of his shoulders. "I'm afraid I've been very busy of late."

"Of course he has," Sanford said. "Andrea, I swear, if every man you see doesn't throw himself at you, you are absolutely crushed. Heaven knows there are always enough men making fools of themselves before you that you should be satisfied."

"Pooh," Andrea said. "Do you really think I consider those dandies men?"

"Well, you leave Lorrin alone. He has enough on his mind without worrying about some addlebrained young woman. Lorrin, have you received word when you will leave?"

"Yes," Lorrin said. "As a matter of fact I have. We shall be leaving for Maui this very evening."

"Tonight?"

"Yes. Kalakaua was on board a short while ago."

"Then we weren't a minute too soon," Ashford opened his jacket and pulled out an envelope. "Would you be able to make a stop in Lahaina?"

"Yes, I shall be stopping there," Lorrin said. "Why?"

"There is a man in Lahaina, Robert Cox. Do you know him?"

"Yes," Lorrin said, frowning. "I can't say that I like him."

"He doesn't have to be liked to be useful to us," Ashford said.

"Useful? In what way will Cox be useful? He is little more than a layabout and a ladies' man," Lorrin said. "He is a social gadfly who can be depended upon to show up at the latest party, but is dependable in no other way."

"Perhaps it is just such a trait which shall make him useful to us," Ashford said. "For such a person meets many people and hears many things." Ashford looked around to make sure none of the Hawaiian crewmen or Marines were within earshot. "Cox shall be our contact in Lahaina. He will keep us informed of events there, and we shall keep him informed of events here. That way, there will be no surprises."

"I wouldn't count on it." Lorrin shook his head. "It is my feeling that Robert Cox may surprise you . . . and it won't be a pleasant surprise."

"I feel you are judging the man too harshly, Lorrin," Dole said. He laughed. "I know that for someone like you, there is little to recommend a wastrel. But he is basically harmless. Don't judge him too harshly."

"We shall see," Lorrin said. "I shall try to keep an open mind."

"Admiral, will I be taking my dinner in your cabin?" Kaiulani asked, suddenly appearing in the hatchway which led below deck.

"Yes, Admiral," Andrea said, sizing up the girl with a look of open hostility. "Answer your wahine. Will she be taking dinner in your cabin?"

4

"WE'RE SAILIN' FULL and bye, at your command, Cap'n," West reported, as Lorrin stepped onto the quarterdeck.

"Thank you, Mr. West," Lorrin replied.

"Did you have a good meal, sir?"

"Most enjoyable," Lorrin said. "And I believe the Princess liked it too." He looked up at the sails. "Mr. West, the mizzen t'gallant is spilling air."

"Aye, cap'n, I should've checked the riggin' myself," West said. "You, there! Get aloft, take in the corner of the mizzen t'gallant!" he shouted to a nearby sailor.

Lorrin watched the sailor start up the rigging to take the slack out of the ropes securing the top gallant sail, so that the sail was sheeted tight against the wind. Then Lorrin turned and walked to the after rail and looked back at the ship's wake.

The moon was hanging like a great silver lantern behind them, and the wake stretched from the ship, back to the horizon like a long smear of liquid silver, shimmering brightly against the oily blackness of the water.

Lorrin had a theory about such a long ship's wake. It was a direct and visible link with his past. Somewhere, he felt, on the other end of that wake, everything that had ever happened to him was still happening. If he had a sailing ship swift enough, perhaps one thousand times faster than the swiftest ship, he could follow the wake backward and reach the other end of it before the shifting sea carried it away. When he got there he would see himself as a young boy on his father's ship, as a college student, as a captain sailing on his own ship for the first time . . . and . . . as Andrea Dole's lover.

Andrea had been inexplicably angry when she saw Kaiulani. The sharpness and intensity of her feeling surprised Lorrin, and even when the girl's presence was explained, and Andrea dutifully apologized for calling her Lorrin's wahine, Lorrin still sensed a smoldering hint of resentment.

Why was Andrea so disturbed by Kaiulani? Surely Andrea did not feel proprietary rights over Lorrin? Or, Lorrin thought, perhaps she did.

Lorrin wondered how he would feel about that. Andrea was a beautiful girl, and was charged with a more overt sexuality than any woman he had ever known. Surely none of the women Lorrin had ever slept with—paid whores, young native girls, and an older woman who was the wife of a college professor—had exuded the tremendous sexual vitality of Andrea Dole. And yet that very characteristic which made her maddeningly desirable, also, strangely, repelled him.

Ding, ding, ding.

Three bells rang out clarion-clear like a fine crystal goblet struck by a silver spoon. The three bells indicated the time; nine-thirty P.M., though Lorrin, who had spent his life aboard ship, never converted bells to time. Three bells wasn't nine-thirty, it was three bells, and he thought of it in that way. In fact, Lorrin often converted time ashore to bells to better grasp it. The ringing of the bells were as much a part of Lorrin's early life as the beating of his mother's heart had been when he was in his mother's womb, and as buried in his subconscious.

"Mr. West, I will take a turn about the deck," Lorrin said.

"Aye, sir," West replied. "The cap'n's off the quarterdeck," he called out, as Lorrin stepped down the three small steps onto the deck and began his stroll.

The *Kahili Pahoa* was a wooden ship. Though sails still ruled the Pacific waves, many of the ships now were built of iron and steel, rather than wood. Most of the new ships were awesome in every dimension. They were at least three-hundred-feet long, and their masts, three-feet-thick at the base, towered as high as two hundred feet above the keel. Some of the yardarms from which the sails flew were more than a hundred feet long, and as much as two feet in diameter at the center. The largest of their sails weighed more than a ton, and they were braced with steel wire and chain, which, if laid end to end, would stretch for miles.

Lorrin's ship had been a proud holdover from an earlier age. Smaller, and more graceful, she could match the steel windjammers for speed, but carried less than half their cargo. Her overall dimensions weren't nearly as impressive either, and the rigging was nearly all manila rope, though there were a few mast-bracing cables of steel and turnbuckle.

Lorrin loved his ship. He loved the feel of the wind filling the sails. It didn't have the plunging, pitching motion of other ships, it seemed instead to literally fly over the waves, as if the ship were alive. The masts bowed under the press of sail, forming graceful arches. Wind hummed through the rigging, and played off the sails in a muted roar like thunder whispering in the distance.

Lorrin's stroll took him amidships on the starboard side. A wink of golden light shone through the air vent which led into the mate's cabin, and he knew that Princess Kaiulani was in there now. Though he felt guilty in doing it, Lorrin stepped into position to allow him to look through the vent.

Kaiulani was totally nude, sitting on the bunk, completely uninhibited by her nudity. Unconsciously, she had assumed a pose which would have delighted the most dedicated artist, for her knee was raised and her arm rested upon it so that her breast on that side continued in a beautiful, unbroken line from her shoulder out to a small, upturned nipple. The other breast blended into the shadow of the rest of her body, highlighted by the golden light of the gimbal lantern. There was an unconscious diagonal tension in the pose which directed the eyes of the viewer right to her face, despite her nudity.

Seeing the girl in total, unabashed nudity, Lorrin was struck with an amazing realization. Kaiulani was more innocent without clothes, than Andrea had been when she visited the ship, even though she had been fully clothed.

And, as Andrea's overt sexuality had both attracted and repelled Lorrin, Kaiulani's sweet innocence made him feel protective of her on one hand, while, on the other, it stimulated an almost irrepressible desire to ravage her.

Lorrin turned away from the vent, then continued his walk around the deck. The night air was clear and sharp, and the sea stretched to the horizon in gently rolling purple, textured by the foam which rose like a candle flame when a wave spilled over. In the water just below the ship, hundreds of brilliant green streaks, phosphorescent fish, glowed like a city of lights.

Lorrin thought of the two women who had so recently come into his life. Andrea, who was fire and ice . . . and Kaiulani, innocent and sensual. One he had known, the other he desired.

Lorrin had never established any relationship with a woman, beyond the momentary relationship of sexual pleasure. He had drifted among them, taking little interest in any of them, believing in none of them. Women had no place in his hopes, dreams or ambitions. They were as unimportant to him as a wave which rolled relentlessly to shore, only to burst and be wasted and uncounted at the end of its journey.

But now his indifference to them had been shaken. Andrea and Kaiulani were haunting presences in his mind. They were the subjects of unbidden thoughts which plagued him and disrupted his peace.

Lorrin's sexual appetite had always been strong, though to him, women were no more than a means of achieving physical release. It was a temporary release to be sure, because the last woman he never remembered, and the next woman he did not know.

Until Andrea . . . and now, Kaiulani.

There was something extraordinary about these two women. Something which had taken root in his mind, and awakened feelings he had thought were impossible.

Lorrin looked out to where the rolling sea seemed to meet the sky. He could almost see a face, just over the horizon, waiting for him. But which face was it? The face of passion, or the face of innocence?

"All guns ready to fire a salute, sir," Lt. Manakaloa reported, and he drew himself to attention, clicked his heels, and saluted sharply.

It was late morning, and the sky above Maui was blue and cloudless. Lush green trees climbed the black volcanoes, while birds of brilliant plumage flitted about, like flowers leaving the branch.

The *Kahili Pahoa* had dropped anchor a little less than an hour earlier, and now the entire ship's company was turned out on deck to receive a courtesy call from Queen Liliuokalani. This was part of the politics in which Lorrin now found himself. His instructions had been to send word to Liliuokalani that he had arrived with Kaiulani. Then, when she came for her daughter, he was to render her full honors with the ship's company.

"Mr. West, has the canoe left the dock yet?" Lorrin asked.

West climbed a few feet into the rigging and

peered through binoculars toward the docks. "Aye, cap'n, she's on her way now. I'll be damned if it don't look like she's bringin' the entire town out to have a look-see."

"I'd best go down to my cabin and put on my Admiral's coat," Lorrin said. He was wearing the loose-fitting white shirt and brown pants tucked into boots, which was his standard shipboard uniform. He climbed down the ladderway, then started for his cabin.

"Admiral?"

It was Kaiulani's voice, and, as usual, it stopped him with its sweet, seductive power.

"Yes, Princess?" Lorrin stopped, but he didn't look around.

"I thought you were going to call me Kaiulani."

Lorrin turned around and saw her standing in the doorway. Her eyes were wide, and shining a rich brown. Her lips looked wet, and her golden skin seemed, somehow, to glow softly.

"I'm sorry," Lorrin said. "I would be honored to call you Kaiulani. What can I do for you?"

"You have already done much for me," Kaiulani said. "I just wanted to thank you for going out of your way to bring me back home. Though . . ." Kaiulani looked down, shielding her eyes with the long, lovely lashes, and the word hung suspended between them.

"Though what, Kaiulani?"

"Though I wish the voyage had not so quickly ended," she said. "Were it to last longer, we might have had the chance to become friends."

Lorrin took a step back toward her, and, without thinking, he reached out to take her hands in his.

Her hands were cool, though they burned against him as if they were irons from a fire.

"I'd like to believe that we are already friends," Lorrin said. "Is there any reason to feel otherwise?"

"No, of course not," Kaiulani said, smiling at him. "It's just that we would have had time to enjoy our friendship. Perhaps someday we will get the opportunity to enjoy one another."

Lorrin recognized the double entendre in her comment, and on any other occasion, he would have taken ribald pleasure over the slip. But not with this girl. With this girl, such thoughts only caused heat to flash through his body.

"Yes," Lorrin said. "Perhaps soon."

"Cap'n, the boat is approachin' fast," West said. "Permission to fire the salute?"

"Fire the salute," Lorrin called back and almost immediately the ship roared with the sound of booming cannon.

Kaiulani smiled broadly, then rushed up on deck to watch the rest of the ceremony.

The air hung heavy with the smell of gunsmoke, and a cloud drifted across the bay. The echo of the salute came floating back from the tree covered hills of Lahaina, and thousands of birds, frightened by the intrusion into their peaceful domain, fluttered up in colorful, living clouds.

Kaiulani stood on the deck with her hands over her ears, watching the cannons as they were fired. It was an exciting moment, and she felt it, deep inside, like the drum beats and the chants during the hula-hula luaus. She knew that her mother would have a luau to celebrate her return to Lahaina, and she wished Admiral O'Lee could be persuaded to stay.

Liliuokalani's canoe bumped up alongside the *Kahili Pahoa* just after the last cannon boomed, and the sister of King Kalakaua stepped on board, smiling broadly. She saw Kaiulani and she opened her arms wide, and beckoned to her.

"Daughter, it is good to have you home again."

Kaiulani went to her mother's arms and accepted a hug, then hugged others of her mother's court. One of the members of the entourage which had come on board with her mother was Robert Cox. He was waiting for his embrace, but Kaiulani merely smiled weakly at him, then moved away to avoid having to embrace him. Of all the people who hung around her mother, Robert Cox was the one she liked the least.

"Is my brother in good health?" Liliuokalani asked.

"Yes, mother," Kaiulani said.

"What is this vessel?" she asked, looking around. "To what nation does it belong?"

"It belongs to Hawaii, my lady," Lorrin said, appearing on deck then. He was dressed up in his Admiral's coat and tricorn hat. He clicked his heels and bowed formally. "I am Admiral O'Lee, at your service."

"*Admiral* O'Lee?" Liliuokalani said. "I am most impressed. Has my brother gone to war?"

Lorrin laughed. "No, my lady. He wishes merely to extend his . . . protection . . . to those islanders who are not now a part of Hawaii."

"Extend his protection? You mean he is going to force them to join Hawaii?"

"I believe he intends to call it the Greater Polynesian Empire, my lady," Lorrin said.

Liliuokalani shook her head, and clucked her

tongue. "Truly, Captain O'Lee, my brother has gone mad. Does the House of Nobles know of this foolhardy plan?"

"It is my belief that they do," Lorrin said.

"Well, what do *you* think about it? Don't you think such a thing is mad?" Liliuokalani asked.

"I am a loyal subject to the legitimate government of Hawaii, my lady," Lorrin answered. "I have no right to comment."

"I see." Liliuokalani sighed, then put her arm around Kaiulani again. "I am glad, my daughter, that you have come home where you belong. Here, you will be safe, and here you will be away from the influence of my brother, the madman. Thank you for bringing her, Captain O'Lee."

"He is an Admiral, mother," Kaiulani said, smiling at Lorrin.

Liliuokalani looked at her daughter in surprise, then she smiled at her. "Of course he is, dear. I forgot," Liliuokalani said. She looked back at Lorrin. "Admiral O'Lee, where does your adventure take you next?"

"To French Frigate Shoals, my lady," Lorrin said.

Liliuokalani laughed. "Perhaps such adventure makes my brother feel as if he is attacking France itself. Very well, Admiral, proceed on your adventure if you must. I shall merely bide my time until my brother proves his incompetency to the rest of the world. Then, I shall assume the throne and we will be free of his madness. Kaiulani, we will have a luau tonight."

"Mother, would it not be nice to invite Admiral O'Lee to the luau?" Kaiulani asked hopefully.

Liliuokalani looked at Lorrin for a moment, then

shook her head in the negative. "I'm afraid the Admiral has too much to do," Liliuokalani said. "He must run my brother's navy. Come, we will go now. We should not keep the Admiral from his duty."

"My lady, would you do us the honor of inspecting the ship's company?" Lorrin asked, indicating the Marines and crewmen who were standing like rows of statues on the deck.

"Very well," Liliuokalani said. "After all, we wouldn't want my brother to think I was unimpressed, would we?"

Liliuokalani started toward the ranks of men, and Lorrin moved over to whisper to Cox.

"Colonel Ashford asked me to deliver this letter to you," he said. "I don't know its contents."

Cox looked around, and when no one was looking, he took the letter and put it in his jacket pocket. "Tell the Colonel I will be in touch," Cox said.

Lorrin stepped back to his place by the railgate and watched as Liliuokalani moved quickly through the ranks. Finally her "inspection" was completed, and she came back to the railgate, preparatory to leaving the ship. She looked at Lorrin and smiled.

"Tell my brother I am struck with fear at the sight of his mighty soldiers," she said. "Come, Kaiulani, we will go now."

"Yes, Mother," Kaiulani said. The young Princess followed her mother down the ramp and onto the royal canoe. Her chair was next to her mother's, and she took her seat and looked back toward the ship. She searched among the faces on the deck until she saw Lorrin O'Lee, and then she fixed her gaze upon him, and looked at him for as long as she was able to keep him in sight.

Kaiulani stood in an open glade on a cliff which overlooked the ocean. The ocean shimmered now with thousands of dancing sun-jewels. The *Kahili* was already on its outward journey, and Kaiulani's heart was on board the ship.

Kaiulani was in love with Lorrin O'Lee. She could not explain why . . . they had spent so little time together, and none of it alone . . . yet when she saw him, or when she heard him speak, or even when she thought of him, her heart grew big and her knees grew weak.

"I knew I would find you here," a voice said quietly.

Kaiulani turned to see her mother. She smiled at her. "I came to watch the ship leave," she said.

"You came to watch Captain O'Lee leave," her mother corrected. "Am I not right?"

Kaiulani turned back to gaze out over the sea. "Yes," she said. She sighed. "I do not understand," she said.

"You do not understand how you can feel love for someone you have just met?"

Kaiulani looked at her mother in surprise. "How did you know?"

"I know, Kaiulani. And to answer your question, it is because you are an Aliï-Nui."

Kaiulani laughed. "Mother, those are superstitions from the old days. No one believes such a thing anymore."

"The ways have changed, that is true," Liliuo-kalani said. "And the secrets and powers died with the last Aliï-Nui, Leilani, who was the daughter of

Kaliolani, who was the granddaughter of the great King Kamehameha. But though the wondrous powers which were passed on for one hundred generations are no longer ours to use, the blood of the Alii-Nui lives on. It is in me, it is in you. That is why it is my destiny to rule this country. That is why you can meet the man you love, and know your love for him at once." She smiled again. "Ah, my daughter, the powers we might have had, if the ways had not changed."

"Is it bad that things changed, Mother?"

"Who is to say?" Liliuokalani said. "Surely all things must change or they will wither and die. Still, to have been an Alii-Nui . . ." she let the sentence trail off. Then, after a moment's silence, she smiled. "But come, some things never change, such as the feast of the hula-hula luau. It has started, and we should be there."

Happily, Kaiulani followed her mother back to the luau. It had started in the late afternoon, and it continued, through the golden blaze of sunset, and into the soft blanket of night. Young pigs had been buried in firepits to be roasted, and as night fell, they were dug up and eaten. Copious quantities of a powerful Hawaiian liquor called *okoleaohao* were drunk, and music was made by tamping the ends of hollow bamboo reeds against the ground, and by blowing on flutes and pounding on drums. The night was full of laughter, singing, and bubbling conversation. Beautiful young girls, with skins of flashing gold, wearing flowered leis, danced passionate and erotic dances.

Kaiulani, moved by the excitement of the moment, joined in with the dancers, showing her ability in a wild, powerful display of energy, with graceful and fluid movements. There were cheers and laughter to greet her flying feet and fluid performance, and she kept up her dance until all others fell out in exhaustion and even the musicians begged her to stop.

Finally, full of food and more of the strong liquor than she was used to, Kaiulani bid farewell to the others and made her way into her mother's palace, and into her own bedroom to sleep.

"If I were an Alii-Nui now, a real Alii-Nui with magical powers," she said quietly, "I would snap my fingers and summon Admiral O'Lee here at this very moment." Then she smiled and lay on her bed. If she could not bring him here in fact, she could bring him in her imagination, and dreaming of him she drifted off to sleep.

5

A BIRD's SONG awakened Andrea. She lay in the bed for several moments after awakening, just enjoying the exquisite feel of silk sheets and pillowcases against her naked skin.

If anyone knew that Andrea slept without clothes they would have been shocked, but it was worth the risk, for it allowed her to exist on the edge of sensuality for hours on end. Even now, as she moved in the bed, the silk against her skin sensitized her, and made her tingle as if the hands of a most skilled lover were upon her.

A bright though not harsh morning sun streamed in through the casement windows, and Andrea got out of bed and walked toward the golden light on the far side of the room. She pushed the window open to better enjoy the song of a bird, then she looked out across the great expanse of lush, green lawn, toward the hedgerows, three hundred yards away. There was a sculptured fishpond halfway toward the hedgerows, and around the pond were bright splashes of colorful flowers. Beyond the hedgerows were the rolling acres of productive farmland; fields of sugarcane and pineapples, for this was Dole's plantation home.

Andrea was about to close the window, when she saw one of the gardeners coming across the lawn. She started to step back into the shadows of her room, then, on impulse, decided to stay right where she was, playing a delightful though wicked game with herself. She was still nude, and she was standing in an open window. If the gardener chanced to look up, he would see her.

Andrea stood there, feeling a sense of sexual excitement, heightened by the realization that she was playing a risky game. If the gardener looked up and saw her, she would, at the least, be embarrassed, and at the worst, be risking the danger of enflaming the simple man's ardor to the point that he might seek some opportunity to rape her.

And yet, the very thought of that only intensified her forbidden pleasure of the moment.

Andrea had long realized that she possessed an erotic nature. Her first sexual experience happened when she was only fourteen, and though it could have scarred the lives of most other girls, it was something which had made a profound impression upon Andrea, not because of trauma of the moment, but because of its unexpected pleasure.

Andrea's father was a San Francisco banker with a waterfront townhouse. The house featured all the latest luxuries, including indoor plumbing, and a large, porcelain bathtub.

As a little girl, Andrea had not particularly enjoyed taking baths, and she did so only at the insistence of the nurses who raised her. Her mother had died when Andrea was three, and Andrea knew nothing but a succession of nurses, some more pleasant than others, but all authoritarian.

By the time Andrea was fourteen, taking a bath was no longer a chore. Instead, it had become a pleasure, and she would luxuriate in the warm soapy water for several long moments, enjoying the caress of the bath against her budding young body. Then, one night, right after she had finished her bath, she stood in front of the mirror examining herself critically. Small mounds of flesh were forming into breasts and, her hips were rounding into the curve of young womanhood.

Andrea felt a sense of excitement over the blossoming, but confusion as well, and questions plagued her. She wondered what was the source of the strange, submerged hunger within her. When she looked at herself, or touched herself, it felt exciting, but not fulfilling. What more did she want?

Suddenly the door to the bathroom opened and Andrea gasped in surprise and looked around to see a man! The man was Mr. Crabtree, a railroad construction engineer, building a railroad in Arizona. He was here to borrow money from Andrea's father's bank, and Andrea's father had invited him to stay with them during the business negotiations.

Crabtree made no effort to leave right away. Instead, he just stared, amazed that the little girl who had eaten dinner with them was not so little after all. But it was more than amazement which held his gaze. His eyes had already become glazed with lust, and, though this was the first time any man had ever looked upon her in such a fashion, Andrea recognized it for what it was.

"I didn't know anyone was in here," Crabtree said. "Your father and the others are all gone. I thought I was alone in the whole house. I didn't realize you were here, too."

During Crabtree's feeble explanation, his eyes stayed riveted to Andrea's most intimate spot, and she felt a burning heat from it which, strangely, began to spread through her body.

"Mr. Crabtree," she said, forcing a calmness which she didn't feel. "In this house, when the bathroom door is closed, it is customary to knock."

"I'm sorry," Crabtree said. He made no effort to leave. In fact, he even came closer to her and Andrea could feel the wheezing of his breath. In the dim light, she could see the beads of perspiration on his upper lip.

"You can see that the bathroom is occupied, so would you please leave?" Andrea said indignantly. Was this buffoon going to stand there all night?

"I'm sorry. Am I disturbing you?" Crabtree asked inanely.

"Yes," Andrea said. "A girl likes a little privacy in her bath."

"Especially if that girl is a woman, eh?" Crabtree said, chuckling softly, as if he had made a joke. "You've been hiding all that under a little girl's clothes. Shame, shame on you."

"Mr. Crabtree, please," Andrea said, fear beginning to creep into her voice. "Go away now. What are you doing?"

"Oh, I'm just going to show you a few things," Crabtree said. "A few things you ought to know about—now that you're a woman."

"What, what are you talking about?" Andrea asked, but already the fear which had begun to creep in was fleeing, fleeing before the more powerful emotion of rising excitement. Her eyes were drawn like a magnet to the bulge in the front of Crabtree's pants, and that was her mistake, because Crabtree saw, and recognized the look in her face.

"Why, you little vixen you," he said, breathing heavily. "You're wanting this, aren't you? You're wanting this as much as I am."

"No," Andrea said. "No, that isn't true! Please, go away now and leave me alone." But Andrea's entreaties sounded weak, even to her own ears.

Crabtree's fingers released the buttons of his pants, then went inside. The palms of Andrea's hands grew sweaty, and she held her breath in fear and fascination, waiting . . .

"Look what I've got for you, little girl," Crabtree said.

He held it in his hand, a one-eyed serpent, fascinating and ugly, revolting, yet tempting, as tempting as had been the serpent which had seduced Eve.

"No," Andrea said quietly. "Please, Mr. Crabtree, don't do this."

Crabtree moved to her and put his hand on her shoulder to pull her toward him. Andrea was unable to control her shaking. It was caused by fear, yes, but there was something else, another emotion just as violent. It was excitement!

Andrea felt Crabtree against her then. His hands found her breasts, and the small mounds of flesh grew hot with a fire which flamed through her, and her barely controlled hungers caused her to react with a response which both thrilled and frightened her.

Crabtree was pushing against her, trying to gain entrance into her tight opening.

For a moment, Andrea's mind regained control of her passions and she held her legs together, refusing to help him. But even while fighting against him, the banked fires threatened to break out, and she felt the overwhelming need of her body beginning to overcome the dictates of her mind.

There was no skill or finesse on Crabtree's part. He was still clumsily trying to effect penetration when it happened. Suddenly and unexpectedly a quick, sharp, spasm of pleasure racked Andrea's body. It was small, and not accomplished under anything like the conditions of her fantasies, but it was the first, and therefore it was bewildering and satisfying, wonderful and frightening, all at the same time. She shuddered violently.

Then, the unexpected slam of the downstairs door reached them, and Crabtree, hearing it, jerked away from her, not knowing what had just happened to her. He turned to leave the bathroom, but before he left, he gave Andrea a warning.

"You'd best say nothing at all about this, girl, or I'll tell as how you were wanting it as bad as me." He smiled evilly. "And there's nothing any worse than a woman who likes it as much as you do."

Crabtree's warning had proved prophetic. Andrea didn't know whether she was cursed or blessed. When she was making love, she was able to experience the rapture of the gods, and surely, she thought, that was a feeling few other women were able to enjoy. And yet she paid for those moments of sublime pleasure, because she had to constantly fight against her sexual hungers. Then, when her affair with a vice-president in her father's bank became common knowledge, she was forced to leave San Francisco.

At first, Andrea had thought being forced to leave, and being faced with the knowledge that she would never again spend a languorous afternoon with Harold was a punishment beyond enduring. Then she met Lorrin O'Lee, and all thoughts of Harold were gone, for at his best, he had never made her feel the way Lorrin had. Until Lorrin, Andrea had never believed she could be satisfied with only one man. Since Lorrin, Andrea didn't think she could ever be satisfied again by anyone but the handsome sea captain.

The gardener walked into the tool house to put away his tools, and never once looked up at Andrea's bedroom. Andrea had gotten away with her little game one more time. She sighed, almost in disappointment, and pushed the windows closed, then went over to her closet to select the clothes she would wear today.

When Andrea went into the dining room for breakfast a short time later, she saw that V. V. Ashford was at the table with her Uncle Sanford. Both men greeted her as she came in, then returned to their own animated conversation. Andrea walked over to the buffet where scrambled eggs and sausages were keeping warm in a silver chafing dish. She put the food on her plate, selected a slice of cool, fresh pineapple, poured a cup of coffee, then sat down to eat.

"How much longer must we play games with Kalakaua?" Ashford was asking.

"You are an impatient man, Colonel," Dole replied. "Give Lorrin a chance to see what he can do."

"It isn't going to work," Ashford said. "I know it isn't going to work. Hell, Lorrin has no real desire to make it work, you know that. He's in it for what he can get, that's all."

"That's good enough for me," Sanford said. And when Ashford started to protest, he put his hand out to stop him. "There is no one here but us, V. V., you don't have to be coy. I know that the sugar tariff is more important to you than any degree of patriotism. If we become a territory of the United States, then the sugar tariff won't apply to us. Isn't that what motivates you?"

"It isn't just that," Ashford protested. "It's the entire Monarchy. Kalakaua doesn't seem to understand that unless the laws are made attractive to businessmen, he won't be able to raise the revenues he needs to run his government."

"That's exactly why I think our plan will work," Sanford said. "Once we get Kalakaua to understand our point of view, we will be able to live with the situation."

"But do we really want to live with it?" Ashford asked. "Wouldn't it be better to just come right out and say let's kill the son-of-a-bitch and take over the government?"

Sanford looked quickly at his niece, and then cut a warning glance toward Ashford. "No," he said. "I am not for that at all, and I would be opposed to harming Kalakaua, even if it does become necessary to overthrow his government. Don't you understand, V. V., that if we were to do such a thing, that is to say, assassinate Kalakaua, then the United States would never accept us as one of their own? We've got to give them the illusion that we are capable of solving our own problems, without having to resort to violence."

Ashford swallowed the last of his coffee. "I suppose you are right," he said. "But I just wish we could get word from Cox. I'd like to know how things are going over on Maui." He stood up, ready to leave. "I'll keep you informed of all the information I receive, and I'll send word the moment I hear from Cox."

"Thank you, V. V.," Sanford said.

Ashford saluted Andrea. "Miss Dole, good morning to you. I hope our frank conversation didn't disturb you."

"I didn't listen," Andrea said, pretenting innocence.

Sanford followed Ashford out to the front door, then he returned to the dining room and sat at the table across from his niece. "You do know what we are talking about, don't you dear?" he asked.

"I have an idea," Andrea said. "You want to get rid of Kalakaua, right?"

"Yes," Sanford said.

"Why don't you just vote him out?"

"It isn't as simple as all that. I suppose Hawaii is what might be called a representative Monarchy, in that Kalakaua was elected to the throne. But the choice was limited to a member of the royalty, so actually, the people had very little voice. Anyway, under the present system of government, it doesn't really make any difference who is the King. The end result is bad for the Americans who live here."

"Where does Lorrin fit in to all this?"

"Lorrin is my friend," Sanford said. "I've asked

him to try the approach he is trying now, though in fact I think he was against the proposal. But, as my friend, he agreed to go along with me."

"I'm glad he is your friend," Andrea said.

Sanford looked at his niece. "Oh? Why?"

"It makes it easier."

"It makes what easier?"

"My campaign to get him," Andrea said, matter-of-factly.

"Andrea, what are you talking about?" Sanford asked. He ran his hand through his hair. "Look, I've already told you he is my friend. Now I don't want you to get involved in anything which might cause him to get hurt."

"It is interesting, Uncle, that you are more concerned with the possibility of your friend getting hurt than you are with your own niece."

"Well, of course, I don't want you to be hurt either," Sanford said. "But somehow I have a feeling that it would be very difficult to hurt you."

"I'm not certain that I understand what you mean by that," Andrea said.

"I think that you do," Sanford replied. "After all, you are not exactly a woman without experience," he said, letting the last word slide out separate and apart from the rest of the sentence.

"I see," Andrea said. She cast her eyes down toward the plate and sat quietly for a moment. "I'm sorry, Uncle Sanford. I didn't realize I had brought such shame to you."

Sanford walked around the table quickly and reached down to put his arms around his niece. "I didn't mean it that way," he said. "It's just that you . . . you are so beautiful, my dear. You could surely have any man you wanted. If you choose to marry Lorrin, I just want you to be certain that you have made the right choice."

"Marry him? Who said anything about marrying him?" Andrea asked.

"But, I thought . . . I mean, didn't you say you were going to launch a campaign to *get* him?"

"Yes," Andrea said. "I want him, and I want him to want me. I want him to ache for me, to hunger so desperately that he can't look at another woman. But I don't want to marry him."

"Then what in thunder do you have in mind?" Sanford asked sharply.

Andrea smiled. "Oh, Uncle, you are a sweet man, but there is so much about life that you just don't understand." Then she softened the expression on her face. "But don't worry, Uncle, I'm thinking only of a harmless little exercise. I don't want to hurt Lorrin, and I don't want to be hurt. That's why I'm keeping everything so light."

"I don't know," Sanford said, rubbing his hand nervously through his hair again. "Sometimes I think I just don't understand the new generation." He shook his head in confusion, then, kissing her lightly on the forehead, left the room.

Andrea walked over to fill her cup with coffee for the second time. She smiled to herself. Perhaps her Uncle didn't understand what she had in mind, but when Lorrin was turned into a lovesick, helpless lump of clay, he would understand perfectly.

But could she really do that to Lorrin O'Lee? Could she really make him want her so badly that he would be totally subservient to her every whim? And, if she could, would he still be the same man who was now so effectively enflaming her ardor?

She didn't know whether she could do that to

him or not, but she was certainly going to try. And it was in the quest of her goals that she found satisfaction. She was facing a challenge which she couldn't afford to ignore.

LORRIN PUT the binoculars to his eyes and studied
the island, taking notice of the hills and vegetation.
Through his binoculars, he could see a waterfall,
and that meant fresh water. From experience, Lorrin knew that it also probably meant habitation.
There was no name for the island, or at least no
charted name. It appeared on his charts simply as
a pinpoint in the Pacific, one of the inkspots of
French Frigate Shoals.

"Have you ever been here before, Cap'n?" West
asked.

"It's hard for me to believe there are any inhabited islands I haven't visited," Lorrin said. He
brought the binoculars down and squinted across
the sun-bright sea. "But truth to tell, I can't recall
having been here before."

"Have you seen any sign of life?"

"No," Lorrin said. He put the binoculars back to

his eyes. "But there is fresh water here. I think we will probably find someone living here. Nearly all the islands with fresh water are inhabited."

"Wonder what this place is called?"

"I shall call it Kaiulani Island," Lorrin said, then he wondered why he said that. He hoped that he hadn't given away some of his secret feelings.

"That's a good idea," West said, smiling. "The little girl will like that, for sure. And bein' as she was a passenger on the first part of this voyage, why it only seems fittin'."

Good, Lorrin thought. West read no ulterior motive in Lorrin's choice of a name for the island. And the fact that he called Princess Kaiulani a "little girl" is surely evidence that he didn't perceive the Princess in the same light as Lorrin. Not as a little girl, but as an achingly desirable woman.

"Lieutenant Manakalano," Lorrin called to his Marine Lieutenant.

"Aye, sir," Manakalano said, reporting to Lorrin with a salute.

"Prepare a landing party and lower a boat away. We are going ashore."

"How many men should we take?" Manakalano asked.

"Four, in addition to the two of us."

"A total of six?" Manakalano asked in surprise. "We are going to attack the island with just six men?"

"Who said anything about attacking the island, Lieutenant?" Lorrin asked. "It is my intention merely to reconnoiter, and determine if the island is inhabited."

"Aye, sir," Manakalano said. He saluted sharply. "I shall prepare the landing party." He turned and moved quickly back to his marines, who were standing in a loose formation amidships.

"Now there's one ambitious fella," West said derisively.

Lorrin chuckled. "I guess we can be thankful about one thing," he said.

"What's that?"

"The little son-of-a-bitch ranks under us, and not over us."

"Cap'n, you just spoke the Gospel," West said, laughing in appreciation of the observation. "What was that?" he suddenly asked, and he reached for the binoculars which Lorrin handed to him without question.

"What is it?" Lorrin asked, as West studied the island with the glasses. "What do you see?"

"I caught something just out of the corner of my eyes," West said. He smiled. "Yes," he said, "there they are." He pointed, then handed the glasses back to Lorrin. "They are hiding in the bushes there, just beneath the point of that cliff. Do you see them?"

Lorrin pointed the glasses to the location indicated, and he saw about a dozen figures. They were all men, the youngest appearing to be not much over twelve, and the oldest one at a pretty advanced age. All were naked, and each was carrying a shield and spear.

"Well, well," Lorrin said. He chuckled. "I'll bet their morning hunting trip was rudely interrupted when they looked out here and saw us."

Suddenly there was the roar of a cannon, and Lorrin saw, flashing swiftly against the white cloudbank, a projectile, speeding toward the island, in the direction of the natives. Less than a second later, an erupting rose of flame and a puff of smoke appeared on the beach, and the dull thump of the beach explosion rolled back across the water to them.

"My God!" Lorrin shouted. "What the hell happened?" He looked through the glasses at the natives, and saw them running away. He breathed a sigh of relief as he saw that none of them appeared to be hurt.

A second cannon roared, and again Lorrin saw the wink of the shell as it raced toward the island.

"Cease fire!" Lorrin shouted, just as the second shell exploded on the island. The second shell exploded in the tree tops, and Lorrin could see palm fronds spinning crazily as they fluttered to the ground.

Lorrin ran from the quarterdeck to the gun captain. "What the hell are you doing?" he shouted. "Why are you firing on them?"

"The gun captain is firing because I ordered him to do so, Admiral," Manakalano said.

"What?" Lorrin asked, turning around to face the young Hawaiian Lieutenant. "Why would you give such orders? I gave you no such authorization!"

"I have the King's authorization, Admiral," Manakalano said smugly.

"The King's authorization? What are you talking about?"

"King Kalakaua issued specific orders, Admiral," Manakalano said. "If we find an inhabited island, we are to provide a demonstration of our strength before we contact the natives."

"Well, did he tell you you had to blow them all to hell?" Lorrin asked angrily.

"No, sir. He merely said I should provide a demonstration of our strength."

Lorrin ran his hand through his hair and sighed. "I suggest to you, you pompous young ass, that the truest demonstration of our strength would be to land a party of men, showing that we have absolutely no fear of them. By firing the guns, you show nothing but cowardice and weakness. Cowardice, because you are afraid to face them, and weakness because, Lieutenant, if we ever encountered a *real* military threat, they would *laugh* at our armament." Lorrin turned to the gun captain. "If you ever fire so much as one gun without first receiving my permission, so help me, I'll stuff you down the barrel of the biggest piece we have and shoot you out to sea. Do you understand that, mister?"

"Aye, sir," the gun captain said in a frightened voice.

"And you," Lorrin said, looking at the Lieutenant. "Prepare the party for landing."

"Aye, sir," Manakalano said. "You'll be wanting more men now?"

"More? No, I want the same size party I requested in the first place. Unarmed."

"Unarmed? But Admiral, surely now, you—"

"Why do you find it necessary to question every order I give you?" Lorrin said. "Now you have that landing party ready in three minutes, mister, or you'll be going ashore as a common seaman, I promise you that."

"Aye, sir," Manakalano said, sullenly. "Four men, unarmed. I'll make ready to go ashore."

Lorrin watched Manakalano select his men, then he walked back over to lean against the rigging and study the lush shoreline of the island. West was looking toward the shore through the binoculars.

"See anything?"

"No, sir," West said. "They've all skedaddled."

"I can't say as I blame them," Lorrin said.

West lowered his glasses and looked around to make certain no one else could overhear him. "Cap'n, are you sure it's wise to go ashore unarmed?"

"I'm going to try and convince them that we fired the guns as a salute," Lorrin said.

"With live ammunition?"

"They appear to be a pretty primitive race of people," Lorrin said. "Maybe they won't realize that we were firing at them."

"How are you going to talk to them?"

"Well, unless they are an exceptionally unusual group of people, they'll speak a Maylayo-Polynesian dialect of some form. All the people on these islands speak a common language; that's why many believe they all started in the same place at one time or another. I should be able to talk to them."

"Admiral O'Lee, the landing party is ready, sir," Manakalano called.

"Is the boat over?"

"Aye, sir."

"Then let's go."

Lorrin, Manakalano, and the others of the landing party climbed over the side, and loaded into the launch. The lugsail was set, and the launch pulled away from the *Kahili Pahoa*, and headed for the island. It didn't skim across the breakers with the surf-boarding finesse of an island outrigger, but rather, plugged through with the dogged determination of a solidly built boat. Finally, it moved through the final bursting wave, then coasted into shallow water. One of the men of the party jumped out, and pulled the boat on to shore.

Lorrin cupped his hands to his mouth, and shouted into the trees.

"*Aloha, aikane.*"

There was no answer to his simple call of, "Hello friend," so he tried again.

"*Aloha! Nei malihini aikane!*" he yelled. "I am a stranger, but I am a friend."

"*Aikane aole hana pu nui!*" a voice floated back from the tree line. "A friend would not use a big weapon."

Lorrin smiled broadly. So, they *did* speak the Maylayo-Polynesian language, though it was in a dialect which was difficult to understand.

"I am sorry," he replied in their language, speaking slowly and distinctly, so they could understand him. "The *pu nui* was fired as a salute, to say *aloha*. It is meant to honor the people of this island." He held his arms up in the air. "Look, we have no weapons. We come as friends."

The group of natives came out of the treeline then, moving slowly toward them, with two or three of the men holding their spears over their heads, the points aimed menacingly at Lorrin and the others. The points of the spears were made from coral and shell, Lorrin noticed. That meant that they probably had no metals on the island, nor had they come into contact with metals. They were a totally isolated people.

"Did you come from the moon?" the oldest of the natives asked. "We have a *kapu mo'olelo*, a holy history, which tells of gods coming from the

moon." The old man reached out slowly and
touched Lorrin's blond hair, then he dropped to
his knees. "Aiyee, the story has come true. You
wear the moon on your head."

"They think you are a god," Manakalano said in
English. "They are an ignorant people," he added,
his face twisted in contempt for the natives.

"There was a time when your ancestors thought
Captain Cook was a god," Lorrin reminded Manakalano.

"As I recall, my ancestors killed Captain Cook,"
Manakalano said hotly.

"Yes, they did at that," Lorrin said. He smiled.
"I guess that means we had better watch our step,
hadn't we?"

"Are all of you gods to speak in a tongue I cannot
understand?" the old native, who was the spokes-
man of the group, asked.

"We are not gods," Lorrin said. "We are friends,
and children of King Kalakaua, who is the great
ruler over all the islands of the sea." Lorrin pointed
to the *Kahili Pahoa*. "King Kalakaua has many such
great ships, and all the ships have big thunder
weapons, *pu nui*, which are very powerful. He
uses his power to help his friends and children."

"How can we become friends and children of
this mighty King?" the native asked.

"It's very easy," Lorrin said. "You just agree to
become a part of the Empire. Would you like
that?"

The old man smiled. "Yes, we would like that.
But such a thing deserves a celebration, does it
not? Come to the village, we will eat and celebrate."

"I will come to the village tonight," Lorrin said.

"First, I must return to the ship, for there I have many presents which the King has asked me to give to his children."

"You have presents for us?"

"Yes," Lorrin said. "I have many wonderful presents, and I shall bring them with me when I return."

"Then we shall have presents for the King as well," the old man said.

When Lorrin returned to the island that evening, he carried a chest of presents with him. The chest contained a few worthwhile items, a few axes, a couple of knives, and a flint-lock lighter, but, in the main, it was composed of hundreds of brightly colored glass beads and fake jewels. And yet it was the jewels which attracted the most attention, and the natives adorned themselves happily with the baubles at the evening feast.

The old man called himself Teoko, and the villagers referred to themselves as the Boka People. There was only one village on the island, and it consisted of less than three hundred people. From Teoko, Lorrin learned that the villagers were completely ignorant of the outside world, and often held long discussions where they argued the possibility that there might be another island somewhere in the vast sea, and on that island, there might be people.

"It is said that the Boka People came here from another island one hundred fathers before now," Teoko explained, and Lorrin knew that he meant generations.

"There are many islands such as this island," Lorrin said. "And beyond the islands, there are continents, which are like islands, but they are as big as the sea."

"And there are people on these huge islands?"

"Many, many people," Lorrin said. "In this world there are more people than there are stars in the sky."

"How can there be so many people?" Teoko asked, looking at the group of sailors and Marines who had come ashore for the feasting. Many had paired off with nude, lithesome young native girls. "There are no *wahines* among you."

Lorrin smiled. "We have many women," he said. "We did not bring them on our ship."

"Do you find our *wahine maika'i?*"

"I find your women very beautiful," Lorrin said, and indeed, there was a degree of innocence to their nude loveliness which reminded him of Kaiulani.

"In your society, does the kanaka and wahine mate?"

"Of course," Lorrin replied.

"Does your society find mating pleasurable?"

"Very pleasurable," Lorrin said with a smile.

Teoko returned Lorrin's smile. "It is good that you find mating pleasurable," he pointed to the young girls who were moving around the food-laden cloth, carrying gourds of liquor and food to the men. The girls were all nude, and their skin shone like gold in the flickering flames of the kukui nut lamps.

"Do you find one more beautiful than the others?"

"I find them all beautiful," Lorrin said diplomatically.

Teoko looked at Lorrin with an expression of surprise on his face. "You mean to mate with them *all*? Truly your society is made of strong men!"

Lorrin smiled. "No," he said. "I didn't mean that. I meant that they are all so beautiful that it is difficult to determine who is the most lovely."

"But you can find one you like?"

A young girl came toward Lorrin and Teoko and poured more liquor into their drinking cups from the gourd she carried. She smiled at Lorrin, and in the exotic atmosphere of the moment, the effect of the liquor, the smell of the flowers, the sight of so many beautiful girls, all of whom were nude, he saw, or else he imagined he saw, a striking resemblance between this young girl and Kaiulani.

Teoko was watching Lorrin's reaction as the girl served him.

"You like Mira, do you not? She is most beautiful. She is the daughter of my daughter. Mira, you are honored," Teoko said. "Take O'Lee to my house." Teoko said the name O'Lee as if it were one word, with the accent evenly distributed, so that it came out sounding strangely Polynesian.

"I am most pleased," Mira said, smiling and reaching for Lorrin.

"Teoko, you don't understand," Lorrin said. "I didn't . . ."

"You do not find me pleasing?" Mira asked with an expression of hurt on her face.

"I find you beautiful," Lorrin said.

"Then we shall mate!" Mira said happily.

Lorrin started to protest again, but realized that his protest would be misunderstood, so he sighed and acquiesced. Finally, he laughed weakly. "Alright," he said. "We will mate." And even as he said the words, he knew that it was more than social decorum which caused him to agree. He wanted this girl, this island surrogate for Kaiulani, and he wanted her very much.

Mira led Lorrin away from the others, toward a small, thatched hut on the edge of the village.

"No," Lorrin said, pulling on her hand and stopping her.

Mira looked at him with questioning eyes.

"Not in your grandfather's house. Let us find some other place. Do you know another place we could go?"

Mira smiled. "Yes," she said. "Come with me."

The Boka village had been built alongside a stream, and Lorrin and Mira picked their way across the stream on a bed of rocks, then they started up a hill on the other side. They reached the top of the hill after a few minutes climbing, and from up here Lorrin could look down one side and see the flickering flames of the luau fires of the village, while looking down the other side, he could see the white sands of the beach, the flickering feathers of foam of the rolling breakers, and the dimly winking lights of the *Kahili Pahoa* at anchor. From here also he could hear the relentless sound of the booming surf.

"I like this place," Mira said.

Lorrin had to agree with her. Though the bright colors of the flowers were dimmed by the darkness, the diamond-brilliance of the stars, the shimmering iridescence of the sea in the distance, the moon-silvered jungle and beach were pure enchantment. The wind blowing through the reed grass, the rattle of palm leaves, the rhythm of the surf, and the songs of the nightbirds all combined to serenade them, while the fragrance of hundreds of unseen flowers perfumed the night air.

"We will mate here," Mira said softly, and she pulled Lorrin down to a soft mat of leaves which would be their bed. There she undressed him, so that he, like Mira, was nude, and then, naked body against naked body, they kissed.

Lorrin lay against Mira's body, feeling the touch of flesh which was so much like that of Kaiulana. He closed his eyes and imagined that this girl was Kaiulani, but he hated himself for doing it.

As they lay facing each other, their body heat transferred from one to the other until they were on fire with desire for each other. Mira took Lorrin's hands and moved them over her own body, along the smooth curve of her hips, and then up across her breasts. She rubbed the palm of his hand across her nipples, which felt so small and hard after the soft feel of her belly, hips, and thighs. As Lorrin's fingers explored her secret place, gently probing and stroking, Mira began whimpering with barely controlled delight, arching her body to present it to him for his supplication.

Lorrin could smell the sea and the flowers, and her musk and his. Then, with a muffled cry of want, Mira lay back and pulled Lorrin down on her.

They began making love then, in a strong, ever-quickening rhythm. It was very physical and immensely satisfying, but it was much more than that. These were two creatures from totally alien cultures, cultures which didn't even know of the existence of each other, but they developed a passion which was perfectly orchestrated to move in harmony, so that there was a tremendous sense of mutual need and longing for fulfillment.

As they clung together, their bodies moving as one in the urgent rhythm that would bring them to the desired climax, they could hear the surf thundering in the distance, and feel the gentle breeze playing across their naked bodies. And then they were no longer aware of anything but their own shared rapture.

7

A HIRED HACK pulled to a stop in front of the Royal Palace, and the driver turned toward his lone passenger. "This is where you said you wanted to go," he said.

"Drive around to the back," the passenger ordered. The passenger was wearing a hat with the brim turned down, and a jacket with the collar turned up. He sat back in his seat, shielded by the landau, so that those who walked by on the street would have little chance to see him, and less chance of recognizing him.

"The only conveyances that use the rear entrance and alleyways are the produce wagons and delivery carts," the driver protested. "Visitors are expected to use the front."

"I said drive around to the back," the passenger said again.

The driver sighed. "Alright, if you say so." He

turned around and clucked at his horse, and the animal, a large bay decorated with feathers of yellow and red, pulled at the traces and the hack moved off the paved street, and onto a small, dirt alley.

The passenger, making certain that he couldn't be seen, studied the grounds of Iolani Palace as the hack circled the capitol building.

"Here you are, sir," the driver said. "The back entrance."

"Thanks," the passenger replied. He stepped out of the carriage, paid his fare, then proceeded along a winding, overgrown path, away from the most traveled areas, and shielded from view by trees and shrubbery. He saw a secluded door, the very existence of which was unknown by most of the citizens of Honolulu.

With no hesitation whatever, he walked right up to it and knocked. The door opened and a servant granted him entrance.

"I must see the King at once," the visitor said, handing a small yellow token to the servant.

The servant looked at the token, then silently beckoned him in, indicating that he should wait in a small anteroom. The mysterious visitor went into the room and sat in a chair to await the King.

King Kalakaua came into the sitting room a few moments later, and the mysterious visitor stood in respect.

"Well, Robert Cox, advisor to my dear sister," Kalakaua said. "I interrupted affairs of state to attend to your call." He handed the yellow token back to Cox, who took it and returned it to his billfold.

"I am honored that you would see me, Your Highness," Cox said.

Kalakaua smiled broadly. "You are a member of the Committee of Five. I vowed to all of you that I would always honor the call of the yellow token. What do you have for me?"

"This, Your Highness," Cox said. He took a letter from his pocket and handed it to the King. "It is from Colonel V. V. Ashford, of the Honolulu Rifles. You may be interested in reading it."

"What does it say?" Kalakaua asked.

"Colonel Ashford has asked that I contact American Members of the Militia in Lahaina, and feel them out for a possible revolution."

"I see," Kalakaua said, running his hand through his coal black hair.

"He has also asked me to see if Liliuokalani would be interested in assuming a role in any new government he might set up."

"And what did my dear sister say to such an inquiry?" Kalakaua asked.

Cox smiled. "I have not yet contacted her. I thought I would contact you first and see what your wishes are."

Kalakaua smiled and put his hand on Cox's shoulder. "You are a good and trusted friend," he said. "I am glad it is your Hawaiian blood which rules your heart." He rubbed his chin and looked at the letter, studying it for a long moment. "How was this letter delivered?"

"Ah, there is the thing, Your Highness," Cox said, holding his finger up as if making a point. "The letter was delivered personally by none other than Admiral O'Lee, of your Navy."

"Admiral O'Lee is also a part of this conspiracy?"

"Yes, Your Highness. What will you do? Remove him from his position?"

"No," Kalakaua said. He smiled. "No, it may serve my purpose to allow him to continue, without his knowledge that I am aware of his treason. Tell me, Mr. Cox, as you are the advisor to my sister, how do you think she will react to this letter?"

"Alas, Your Highness, it is sad to say that she will be taken in by it."

"Liliuokalani will accept their treason?"

"Yes," Cox said. "Forgive me for bringing unpleasant news, but I must report that never in her conversations of you does your sister speak well. She will willingly play a role in your betrayal."

"And Princess Kaiulani? She will do so as well?"

Cox smiled. "Kaiulani knows no politics," he said. "She does little but pine after Admiral O'Lee."

"What? Kaiulani is taken with O'Lee?"

"Yes. Every day she walks out on the cliffs to look out over the sea in search of O'Lee's sails."

Kalakaua smiled. "Perhaps there is a way I can use that," he said. "Yes, I know what I will do. I will order that O'Lee return for Princess Kaiulani. He will return for her and take her with him on his journey to the outer islands."

"Why would you do that?"

Kalakaua smiled again. "I have absolute trust in Lieutenant Manakalano, the commander of the Marines on board the *Kahili Pahoa*. I will send him a message that Kaiulani is to be his hostage, though neither Kaiulani nor O'Lee will realize that. With Kaiulani under my control, I shall have control over my dear sister. Should she decide to start anything, I can bring it to a quick halt, by threatening to kill Kaiulani."

"King Kalakaua, would you really kill your own niece?" Cox asked in surprise.

"Of course," King Kalakaua said with a shrug. "If I thought such an action was necessary to preserve the stability of my government."

"Under what ruse will you get Kaiulani aboard?" Cox asked.

"She will be an ambassador," Kalakaua said. "Yes, that's it. She will be my good-will ambassador. Perhaps her presence will be as effective in bringing new islands into the Greater Polynesian Empire as are O'Lee's cannons."

"That is a brilliant plan, Your Majesty," Cox agreed. He took the letter back from the King. "I will return to Maui with the next ship, and await further development."

"I will send the order to have Kaiulani appointed as an Ambassador."

"Your Majesty," Cox said, getting an idea and holding his finger up again. "Suppose you let me handle that? I will speak to Liliuokalani, and I will convince her that it would be to her interest to have her daughter travel with Admiral O'Lee. That way, she won't suspect anything."

Kalakaua looked at Cox for a moment, then as he figured out what Cox was saying, he laughed. "Yes," he said. "Yes, that would be a fine, fine plan. Very well, this you shall do, Robert Cox. I will wait in my Palace until I receive word from her, asking me to appoint my lovely niece as good-will ambassador. I will pretend that I do not think this is such a good idea, but I will be persuaded." He laughed again. "Your ways are devious, Robert Cox. You are the closest advisor to my sister, and yet you are a member of the Committee of Five. It makes one wonder, sometimes, whose side you are really on."

"You need never trouble yourself about such wonders, Your Majesty," Cox said easily. "I am on your side."

Kalakaua laughed again. "To be sure, Robert Cox, to be sure," he said.

V. V. Ashford came into the living room to greet his guest, and when he saw Robert Cox he smiled and extended his hand. "Mr. Cox, how good to see you," he said. He indicated a chair. "Sit down, sir. Please, sit down. Would you like a whiskey?"

"Yes," Cox answered. "I think I would, if you don't mind."

Ashford clapped his hands, and a servant girl glided in silently on bare feet.

"Two whiskeys, please," Ashford ordered, and the girl bowed, then turned and left.

"Chinese," Ashford said, after the girl was gone. "I trust them a hell of a lot more than I trust the *kama 'ainas*, the native Hawaiians."

"I don't blame you," Cox said. "There is so much intrigue going on that there are few people you can trust today, and fewer Hawaiians."

"My sentiments exactly," Ashford said. He rubbed his hands together in anticipation. "Speaking of sentiments, what are the sentiments of the Americans on Maui? Are they ready to stand with us, if we move on the King?"

"Yes," Cox said. "I have spoken to every one of them, and they all stand by, waiting to join with any army which would bring down the Royal Government."

"Bring down the Royal Government?" Ashford said. "No, I mean Kalakaua."

"Why not the entire Royal Government?" Cox asked. "Why replace a king with a queen? Why not establish a republic?"

"Because Dole would never go along with anything as drastic as a complete overthrow of the system."

"Then we shan't tell Dole," Cox said.

"What do you mean? Of course we will tell Dole. He is necessary to the success of anything we do."

"You may have regarded him as necessary at one time," Cox said. "But such is no longer the case. Not as long as you have me working with you. Together, Colonel Ashford, you and I can establish a new republic!"

"Yes," Ashford said, getting caught up now in the enthusiasm of the moment. "Yes, perhaps you are right."

The servant brought the whiskey then, and Ashford took both glasses from the tray and handed one to Cox. "I propose a toast," he said, holding forth the glass. "To the Republic of Hawaii."

"And to the men who will lead it," Cox replied. He smiled and took a drink, then holding his finger aloft in the gesture common to him, he went on. "I would warn you, Colonel, to say nothing to Dole about this. I fear he would be against it and would work to prevent it."

"Perhaps you are right," Ashford said. "And you were right to say nothing to Liliuokalani as well. But tell me, where will she stand? Will she team with her brother and thus prevent our coup?"

"No," Cox replied. "She is so busy fighting against her brother that she could never ally herself with him. We shall have no difficulty along those lines, Colonel, believe me," he said, with the glint of ambition in his eyes."

The entire ship's company was above. Some were on the deck, leaning against the rail, some were aloft, hanging in the rigging from the spars which were now without sail. The *Kahili Pahoa* was at anchor a hundred yards or so off shore, riding a gentle swell just seaward of the crashing breakers.

The beach was of black sand, dotted here and there with driftwood which had been twisted by the sea and bleached white by the sun. Just beyond the beach, palms waved gently in the wind. A dense jungle was just beyond the palms, and beyond the jungle, the black cones of volcanoes.

The ship's launch was nearly to the breakers now, and it was the launch which held the attention of those on board, for this was the first contact being made with yet another island.

Mr. West was commander of the shore party, while Lorrin O'Lee and Lt. Manakalano remained on board. As before, the shore party was unarmed.

"I still think this is a foolish way to make a show of strength," Manakalano said.

"It is a matter of little importance that you think so," Lorrin said, all the while looking through his binoculars. "The point is, *I* think it is the proper way to approach them, and that is all that matters."

Lorrin had seen a party of men coming through the jungle, and he was keeping a wary eye on them. He had, as a precaution, ordered the guns loaded and run out, but he had no intention to use them.

The boat ploughed through the final breakers and the lugsail was dropped, then West and the others leaped out and towed the boat up onto the shore. By following the activity through his binoculars, Lorrin could tell that Mr. West had seen the natives as well, for West waved in their direction, and called to them, though of course there was no sound from this far out. West and the others held their arms over their head, to indicate that they were without weapons.

This was the critical moment, and Lorrin stared hard at the natives. Then he saw them stacking their spears and war clubs as they began to come out of the bush, and he smiled because it appeared as if contact had been established with one more group. He lowered his glasses and smiled. Yes, this was the best way to approach them.

"West is surrendering to them, the coward!" Manakalano suddenly called out. "Look, he has his hands up! Fire! Open fire!"

"What the hell are you talking about, he hasn't—"

Suddenly Lorrin's response to Manakalano's outburst was interrupted by the explosion of cannon fire, as the guns of the *Kahili Pahoa* opened up.

"My God, what are you doing?" Lorrin yelled. The ship was rocked by the recoil of six guns firing at one time, and Lorrin looked back to see the rounds exploding in the tree line. One of the natives fell, and the others started back toward their cache of weapons.

"West, get the hell out of there! Get out of there!" Lorrin shouted, waving at his friend frantically, though he knew that West could neither see or hear him.

West didn't need Lorrin's shouted warning. He had already perceived the danger and was trying to herd his men onto the boat.

The natives reached their weapons, then started toward the landing party. One of them threw a spear and a sailor went sprawling in the surf with the shaft sticking from his back. Another went down under a war club. Another was captured by two of the natives and dragged away. That was when West, who had already reached the relative safety of the boat, climbed out and went back. He managed to free the hapless sailor, but he caught a spear in his back as he did so. With apparent disregard for his wound, West fought, barehanded, with the natives, providing time for his men to make it to the boat, and start back toward the ship.

Lorrin watched his friend with a sinking heart. West fought valiantly, buying precious time for his men, until finally, with no less than three spears sticking out of his body, he went down. The natives, unable to reach the retreating seamen now, took their frustrations out on West, swarming around his body, kicking and slashing at him, until finally, with a grotesque heave of his stomach, Lorrin saw that one of the round objects the natives were kicking through the black sand was West's severed head.

"Manakalano, you ignorant fool!" Lorrin swore. "Do you realize what you have done?"

"What *I* did? Admiral, I think you are mistaken," Manakalano said. "You are the one who sent the landing party ashore without weapons. You are the one who got those men killed."

"Mr. West had established peaceful contact with

the natives," Lorrin said. "It was only your stupidity that turned success into tragedy."

"I don't consider it that way, sir."

"*You* don't consider? Lieutenant, it isn't your place to consider," Lorrin said. "As of this moment, you are under arrest without restraint." Lorrin turned toward the shore and saw the boat returning to the ship. Two of the party were injured, one was holding a bleeding head, the other suffered a severe cut on the shoulder.

"Request permission to help with the boarding of the landing party?" Manakalano asked.

"Of course you can help," Lorrin replied. "Why would you even think you have to ask?"

"Since you have placed me under arrest," Manakalano said. "I thought it ill-advised of me to act independent of your orders at this point."

"That's a good thought," Lorrin said. "It is too bad you didn't have it earlier."

"Aye, aye, sir," Manakalano said. He walked over to the rail and began helping the returning seamen aboard the ship.

"Beggin' your pardon, sir," one of the seamen asked. "But why did you shoot? They was actin' real friendly until the big guns opened up." The seaman who asked the question was holding a wadded up shirt against the wound of the one with the shoulder injury.

"I'm sorry," Lorrin said. He glared at Manakalano. "There seems to have been a breakdown in communication."

The men were loaded aboard, and the boat was placed on the winch, preparatory to being lifted out of the water.

"Belay that," Lorrin said, holding his hand out. "I'll be needing that to go back ashore."

"Cap'n, *you're* goin' ashore?" one of the men of the boarding party asked.

"Yes," Lorrin said. He looked through his binoculars at the natives on the shore. They had taken West's head and placed it on a pike, and were now waving it defiantly toward the ship. "I don't intend to leave the bodies of my men there for those savages to use as play things," he said. "Gun captain?"

"Aye, sir."

"Are the guns still laid in from the first volley?"

"Aye, sir," the gun captain answered.

"Drop one hundred yards and fire again."

"Aye, aye, sir!" the gun captain said, and the men on the ship cheered, then rushed to the rail to watch.

"Gun number one ready to fire, sir," the first gun crew chief called.

"Gun number two ready to fire, sir."

One by one, the crew chiefs announced their weapons as ready until six crews had reported. "Ready to fire, sir," the gun captain announced to Manakalano.

"Lieutenant Manakalano isn't giving you your orders, I am," Lorrin said quietly. He was still looking through the glasses toward the shoreline. "You boys are in for a little surprise," he said under his breath, meaning the remark for the natives ashore.

"Excuse me sir," the gun captain said. "The guns are ready to fire."

"Fire," Lorrin said quietly.

The gun captain turned and faced the guns. All

gun crews were standing by, looking anxiously toward him. The gunner of each gun was holding the lanyard, waiting for the order. The gun captain cupped his hands to his mouth.

"Fire!" he called.

The guns roared as one, and ship rocked with the recoil. Smoke and shock waves rolled across the water, and six projectiles screamed toward the beach. They exploded on the beach itself, and two of them were exactly on target, bursting in the middle of the dancing, celebrating warriors. Six of the natives went down, and the remainder turned and ran from the beach, disappearing into the trees. The men on board the *Kahili Pahoa* let out a cheer.

"I need eight volunteers for a landing party," Lorrin shouted.

Lorrin was besieged with volunteers, and he was gratified by their willingness to go ashore, even though this had proven to be a dangerous island. One of the volunteers was Lieutenant Manakalano.

"You are under arrest," Lorrin reminded him.

"But by your own orders, sir, it is arrest without restraint," Manakalano said. "I'll go as one of the able-bodied seamen if need be."

Lorrin cupped his chin with his hand and studied the face of the eager young Hawaiian. "No," he finally said. "No, that won't be necessary. You may lead the party, Lieutenant."

Manakalano's face was expressionless. "May I select the members of my landing party, sir?"

"Yes," Lorrin said. Manakalano turned to pick his volunteers, and Lorrin called to him. "Lieutenant?"

"Yes, sir."

Lorrin sighed. "You may consider the arrest terminated."

"Thank you, sir," Manakalano said.

Lorrin watched as Manakalano selected his volunteers, Marines all, and all Hawaiian. Then, as the men climbed over the side to get into the boat, he turned and went below decks to see to the condition of the two wounded men who were returned.

Lorrin was writing in the ship's log when Manakalano knocked on the door some time later. Lorrin looked up.

"Did you have any trouble?"

"No, sir," Manakalano said. "And I doubt if we will ever have trouble with any of these people again."

"What do you mean?"

"Nothing, sir," Manakalano said. "Except that we gave them a most adequate demonstration of our strength."

"At a fearsome cost, Lieutenant. At a fearsome cost," Lorrin said. He closed the log and stood up. "I'd better appoint a new First Mate," he said. "The wind is freshening. We should weigh anchor and get underway."

"The bodies are on deck, Admiral," Manakalano said. "There's little left of Mr. West."

"I know, I know," Lorrin said. He started up the ladderway and when he reached the deck he saw several men standing around, looking down at what appeared to be a couple of sea bags. He took a deep breath before he walked over, but even so, seeing what was left of his friend, the armless, legless, disemboweled torso, and the head, lying against the rail scupper like a rotting melon, caused an instant revulsion in his stomach, and he had to fight hard to keep from throwing up.

"Mr. Adams," he said.

"Aye, aye, Admiral?" An older, gray-haired man said.

"Mr. Adams, you are the new First Mate. Have the sail maker prepare burial shrouds, then make ready in all respects to get underway."

"Aye, aye, sir," Adams said.

Lorrin closed his eyes tightly for a moment, then walked away from the macabre scene and stood on the opposite side of the ship, gripping the rail with his hands, staring out to sea. He stood there for a long moment, until he heard the activity of the men going aloft, and he knew the sails were being set. The movement of familiar things around him helped calm him somewhat, and after several deep breaths, he was ready to play the cards life had dealt him.

"Goodbye, Mr. West, my friend," he said quietly. "May there be no stinking smudgepots on the sea you are sailing now." And Lorrin smiled as he thought of his friend's hatred for coal-burning ships . . . "stinking smudgepots," West had called them.

"Course, sir?" Adams called.

"East, Southeast," Lorrin said. "We're returning to Honolulu."

8

HONOLULU HAD NOT always been the capitol of the
Kingdom of Hawaii. For some time, the capitol
was in Lahaina. It was moved to Honolulu, because Honolulu was the most logical place for it to
be, for Honolulu was home to nearly fifty per cent
of all Hawaiians, and it had long been an economic
center.

Honolulu is the Hawaiian word for sheltered
bay. It was already being used as such by the Hawaiian seamen when Captain William Brown of
England sailed into the harbor to discover a thriv-
ing fishing village in 1794. Nearly one hundred
years later, it had become the crossroads of the
Pacific, and from all nations, ships which were traversing the Pacific stopped in Honolulu.

Lahaina had always been cool toward the sailors,
but Honolulu welcomed them with open arms, for
with the flags of several nations in the harbor,

Honolulu felt itself truly a part of the world community. The *Kahili Pahoa*, as the flagship of the Hawaiian Navy, was visible evidence of the Hawaiian's proud entry into the world community.

King Kalakaua ordered a day long celebration to be held shortly after the *Kahili Pahoa* returned. The celebration would consist of a parade through the streets of the city, complete with flower-bedecked carts and carriages, and it would end before a reviewing stand which was built in front of Iolani Palace. There several honors were to be bestowed, and Lorrin, Lieutenant Manakalano, Sanford Dole, Walter Wilson, and others were on the stand. One of the reviewers on the stand was Princess Kaiulani. It was only because Kaiulani was a part of the reviewing party that Lorrin O'Lee agreed to sit there.

Several times, Lorrin thought he caught Kaiulani looking at him, but when he looked toward her, she would always look away, thus he could never be certain. The game did help to occupy his time, though, and with that diversion, he was able to sit through the entire parade. The last band and the last flower decorated unit, which he heard someone call a "float," passed by, and the King got up to make a speech to those who were assembled around the reviewing stand.

"My loyal subjects and friends," Kalakaua said, holding his hands out in a grand gesture toward them. "This is indeed a wonderful day in the life of our nation. On this day, we celebrate the fact that Hawaii has become one of the major countries of the world, and, on this day, we shall welcome a new island into the Greater Polynesian Empire."

The crowd applauded, and Kalakaua beamed.

Then he turned and looked toward Lorrin and Lieutenant Manakalano.

"I have two medals to award," he said. "Medals which I designed myself, and which are tokens of love and esteem from our Empire, to two deserving subjects. The first medal is the Award of Merit, which I am giving to Admiral O'Lee, such award given because Admiral O'Lee discovered the new island we are annexing today. Admiral O'Lee?"

Lorrin was embarrassed to walk across the platform and receive what he considered to be a perfectly worthless and totally undeserved award, but he was more embarrassed to remain in his seat. So, as quickly as possible, he walked across, received the medal, mumbled a thanks as the King pinned it on his tunic, then returned to his seat, amidst a smattering of applause.

"The next medal is the highest award which can be given by our government," Kalakaua said. "I had it struck especially for a brave warrior, who, along with the medal, is receiving a promotion to the rank of General. Our own brave, Manakalano. General Manakalano, you have received the King's Cross for bravery, for your part in the Battle of Bloody Island."

Manakalano smiled broadly and walked across with quick, proud steps to receive his medal. Lorrin looked on the scene first in shock, and then in anger. He had known nothing about this, and now he was discovering that the very thing which he intended to use to persuade Kalakaua to remove Manakalano from his ship, was being used instead, to justify Manakalano's promotion and medal. He wanted to shout out in protest, but Dole caught his attention, and with a warning glance, told him to say nothing. Dole knew the story, for Lorrin had gone to visit him the moment the ship returned. Lorrin had hoped Dole would see thereby that the noble naval experiment simply wasn't working.

But it was working, at least in so far as to feed Kalakaua's ego, and that was exactly what Dole had intended in the first place.

Lorrin, with the greatest of effort, managed to hold his tongue, and he listened to the King extol Manakalano's virtues as the medal was presented. Finally, Manakalano returned to his seat, and he looked over at Lorrin.

"Now, Admiral," he hissed. "Our ranks are equal, and *I* will make all the military decisions. You will merely provide me with transportation."

"You can swim to the next island as far as I'm concerned," Lorrin whispered back.

"And now," Kalakaua said, looking back over his audience. "I have, this day, by royal decree, accepted into the Greater Polynesian Empire the island known as *Kaiulani*." Kalakaua looked over at his niece and smiled. "I am told, Princess, that it is a beautiful island, and it was its beauty which inspired our intrepid Admiral to name the island after you."

Kaiulani blushed, and studied the platform from beneath long, silken eyelashes, but the focus of attention on her was enough to cause Lorrin to momentarily forget the disgust he felt over the Manakalano episode.

"And to govern the new island, I have appointed my trusted friend and religious advisor, Walter Wilson," Kalakaua said, pointing to the American missionary.

Wilson smiled smugly at the crowd, and listened

to Kalakaua sing his praises, telling how it was important to provide a Christian environment for the new subjects as soon as possible. Thus, he appointed Walter Wilson not only the Governor but Official Missionary as well.

Lorrin had not wanted to see that, either. He had hoped that Teoko would be allowed to continue to rule the Boka People. After all, Teoko was doing a magnificent job with them, and he really needed no outside interference. But even as he thought that, Lorrin knew that it was a thought inspired by naivete. There would be no purpose in bringing new lands into the Empire if those new lands were not going to be governed by the Empire. He could only hope that Teoko would understand.

"And so, finally, the appointment which brings me the most pleasure," Kalakaua said. He looked over toward his niece again. "My beloved sister, Liliuokalani, has recommended to me that I use her daughter, Kaiulani, as a good-will ambassador. Kaiulani would travel from island to island on board the *Kahili Pahoa* acting as an emissary of friendship, inviting new peoples to join with us in the Greater Polynesian Empire, to create a co-prosperity sphere of influence throughout the entire Pacific."

The audience applauded the choice of the popular and beautiful young Princess, and she shyly walked over to the King to accept her letter of appointment.

"And now," Kalakaua said, "we will all stand and sing our National Anthem, which, in case some of you have forgotten, I wrote myself."

The audience began singing the anthem, which

Kalakaua really did write. Kalakaua was a talented man, gifted in the arts, and with a flair for the dramatic. He was also a fun-loving man, who would give a party at the drop of a hat, and as it was said, "he would supply the hat." Kalakaua enjoyed food, drink, and most of all, women. His sexual appetite mortified some, while it provided others with a ribald, if vicarious, pleasure. Kalakaua earned his nickname, "the merry monarch."

"Come out to the plantation, Lorrin. I want to talk with you," Dole whispered, as the ceremony was breaking up.

"And I want to talk to you as well," Lorrin said. "This isn't going at all the way we planned."

"It will all work out," Dole promised. "Believe me, it will all work out."

Dole left the reviewing stand and joined his niece in walking toward one of the many carriages parked nearby. Lorrin smiled at Andrea, but she returned a look which was difficult for him to discern. Then she looked away toward the other side of the platform and Lorrin followed her eyes. There, on the other side, talking to reporters about her new appointment, Lorrin saw Kaiulani, and he realized then, that the look on Andrea's face was one of jealousy.

The music of a Bach fugue filled the room as Lorrin sat with Sanford Dole to listen to Andrea play the organ. Andrea's ability to play had been unknown to Lorrin, and as he sat there listening to the notes weave a tapestry of gold, he knew that he was listening to someone with a great talent.

Lorrin did more than just listen to the music. He watched, and he studied Andrea's face, and he saw with some degree of surprise that the Andrea who played the organ was not the same Andrea he saw under other circumstances. This Andrea was more ethereal, more detached from worldly things. The Andrea at the organ was almost spiritual.

Finally, the last note drifted off to linger only as an echo in the chambers of the great plantation house, and Lorrin, Sanford, and even Andrea sat spellbound for several seconds afterward. Sanford broke the spell by speaking first.

"Lovely, my dear. That was absolutely lovely."

"Yes, it was," Lorrin said. He got up and walked over to the bench where Andrea was sitting. "I've never heard anything more beautiful in my life," he added.

Andrea looked into Lorrin's face, and for an instant, he saw an innocence which he didn't know Andrea possessed. She was a little girl, anxious to please, a musician in a choir of angels, soft, and vulnerable.

"Did you really like it?" she asked.

Lorrin reached down to take her hands into his. "I loved it," he said. "I could sit for hours and listen to you play."

Andrea smiled, and even as she smiled the aura of innocence began to drift away. Her hands which had but moments before been instruments capable of evoking the most beautiful music from the organ once again became an intimate part of her body, and they warmed with a quick, building heat. The innocence left her eyes, to be replaced with an unbridled look of desire, and Lorrin could almost see tiny red lamps of lust deep in them. She leaned forward slightly in what appeared to be an unconscious move, but was in reality a studied pose, designed to offer Lorrin a most intimate view of the cleavage which the dress exposed.

"I would be glad to arrange a private concert for you," Andrea said in a husky voice. She looked over at her uncle. "Lorrin will be staying the night, won't he?"

"Of course," Sanford said. "Of course he will."

"I don't know," Lorrin said. "I really should be getting back to my ship."

"How foolish of me to forget," Andrea said, and as she spoke, Lorrin could literally feel the heat escaping her hands as they cooled to match the sudden change in her mood. For her mood had abruptly changed with surprising suddenness. One moment she was fire in his presence, and the next she was ice. "I imagine you shall want to make certain that Princess Kaiulani is properly looked after."

"No," Lorrin said sharply. "I mean, uh, of course I want to make certain that she is properly looked after, but that is the normal consideration I would show any passenger. I've no intention of going to see her now."

"Good," Andrea said, and she smiled so broadly that the ice melted and her mood was fire once again. "Then you will stay the night here."

Lorrin sighed helplessly, then he smiled. "Yes," he replied. "Yes, I suppose I will."

"I shall see you then," Andrea said. "In the meantime, I know that you and my uncle have several important things to discuss, so I will leave you to your business." She got up and as her uncle approached, she leaned toward him to kiss him. As she leaned forward, her lips brushed against Sanford's cheeks, but her body leaned against Lorrin, and she prolonged the contact, letting him know in no uncertain terms that it had not been an inadvertent move.

"Your niece is a most remarkable woman," Lorrin said a moment later as Andrea left the room.

"Yes, I dare say she is," Sanford said. He walked over to the door through which Andrea had just exited, then returned and sat down, motioning for Lorrin to do the same. "What did you think of the Battle of Bloody Island?" Dole asked.

Lorrin let a snorting laugh escape from his lips. "I would scarcely call a few rounds of artillery a battle," he said. "What fighting there was we lost."

Lorrin told Sanford of the unarmed landing party and of the rounds which were fired inadvertently. Then he told the story of the brief but bloody fight which had taken the life of West, along with three other valuable men.

"I suppose such a thing could have inspired the retaliatory massacre," Sanford said. "But to have killed so many of them, women, children, old men, and little boys . . ."

"What are you talking about?" Lorrin interrupted.

"I'm talking about the raid for revenge," Sanford said.

Lorrin laughed lightly. "There was no raid for revenge," he said. "I sent a landing party ashore to recover the bodies, and that's all. After the bodies were on board, we weighed anchor."

"Could it be that you *don't* know?" Sanford asked. He looked at Lorrin with a puzzled expression on his face. "Lorrin, were you with the landing party?"

"No. I sent Manakalano."

"Then it figures," Dole said. He walked over to a roll top desk. "Here is the story on it in today's *Mail*." He tossed the paper to Lorrin.

ROYAL NAVAL EXPEDITION IN TERRIBLE BATTLE

Word has reached this newspaper of a battle engaged in by Hawaiian Marines, under the command of Lieutenant, (sources close to His Majesty say soon to be General) Manakalano, and armed savages of an island known only as Bloody Island.

"Our first contact was the landing of an unarmed band of men," Manakalano told this reporter. "But those poor souls were suddenly and without provocation attacked by a large number of armed warriors. Four of the landing party, including the First Mate of the ship, a man I knew only as Mr. West, were killed. The Captain of the *Kahili Pahoa* was a close friend of Mr. West's, and he was so grief-stricken that he went below decks to be alone with his sorrow. It was up to me to recover the bodies, so I took an armed party of Marines ashore. In order to provide security for the landing party, I attacked the village, and there discovered that in such savage societies as this, all are warriors; men, women, children, and old people. They set upon my men in a most fearsome manner, but we joined in the fight and a short time later left the dead and dying; men, women, and children, strewn about the streets of the destroyed village. I recovered the bodies of our own dead, and returned to the ship, where I found the Captain, still incapacitated with his grief. I informed him of the recovery of our bodies, and he ordered that we return to Honolulu."

The battle, known as the Battle of Bloody Island, is the basis for the highest decoration of bravery, the King's Cross, which is to be given to Manakalano in a special ceremony today.

Lorrin looked up after he read the article.

"Of course, the medal they are talking about was given today," Sanford said. "The story was no doubt written last night." Sanford took a cigar from his inside pocket and prepared it, then lit it and blew out a puff of smoke before he went on. "Well?"

"Well, what, Sanford?"

"What is your reaction to this story?"

"I have no idea what they are talking about," Lorrin said. He looked at the story. "There was no battle."

"Are you certain of that?"

"Well, I'm reasonably certain," Lorrin said. He ran his hand through his blond hair. "I'm sure if anything like that happened, one of my men would have . . . wait a minute," he said. "Wait a minute. None of my men were with the landing party. Manakalano asked for permission to select his own."

"Then the battle could have taken place?"

"He told me we had given the natives a most adequate demonstration of our strength," Lorrin said. He slapped his fist into his palm. "Damn, that was what he was talking about. It *must* be."

"Then it *is* true," Sanford said.

"It could be," Lorrin said. "I don't like to think so, but I'm afraid that it could be true."

"Lorrin, it is imperative that nothing like this happens again," Sanford said. "We cannot afford to lose the support of other islands."

"I wouldn't have let it happen this time," Lorrin said. "It happened without my knowledge. And now, with Manakalano equal to me in rank, it will no doubt happen again." He sighed. "That leaves me no recourse but to resign."

"No," Sanford said. "Lorrin, you can't do that. At least not yet."

"But why not?" Lorrin asked. "Sanford, this isn't working out at all the way we had planned."

"You can't resign because you must act as a stabilizing influence over this young fool Manakalano."

"I was unable to stabilize him when he was a mere Lieutenant and I held a much higher rank," Lorrin said. "How would you propose that I stabilize him now that his rank is equal to mine?"

"I don't know," Sanford said. "I only know that somehow you must. We have here a golden opportunity to help shape the government of Hawaii now and for all future generations," Sanford said. "I only ask that we don't blunder our chances away."

"Uncle, Lorrin," Andrea's soft voice said from the door of the room. "I've come to tell you that dinner is ready."

"Wonderful," Sanford said, rubbing his girth. "I don't mind telling you that I am absolutely starved." He stood up and offered his arm to his niece, who had come into the room with her announcement only to see her walk by him and take Lorrin's arm. He chuckled. "It was foolish of me to think I could compete," he said quietly.

"I beg your pardon?" Lorrin asked, unaware of the fact that Sanford was referring to Andrea passing her uncle for the young Admiral.

"Never mind, Lorrin," Sanford said. "I was merely making an observation aloud which I should have confined to my thoughts. Shall we go?"

Lorrin, with Andrea on his arm, followed Sanford out of the room toward the dining room. He felt Andrea's fingers on his arm, and the brush of her hip against his as they walked. And he felt the tremendous heat which emanated from both spots of body contact. She was, he decided, fire again.

"I am glad you will be spending the night with us, Lorrin," Andrea said in her deep, sultry voice. "You have been so long at sea that you need a restful sleep ashore."

"Yes, I'm looking forward to it," Lorrin replied, and as he spoke the words, he knew that he did not mean he was looking forward to a night of sleep, and he knew that she wasn't, either.

9

LORRIN STOOD in the night breeze of the open casement windows and looked out over the gently rolling acres of the Dole Sugar Plantation. Near his window a cluster of coconut trees waved gently, and the palm fronds of one of them caught a moonbeam and scattered a burst of silver through the darkness. The sweet scent of flowers floated in, both from the carefully nurtured garden and from the blooms which grew in wild and fragrant profusion beyond the lawn.

Lorrin had lived most of his life in the close confines of a ship. He had experienced moments alone, during the dog watch when the ship slept, but privacy such as he had here, with a large room all to himself, was a luxury which he was seldom able to enjoy. And he was celebrating this privacy in a most unique way. He had removed all his clothes, and was allowing the air to pass over his skin, feeling the delightful sensuality of being totally nude, and totally alone.

But he wasn't to be alone long, for even as he stood there looking out across the moon-silvered landscape he heard a soft knock on the door. He knew who it would be, and he looked around quickly to find something to cover his nakedness. Then, with a feeling of wild abandonment, he decided not to bother. After all, Andrea had seen him before, and unless he was terribly mistaken, it was her plan to repeat the intimate scene. Lorrin smiled. He didn't intend to upset her scheme.

"Come in, Andrea," he called softly.

The door opened and closed, and Lorrin, staying for the moment in the shadows, looked over to see her standing just inside. Her legs were bare beneath a cape she was wearing.

"You won't need that cape," Lorrin said.

"I just used it to walk through the hall," Andrea said, and he could see her smiling in the moonlight as she let the cape fall from her shoulders exposing her nakedness. "Well, I see you were expecting me."

"Do you feel it presumptuous of me?"

"Presumptuous? Of course not," Andrea said. "I think practical is a better word. It saves time, don't you think?" She walked over to him then, and he could smell the scent of her mingled with the fragrance of the flowers outside. As she leaned against him, transferring her heat to him, his body readied itself for her, and he felt her hand close around his maleness.

"Oh, my," she said, whispering in his ear so he

could feel her hot breath as well as hear her words. "Oh, my, you really do want to save time, don't you? Do you want me now?"

"Yes," Lorrin said, and he found that his tongue was so thick that it was difficult for him to speak, even in words of one syllable.

"Do you think I'm beautiful?" Andrea asked, and she ground herself against the muscles of his leg so he could feel the moist eagerness of her.

"Yes," Lorrin said.

"And you want me now, more than anything in the world?"

"Yes," Lorrin said again. Her game was maddening to his senses. Every fiber, every nerve in his body was now poised, drawn to the edge of the agony of the quest. He wanted to tell her to stop teasing, to stop asking the questions which in fact required no answer, but he could do no more than mouth the one-word answer he knew she wanted to hear.

Andrea played with him, teased him with the silken touch of her tongue, and the skilled movement of her fingers. She overwhelmed him with the sight, touch, taste, sound and smell of desire, until finally he found himself on the bed with her, following her skillful manipulation until their naked bodies were pressed together, and he found himself in her, indeed, a part of her.

During their moments together, it was as if Lorrin could hear Andrea's music being replayed in his head, and as the ageless melody weaved its magic upon him, Andrea's hands, the hands which elicited the beautiful music from the organ keyboard, now found other pursuits, and her long, cool fingers were able to evoke sensations of pleasure which matched the chords of beauty from the earlier music.

Lorrin felt Andrea reaching her own pinnacle, going from peak to peak with such rapidity that he couldn't tell from her actions if it was one sustained rapture, or several exquisite bursts of delight which brought her such pleasure. Finally, with a shuddering moan, Lorrin abandoned himself to the maelstrom of sensation, and he felt himself dissolving into a white, liquid heat at the center of his being.

Andrea lay beneath the pleasant weight of Lorrin, holding him in her, feeling the last, twitching spasms of muscular release which had but seconds before thrust her into the heavens with exquisite delight. The rapture had not yet passed for her. It had begun even before Lorrin attained his release, kept going through his frenzied thrusts of pleasure, and now, though receding in intensity, continued in longer, slower, though in their own right just as delightful, sensations.

It was at such a time that Andrea was able to close her mind and heart to any possible recriminations about her nature. In truth, she had literally seduced Lorrin, not only this time, but the time before. And Lorrin wasn't the first. There had been many, many men before Lorrin, and though she in times of introspective reflection felt guilty, that guilt could be swept away by the first faint twitchings of desire, for nothing in her life was as important as the sensations she could give herself over to when she was making love.

For these moments of pleasure, Andrea knew she would sacrifice anything, accept any criticism, commit any sin.

Andrea had even committed adultery.

Harold Poindexter was a case in point. He was thirty-seven-years-old, the father of four, a deacon in the church and a pillar of his community. He was Andrea's father's most trusted bank officer, and all agreed that Harold had a brilliant future ahead of him.

Then Andrea, sixteen when she first decided that she would like him to sleep with her, moved into Harold's life. Harold never had a chance. Andrea used every sexual weapon at her disposal, and against such an arsenal Harold was virtually unarmed. She practically raped him one evening when he stayed to work late at the bank, and the taste of the young girl's considerable charms worked their magic on Harold until he gave up everything for her.

Andrea took a particular and perverse delight in seducing him one afternoon during the celebration of his fifteenth wedding anniversary. Her father had given a special anniversary party for his favorite employee, and Harold, his wife, and their friends and family had all come to Andrea's father's house for the party. Andrea took Harold into the library, and teased him into making love to her on the sofa, while just on the other side of the door which Andrea had daringly purposely left unlocked, guests walked by, laughing and talking, never suspecting the scene of passion which was taking place less than twenty feet away.

But the idyll ended when they were caught by Andrea's father one afternoon, ironically after taking special precautions to avoid being caught. He had returned home unexpectedly. Given Andrea's tender age, and her insistence that Harold was "the only one who had ever known her," Harold was immediately blamed for ruining the young girl. He was fired, his wife left him, and he became so discredited that no other firm would hire him. Everywhere he went, he bore the sobriquet of "despoiler of young girls," a particularly vile thing to have to live with, and all who heard the story shunned him.

Andrea, whom most considered innocent in spirit if not in deed, was sent to Hawaii, there to live with her wealthy uncle and to salvage her innocence.

But Andrea had been bored by the island paradise. She missed Harold . . . perhaps not Harold particularly, but the *availability* of Harold when she needed her sexual hungers satisfied. She had tried in every way she knew to let Victor and the other young "gentlemen" callers her uncle welcomed into the house know that she would be willing to engage in the ways of the flesh. But none had taken her hints, and Andrea found none of them appealing enough to her to take the iniative.

Until she saw Lorrin O'Lee. From the first time Andrea saw him, she knew that she must have him, and she would have him in whatever way it took. If she could entice him into taking the initiative, she would. If she had to be more overt in her relationship, she would do that, too. As it turned out, she took off her clothes and literally threw herself at him, and that had been successful, but even as she lay naked beneath his nakedness, she knew that she didn't control him as she had controlled Harold. And until she controlled him, she would never feel secure in their relationship, and without that security, she knew that she would not be able to count on satisfying her sexual hunger any time she wished.

As Andrea saw it, there was only one stumbling block in their path. There was only one thing which kept Lorrin from totally abandoning himself to her, and than one thing was the Hawaiian Princess, Kaiulani.

"Have you done this with Kaiulani?" Andrea asked.

Lorrin had been lying on her, totally relaxed from the lovemaking, and when he heard her question, he stiffened—not abruptly, in fact, quite subtly—but Andrea had felt it.

"I have not asked you about the others who have been with you," Lorrin said.

"Ask," Andrea replied.

Lorrin lay there for a few seconds longer, saying nothing but feeling all the tenuous connections of spirit and emotion which stretched between the two of them being severed. Then, with a sigh of resignation, he physically severed the last connection, the conduit through which all other sensations had traveled, by withdrawing himself and rolling away from her. It was significant, he thought, that she had not denied that there were others. On the contrary, she had even invited his inquiry.

"I prefer not to know," Lorrin said.

Andrea raised up on one elbow and looked down at him. Lorrin could see her quite clearly in the splash of moonlight, and if ever a creature could be said to be Aphrodite's child, here was that creature.

"Why are you afraid?" Andrea asked.

"Why am I afraid of what?"

"Why are you afraid of what you feel? I'm not afraid."

Lorrin smiled and reached his hand up to trace the outline of her face, shoulder, and breast. He felt her shiver involuntarily as his fingers passed across her nipple, and he felt a small twinge of regret that his recuperative powers were not as fast as hers. She could make love again, right now.

"I'm not afraid of what I feel either," Lorrin said, though, even as he spoke the words, he wondered about the truth of the statement. "But some of those feelings are private, and I don't want to share them."

"If you loved me, you could share them with me," Andrea said.

"Andrea, are you trying to tell me that you are *in love* with me?" Lorrin asked.

Andrea was quiet for a moment. Finally she answered, and when she did, she answered with the candidness which Lorrin was learning to expect from her.

"When we have sex, you make me feel better than anyone else ever has," she said. "I love making love with you."

"One can scarcely build a relationship on sex alone," Lorrin said.

"One could try," Andrea suggested. "That is, if if you feel the same way about me. That's why it is so important for me to know if you have had sex with Kaiulani. Do you enjoy it as much with her, as you do with me?"

Lorrin sighed. "I haven't had sex with Kaiulani," he finally said.

"But you do want to?"

"I haven't given it that much thought," Lorrin lied.

Andrea smiled, a slow, knowing, sad kind of smile. "Oh, you've thought of it," she said. "You've thought of it many times. I just hope that when you finally do make love with her, you are disappointed enough to come back to me forever."

Lorrin laughed. "Andrea, correct me if I'm wrong, but I don't think you *could* be with any one man forever."

"I didn't think I could," Andrea said. "But now that I've met you, I've changed my mind. I could be satisfied with you forever, Lorrin. I know I could," she said, and the tone of her voice and the expression in her eyes were almost enough to make Lorrin believe what she said.

Kaiulani was awakened by the shrill whistle of the boatswain's pipe.

"All hands," she heard a voice call. "All hands turn out for the arrival of the Admiral."

There were more shouts and a great deal of activity on deck, and Kaiulani, with a feeling of joy that Lorrin had at last returned to the ship, hurried topside to see his arrival. She had come to the ship within hours of her appointment, because her mother had returned to Maui and she had no wish to stay with her uncle. Walter Wilson, the new Governor of Kaiulani Island, was also on board the ship, as was General Manakalano. Only Lorrin O'Lee was absent, having spent the night ashore as a guest of Sanford Dole.

"Well, Princess," Manakalano said, as Kaiulani stepped on deck. "You have at last ventured forth from your room. Is it the haloe admiral which stirs your heart so?"

Manakalano's sidelong glances had unnerved Kaiulani in the past, but now that he had been promoted to the rank of general, he seemed to think his new status entitled him to liberties with her, and Kaiulani felt that disturbing. There was something about Manakalano that Kaiulani didn't like, something she couldn't put her finger on. She smiled to herself. Perhaps that was but more proof of the mystical quality of the Alii-Nui her mother was always talking about.

Manakalano saw her little smile and misinterpreted it. He thought she was smiling in reaction to his mention of the haloe admiral, and it angered him. He had misinterpreted her smile and reaction, but in fact he had not misinterpreted the way she felt about O'Lee.

"So," Manakalano said. "You would abandon your sacred duty to your people and your blood and feel love for an outsider." He accused her loudly.

Kaiulani had been alone with her own thoughts, and now she looked over at Manakalano, a little surprised as to the cause and severity of his anger.

"What is troubling you, Manakalano?" she asked.

"I am concerned about your responsibility to your position," Manakalano replied.

"My responsibility is none of your concern," Kaiulani said quietly. "And I find your remarks impertinent."

Kaiulani was a princess, the daughter of one of the most powerful people in Hawaii, and the niece of the King. Besides that, her beauty and popularity made her a much-loved personage in her own right, and she wielded an inordinate amount of power among the people. Manakalano suddenly realized that and almost belatedly realized his own position, its precariousness in the overall scheme of things. That realization, coupled with his personal ambition, suddenly sobered him, and he withdrew quickly lest he overstep his bounds.

"I'm sorry, Princess," he apologized, bowing slightly. "I meant no offense by my remarks. It was merely the love of a subject for his Sovereign which caused me to speak improperly."

"I accept your apology," Kaiulani said. She smiled inwardly and with gratified surprise at Manakalano's sudden change of heart. Kaiulani was not one to press her position. In fact, her "position" as such often embarrassed her. But if it would provide her with a degree of protection from the likes of General Manakalano, then she would gladly utilize its advantages.

"I must go to see to the arrival of the Admiral," Manakalano said, and he turned and walked back to mid-deck, where his Marines were standing at attention.

"Admiral coming on deck," someone called, and Kaiulani saw Lorrin's head and shoulders as he climbed up the ladder, then stepped through the siderail and received the salute of his first officer.

"Marines, attention," Manakalano said. "Present arms!"

The marine guard came to attention and raised their rifles in salute. Lorrin glanced toward them, returned their salute, then walked to the quarterdeck. "Mr. Adams, make ready to get underway," he ordered.

"Aye, aye, sir," Adams replied. "Weigh anchor. Loose the topsails," he called, and half-a-dozen sailors scrambled aloft, then crawled out on the yardarms to do his bidding, while others began turning the winch to raise the anchor.

Kaiulani started to walk toward Lorrin, to speak to him, but Walter Wilson reached Lorrin before she could get there.

"Admiral, I will require you to stop at Molokai," Wilson said.

"Very well, Governor, if such are my sailing orders," Lorrin said.

Wilson smiled. "We shall indeed have a pleasant voyage, I feel."

"The more pleasant, sir, if you remain off my quarterdeck," Lorrin said rather sharply.

"I only wished to pass pleasantries," Wilson said.

"I've no wish to pass pleasantries with the passengers," Lorrin replied. "Mr. Adams, loose the forecourse and the mainsail," he called, turning his back to Wilson.

Wilson stood there for an awkward moment until the new sails were released. The canvas billowed and boomed like thunder and the ship leapt forward under the press of the sails.

"What is our course, Admiral?" Adams called.

"We're bound for Molokai," Lorrin said. He turned and looked back at Wilson. "To what part of Molokai, sir?"

Wilson smiled. "First, I shall want to pay a call upon my brother at the leper colony," he said. "And then I shall accept a delay in my journey for you to survey your lands."

"Survey my lands?"

Wilson smiled more broadly now. "Yes. The four thousand acres the King has granted you are on Molokai, immediately surrounding the leper colony," he added, and he couldn't help but break into a victorious laugh.

"Thank you, Governor," Lorrin said. He turned and walked back to the afterrail, there to stare over the stern of the ship toward the rapidly receding city of Honolulu.

Kaiulani had watched the exchange between Lorrin and Governor Wilson with some apprehension. Lorrin had been most rude to the Governor. Was that due to some personal dislike, or was that because the Governor was a passenger and Lorrin didn't want passengers? If so, what was her status? As a good-will ambassador, was she but a passenger, and thus subject to Lorrin's same ill-will? Or was she to be afforded a more permanent status on board the ship, and therefore spared Lorrin's dislike?

Whatever it was to be, Kaiulani had no intention of challenging it now, so, disappointed by the turn of events, she decided to return to her cabin, to await a more opportune time to approach Lorrin.

Kaiulani stayed in her cabin for the rest of the day, listening to the constant roar of the wind in the sails, the singing of the ropes, the creaking of the masts and the rushing of the water. Finally, as the dinner hour approached, she went up on deck hoping Lorrin was in a better mood so she could ascertain what the eating arrangements would be.

When Kaiulani regained the deck after her hours

in her cabin, she saw that they were now far out to sea, and she inhaled deeply, enjoying the clean, fresh smell of the salt air, far away from the fetid odors of shore. Lorrin was standing near the rail, and she walked over to speak to him.

"Are you of a more friendly disposition?" she asked timidly.

Lorrin looked at her in surprise. "Princess, did you think me in an unfriendly disposition?"

"I thought so, yes, when I observed the way you spoke with Governor Wilson."

Lorrin smiled. "Oh, so *that's* why you have remained below-deck," he said. "I'm sorry if my temperament seemed ill-disposed to you. There is always much to do when getting underway, and Governor Wilson," Lorrin let the word "governor" slide out with a twist of his mouth to show his disdain, "is not a person to whom I can easily warm. I'm sorry, however, if I was so rude as to offend you."

Kaiulani laughed. "Perhaps each of us has a person on board with whom we would have a difficult time being friendly," she suggested. "For me, it is Malakalano."

"I don't like that son-of-a-bitch, either," Lorrin said, then when he realized what he had said he flushed red and apologized profusely for swearing before her.

Kaiulani laughed again. "Please, Admiral, don't apologize. Can't we be allies and friends without the necessity for apologies? Besides, you were calling me Kaiulani when we last sailed together!"

"Right," Lorrin agreed. "And you must call me Lorrin."

"We will seal it with a handshake," Kaiulani

said, and she reached out to take his hand in hers. Again, Lorrin felt the wonder of the cool heat of her fingers. And for the brief moment there was contact between them, he felt a quick dizziness and a shortness of breath. He cleared his throat, forcing himself back to rationality, and on the pretext of testing the tautness of a nearby rope, he pulled his hands from hers. "Dinner shall be ready soon. Would you join me?"

"I would love to," Kaiulani said. "Where shall we eat?"

"In my cabin," Lorrin said. He smiled. "I shall let Mr. Adams entertain the General and the Governor in the wardroom mess. I think they will do splendidly without our company, don't you?"

"I don't know," Kaiulani said. She laughed. "I know *I* shall do splendidly without theirs."

10

THE CHART TABLE in Lorrin's cabin had been
cleared of maps and instruments, covered with a
clean, white tablecloth, and set with fine china,
crystal and silver. The china, crystal and silver, as
well as the tablecloth itself, came from a trunk
which was rarely opened. That trunk had been
shipped to Lorrin from Hong Kong after his parents had died, and in it was the sum total of his
mother's possessions.

The little things Lorrin's mother had done to try
to make a ship's cabin a home were in that trunk.
Curtains, bedspreads, a handful of books (*none* of
which were about the sea), some sheet music, and
a handful of framed photographs—browned, en-
circled heads of men and women, representing the
family Lorrin had never known or seen.

Lorrin had never used any of his mother's things

before, though he had of course frequently eaten in his cabin, and had in the past entertained guests. He told himself that he was going all-out now because Kaiulani was a princess, royalty, and thus deserved treatment as royal as he could provide. And yet, deep down he knew there was another reason, though he dared not articulate the thought.

Lorrin turned the gimbal lantern down very low, then lit the two candles on the table. The candles and the candlesticks were also from his mother's trunk, and after the candles were lit and he stood back and looked at the tiny golden flames which danced above the slender white tapers, he thought the scene was quite well-set.

The cook had prepared a small roast beef cooked in red wine, and its bouquet, coupled with the appetizing aroma of a loaf of freshly baked bread, made the atmosphere of the cabin very pleasant indeed. Lorrin took out a long, thin cheroot and stuck it in his mouth at a jaunty angle, preparatory to lighting it, then, because he thought the cigar smoke might spoil the effect, he put the cigar aside.

Kaiulani knocked on the door, and Lorrin opened it, then sucked in his breath.

"Am I too early?" Kaiulani asked, surprised by his reaction.

"What?" he said. "Uh, no, no, not at all. It's just that I've never seen anyone as beautiful."

Kaiulani was wearing a white silk gown. It was high-necked, but close fitting at the bosom and pinched in at the waist, flaring out into many tiers. Her golden skin glowed in contrast to the purity of the white dress. A flash of light sparkled from the dancing ear-bobs she wore.

"I hope you don't mind," she said. "It is a dress

from England. I've never worn it before, but I thought I would like to wear it tonight."

"Please," Lorrin said, when finally he found his voice again. He stepped back and motioned for her to come into the room. "Come in."

Kaiulani came into the room, then looked toward the table. "Oh," she said. "I had no idea one could set such a lovely table on board a ship."

"These things belonged to my mother," Lorrin said, pulling a chair away from the table for her.

"Yes," Kaiulani said. "Your mother lived on board ship with your father. You must have many beautiful memories of her."

"She was a remarkable woman," Lorrin said. "I don't think I ever appreciated just how remarkable a woman she was until it was too late." He sighed. "There aren't many women who could do what she did. Who could make a life for themselves at sea?"

"It would be easier for her if she loved the man who brought her to sea," Kaiulani said. "When you are with the one you love, you don't care where you must go."

Lorrin laughed. "You are a young and terribly inexperienced young girl to have such deeply held convictions about love, Kaiulani."

"Do you find it impossible to believe that I could be in love with someone?" Kaiulani asked.

The sincerity of her statement surprised Lorrin, and stung him a bit, too. Was she in love with someone? Of course, as beautiful and popular as she was, that seemed most likely, but that was a possibility he had failed to consider.

"No," he said. "I guess I wouldn't find it impossible to believe. After all, you are a very desirable woman, Kaiulani, young though you may be."

"I *am* in love with someone, Lorrin."

"That someone is a lucky man," Lorrin said. He poured a glass of wine for Kaiulani, another for himself. He didn't want to talk about it any more, because he didn't want to think about Kaiulani with anyone else. "We should eat now," he said. "It's best before it gets cold."

They ate then, and the meal, as the first meal at sea always was for Lorrin, was truly delicious. It was made even more delightful by the quality of his company, but, through it all, a shadow hung over them. Finally, when the meal was concluded, and Lorrin had poured each of them another glass of wine, he could take it no more. It was like a sore which he wanted to avoid, but couldn't stay away from.

"I have little respect for the man you love," he blurted out.

Kaiulani smiled, as if amused by it all. "Why have you no respect for him?"

"Because if he had any sense at all, if he had any regard for you at all, he wouldn't let you run off with another man."

"Oh? And have I run off with another man, sir?"

"Yes," Lorrin said.

"Who?"

"Why, me, of course," Lorrin said, and the tone of his voice was almost angry. Exasperatingly, Kaiulani's smile seemed to grow brighter, and she seemed to enjoy the situation all the more for his anger.

"What makes you say I have run off with you?" she asked.

"Well, look at this," Lorrin said, sweeping his arm around his cabin. "You've eaten with me, you've drunk wine with me, we are alone in my cabin at sea. You are a beautiful woman, I am a man strongly attracted to you. The situation isn't safe!"

"Lorrin, I would hope I am safe with you," Kaiulani said.

"Well, of course you are *safe*," Lorrin said. "I mean you are safe in that I would never ... that is to say, I wouldn't—"

"Seduce me?" Kaiulani said.

"Well, I would not force myself on you," Lorrin said. "I can promise you that. But, Kaiulani, I won't promise that I wouldn't try and make love to you if I had the chance. Because I would."

"I would hope that you wouldn't," Kaiulani said. She looked at the table, and her long, silken eyelashes shielded her eyes demurely. "I am still a virgin," she said. "And it is important that I stay so."

"Yes," Lorrin said. "No doubt the man you love would wish it that way."

"Would you not wish that for the woman you love?" Kaiulani said.

"I would set less store in that than in other things," Lorrin said. "A woman's past is her own business."

Even as Lorrin uttered the words, he wondered if he was telling the truth, or if he was lying. He was certainly cognizant of Andrea's past, and that cognizance certainly colored his perception of her.

No, it wasn't her past which bothered him, he told himself. It was her present, and her exceptionally loose attitude. And yet, it was precisely that attitude which had attracted Lorrin to Andrea. Andrea was a delightful creature, a totally sexual

being who could bring Lorrin to the summit of
pleasure. Surely she couldn't be such a person, if
she didn't have such an open attitude toward sex.

Did he want Kaiulani to exhibit the same attitude? It was a puzzling question. He had every
desire now to throw her onto his bunk and rip the
virginal white dress from her body, that delicious,
golden, innocent body which he had looked upon
in all its naked glory, and attack her, with her con-
sent if possible, against her will if necessary.

But even as Lorrin entertained these lascivious
thoughts, he knew that he would do nothing to
harm her. He could never willingly cause her the
slightest amount of pain or suffering. He felt rough
and uncouth before her, an unpolished buffoon who
had no right to be in her presence, while at the
same time he felt equal to the task of being her
lover and her protector. It was a tumult of conflicting emotions, each vying for supremacy, and
in a way, not unlike the strange sensation of feeling both heat and cold at her touch.

A sudden knock at the door of his cabin interrupted his reverie.

"Yes," Lorrin called. "Who is it?"

"Beggin' the Admiral's pardon, sir, but we have
a sail contact."

"That's not too unusual in these waters," Lorrin
said. "We are in the intra-island shipping lanes."

"Yes, sir, I know. But this ship is flying signals,
sir. She's requesting permission to send a boarding
party."

Lorrin sat there for a moment, and looked across
the table at Kaiulani. Then he let out a low, mysterious chuckle.

"What is it?" she asked. "Why are you laughing?"

"Do you believe in fate, Kaiulani?"

"Yes, of course I do," Kaiulani said. "I believe that everything is ordered."

"Then your fate has just intervened, for if I were to stay in this room with you alone much longer, I fear I would have a most difficult time acting as your protector." He slid the chair back. "I leave you, madam, with your virginity intact."

Lorrin started to leave, then, on impulse, he walked over to her and put his hands under her arms and picked her up from her chair, then pulled her to him for a kiss.

It wasn't a tentative kiss, hesitant and unsure. It was a lover's kiss, with an open mouth, and a tongue which probed the senses, and set Kaiulani's head to spinning.

Once, when Kaiulani had been a child, she fell from a tree, and she lay beneath the tree for several seconds, unable to breathe. It was a terrifying, mystifying experience, not knowing when she would breathe again, or even if she would breathe. And now this kiss was affecting her the same way. She was breathless and dizzy, and she felt her knees grow weak and her blood run hot, and for one, wild, insane moment, she would have willingly ripped her dress off and given herself to him here, now, without regard for time or place or anyone else on the ship.

Finally the kiss was broken off, and Lorrin looked at her. He may have meant the kiss as an affirmation of his control of things, as a statement of his power over the situation. But if that was the case, it backfired on him, for he was clearly as moved and as confused as Kaiulani. "I . . . I must go," he finally said.

"Yes," she answered. "You must."

Lorrin kissed her again, with slow, hot lips, and when the first mate knocked on the door from the other side, it didn't hurry him one bit, for he acted as if he had the night without interruption, and Kaiulani wished, in the secret, innermost chamber of her heart, that they could share the night.

And she wondered if she should tell him that the man she loved was him.

And then the kiss was ending again, leaving her as dizzy as did the first one.

"Will we be answering the signals, Admiral?"

"I'll be right there," Lorrin said, though he was still holding Kaiulani, and he made no effort to release her. Finally, he kissed her a third time. This kiss was bittersweet and poignant, for even as she felt his lips pressed to hers she knew that the moment had arrived when he must leave, for though it was as sweet as the other kisses, it was less demanding in its urgency, announcing by its very conduct that it was a kiss of surrender to the situation.

Lorrin broke off the kiss and smiled at her, then he turned and walked through the door, leaving Kaiulani to reel in the dizzy sensations of her experience. She felt hot and cold and shaky all at the same time, and her resolve to play the game of propriety, to beckon him to her, while denying him total fulfillment until he was committed to her, was weakened. She wanted him to take her to his bed then, that very moment, and make love to her.

But she was determined to deny her body to him, for she reasoned that favors which were too easily granted would lose their sweetness. And she would use whatever method she could to win the heart and mind of the *haole* admiral, even if it meant tempting him, only to deny him, in order to sustain his interest. It was a carefully worked-out plan, one she was certain would not fail.

But, as in all well-laid plans, there was a flaw which nearly doomed it from the beginning. Desire and sexual hunger was a two-edged sword. She was instilling in him an insatiable want for her, but that want cut both ways. She had not realized that she would have just as much trouble in controlling her own desires as she would in controlling his.

Kaiulani was a virgin, a condition which was relatively rare among girls her age in her culture. Sex among her people was a form of relaxation, indulged in openly and freely by all unmarried young adults.

But Kaiulani wasn't just an unmarried young adult, she was an unmarried princess, third in line of succession to the throne. By the law of the land, she must remain a virgin while unmarried if she would remain in the line of succession to the throne.

Thus far, Kaiulani had maintained her virginity, primarily because it was the law of the land that she do so. She had not developed an inhibited outlook toward sex, but she regarded it with the same healthy enthusiasm as did most of her peers. But for her, she knew, it was not the same thing.

Now Kaiulani was glad she had maintained her virginity, for she was certain that it would please

Lorrin, and pleasing him was all she cared about. She was no longer concerned about her position in the line of succession to the throne.

Kaiulani left Lorrin's cabin, and started for her own so she could change from the regal dress into something more comfortable. As she opened the door into her own cabin, she felt someone looking at her, and she turned to see General Manakalano standing just at the foot of the ladderway. He had his hands on the ladder rungs, preparatory to climbing above, but for a long moment he just stared at her.

Kaiulani wanted to say something to him, but she felt it would be better if she just ignored him, so she shrugged her shoulders and went on into the cabin which had been assigned to her. Once inside, she left it dark and looked through the door's venting slats to see what Manakalano was doing. She breathed a sigh of relief as she saw him climbing the ladder to go topside.

Lorrin handed the binoculars back to his first mate. "It's a mail exchange," he said. "We've only left port today. We've nothing to send them."

"We'll not likely do them any good either, I'm afraid," Adams said. "No one will be sending mail to Molokai, or Kaiulani Island, or any place else we are likely to go."

"No, I think not," Lorrin said. "Though it would be discourteous not to hear them out." Lorrin was aware of the importance speaking to another ship at sea played in the life of seamen. And, as he had been thinking of his mother earlier tonight, he remembered that she, more than anyone on board, looked forward to these chance encounters, in hopes that she would meet another woman.

The ship which hailed them was one of the giant windjammers, carrying several acres of sail on five towering masts, though of course the masts were now bare of sail. A cutter was traversing the distance between the two vessels, and the cutter was one third as large as the entire *Kahili Pahoa.*

"It's the *Adrian Goodman,*" Lorrin said. "I wonder if Amos Hodge is still her skipper?"

"You know the ship?"

"Yes," Lorrin said. "She's out of San Francisco, and she'll be going straight through for the Philippines. She'll leave us mail to be dropped off next time we are in Honolulu. We'll be able to help her out at that."

The cutter steered skillfully alongside the ship. She dropped her sail and anchor. Sacks of mail were tossed onto the deck of the *Kahili Pahoa,* while a man in a uniform climbed the ladder.

"Lorrin, it is you!" the man said, seeing Lorrin approach him.

"Michael Post! I thought you were going to get a ship of your own."

"I'd rather be mate for Cap'n Hodge on the *Adrian Goodman* than master of my own vessel," Post said. He looked around the ship, at the marines in uniforms, and at the gun positions. "What is this?" he asked. "Isn't this the *Centurian?*"

"It was," Lorrin said. "It's the *Kahili Pahoa* now. A ship-of-the-line of the Royal Hawaiian Navy."

Post laughed. "The what? The Royal Hawaiian Navy? Lorrin, are you kidding?"

"Why should the Admiral tease you?" Manakalano asked hotly.

Post looked at Manakalano, who was standing there in full uniform, complete with his recently awarded decoration, and a confused look crossed his face. "I don't understand," he said, looking at Lorrin. "What's going on here?"

"It's simple enough," Lorrin said. "A simple plan, conceived by a simple man. We now have a Navy. May God grant that we never have to use it."

"Wait a minute," Post said, snapping his fingers. "Wait a minute! This is the ship . . . this is the ship that was involved in the incident at Bloody Island, isn't it?"

"Good Lord, you mean you have already heard about it?"

"Yes," Post said. "We spoke to a ship three nights ago, a British ship, as a matter of fact. Their crew seemed quite upset by the fact that a pirate vessel had attacked a defenseless island and killed several of the natives. But Lorrin, that couldn't be you. I've known you for your entire life. You would never do such a thing."

"I must plead guilty," Lorrin said. "At least as far as my ship is concerned. *General* Manakalano was in charge of the landing party, but that doesn't dilute my responsibility."

"Oh, no," Manakalano said angrily. "You can't take credit for that battle. You were below decks and knew nothing about it. It was *my* victory, and *I* received the medal."

Post looked at Manakalano in shock, then he looked right at Lorrin and spoke, as if Manakalano wasn't present. "Is this son-of-a-bitch *bragging* about it?" he asked in surprise.

"Yes," Lorrin said.

Post sighed and looked around the ship. "Lorrin,

I don't know what you've got yourself into here," he said. "But my advice to you, my friend, is to be awfully careful. The British ship we saw will be arriving in San Francisco soon, and then they will be sending a cablegram to the Queen, asking for permission to protect the islands against further attack. The United States and France are sure to follow. You are likely to sail into some quiet harbor one morning and find yourself looking down the barrels of sixteen-inch guns." Post looked at the armament of the *Kahili Pahoa.* "One shell from a sixteen-inch gun would blow you out of the water, whereas a broadside from this bucket wouldn't make a scratch on a ship-of-the-line."

"I know," Lorrin said. He sighed. "I'll just have to be careful, that's all."

"Will you have a chance to drop these mail bags off?"

"Yes. We're going into Molokai now, we can drop them off there for the next island mail service which will return them to Honolulu. They should be on their way in less than a week."

"Good, good," Post said. "Our lads will be glad to hear that." Post turned and started back to the cutter, then he stopped and took a small package out of his inside jacket pocket. It was a package of cheroot cigars, and he tossed it across the deck to Lorrin. "I almost forgot," he said. "Cap'n Hodge sends his regards."

"And mine to the Captain," Lorrin said.

Lorrin walked over to the rail and watched the cutter going back through the waves, headed for the *Adrian Goodman,* and for one long moment he wished that he was going with her, to quit himself of this ship, of Manakalano and Wilson, and King

Kalakaua and Sanford Dole and V. V. Ashford and all the political intrigue of Hawaii. And then he thought of Kaiulani, and he knew that he would stick it out, wherever it led.

"Mr. Adams," he called.

"Aye, aye, sir?"

"Resume the passage to Molokai."

"Aye, aye, sir."

11

KALAUPAPA PENINSULA PROTRUDES like a thumb into the sea from the northern coast of the island of Molokai. A ring of volcanoes isolates the peninsula from the rest of the island, and the island itself is isolated by the sea from the other islands, so that it makes a secluded place to which lepers may be sent to live out the remainder of their lives in the supportive company of other lepers.

Leprosy as a disease is seldom fatal, though it does create a condition whereby the victim can more easily catch pneumonia and other fatal illnesses. Therefore, the care of leper patients consists primarily of shielding them from such illnesses. But leprosy destroys the nerves of the skin, muscle, and often causes grotesque disfigurement. It is a hideous disease which frightens people out of proportion to its real danger. Leprosariums, such as the one in Kalaupapa, are often constructed as much for the peace of mind of the non-sufferers, who don't wish to be exposed to the patients, as for the patients themselves.

Walter Wilson's brother Matthew had come to Kalaupapa several years before to work with the patients, and it was to see Matthew that Governor Wilson had ordered the *Kahili Pahoa* to stop at Molokai.

The boat which went ashore carried only the helmsman and two oarsmen, plus Governor Wilson, Lorrin O'Lee, and Kaiulani. All others stayed aboard because they were frightened to come into contact with the lepers. Kaiulani came ashore because she felt it was her duty.

A man stood on the point watching the boat as it was beached, and when the occupants stepped out of the boat, he started down to meet it.

"Have you a new patient for us?" he asked.

"A new patient? No," Wilson replied. "I'm Governor Walter Wilson. Who are you?"

"I am George Mason," the man said. "I work with Father Damien and Reverend Wilson. I am their assistant." The man suddenly smiled. "You must be Reverend Wilson's brother!"

"Yes. I would like to see my brother, please."

"Yes, of course. I know he will be happy to see you. Come along, I shall take you to him." The man turned and started back up the path toward the large white building which housed the lepers.

"Couldn't he come down to the beach to meet me?" Wilson asked, balking at the thought of going to the hospital.

"If I see him, I'll send him down to you," Lorrin said. "Mr. Mason, I'll return with you. I know your patients enjoy seeing someone from the outside world on occasion."

"Oh, yes, indeed they do, Captain," George Mason said, beaming broadly at Lorrin's offer. "Indeed they do. You are most kind to consider coming!"

"I shall come as well," Kaiulani said.

"Miss, are you certain you are up to it?" Mason asked. "It can be pretty unnerving."

"I will be all right," Kaiulani said.

"This is Princess Kaiulani," Lorrin said, introducing her. "She is here as a representative of the King and the government of Hawaii."

"Oh, you are most welcome," Mason said, taking her hand and shaking it gladly. "Most welcome indeed." He got a sad look on his face. "Too often, I'm afraid, some of our patients are forgotten, even by their own families. To think that a princess would call on them is quite wonderful indeed. Come, I shall lead you to the hospital."

"I'll come, too," Wilson said reluctantly. "I merely thought it would be best if I didn't interfere with my brother's busy work schedule."

"Good," Mason said. "We have a reception room which is quite lovely. I will take you there, first, then after Father Damien and Reverend Wilson meet with you, you can plan whatever else you might do."

"I've no desire to meet with the representative of Rome," Wilson said coolly.

"Oh?" Mason said. "Well, if you say so, though poor Father Damien gets so few visitors and he does like to meet with new people."

"I've never been able to understand how the son

of my father, a dedicated man of the Protestant God, could work so closely with a Roman Catholic," Wilson muttered as they climbed the path toward the hospital.

"You are the preacher," Lorrin said quietly, "and you have the religious training behind you. But I always thought the Catholic God and the Protestant God were one and the same."

"Well, of course, there is but one God," Wilson said. "It is merely a matter of how one perceives Him, that's all."

Two women were walking down the path, talking animatedly to each other. As they saw Lorrin and his party approaching, they quickly drew shawls around their faces, so that only their eyes showed through the opening. They moved off the path and looked down at the ground as the group came up to them.

"Hello," Kaiulani said. She stuck her hand out to offer to shake hands with them. "I am Princess Kaiulani."

"We are unclean, madam," one of the women mumbled through the shawl. Neither of them made any effort to take her hand. Both turned then and walked away quickly.

"Oh," Kaiulani said after they were gone. "I'm sorry they felt that way."

"Princess, it is easier if you don't try to force yourself on them," Mason explained. "Some will accept you, and some will not."

"Thank you," Kaiulani said.

They reached the hospital, then stepped inside. "The reception room is in there," Mason said. "If you will just wait, I'll send Reverend Wilson right along."

There were three people standing over in the corner, and Kaiulani went over to talk to them. Lorrin settled into a chair and began reading a newspaper; then he noticed the headline.

BRITISH FILE PROTEST OVER ATTACK
ON UNINCORPORATED ISLAND

Lorrin read the story. As a retaliation against the attack on Bloody Island, the British were threatening to annex all unclaimed islands in the Pacific and offer protection to them. The reporter who wrote the story doubted that it would happen, though, because he felt that action would be extremely provocative to the United States.

"Walter, how good to see you," a man's voice said, and Lorrin looked up to see another tall, skinny man, a carbon-copy of Walter, walk into the room. And yet, though the two men were superficially similar, there was a very discernible difference between them. Whereas Lorrin disliked Governor Walter Wilson, there was something about Matthew Wilson which made Lorrin like him immediately.

"And Princess Kaiulani," Matthew Wilson said, walking over to her and bowing slightly to her. "I know many of the sick will be thrilled at a visit from you."

"I just met two ladies who seemed uneasy by my arrival," Kaiulani said. "I don't know. I fear I may have done the wrong thing by coming ashore."

"It is your beauty, Princess," another voice said. "You see, everything here is ugly, so ugly becomes the norm. When an outsider arrives, one who is not only clean but beautiful as well, then that very beauty becomes grotesque."

The man who spoke was standing in the shadows of the hallway just beyond the door.

"Father Damien," Matthew said, smiling. "Joseph, you must come and meet my brother!"

Father Damien stepped into the room, and Kaiulani, despite her best intentions, gasped. Father Damien was clearly afflicted with the disease.

"You . . . you have it?" she asked.

"Yes," Father Damien said, and he smiled, not sadly, but almost proudly.

"When Joseph discovered that he had the disease, he held a solemn High Mass of Celebration," Matthew said. "And he gave praise to the Lord for the affliction, so that he would better understand the Lord's children who were suffering from the malady."

"I dare say, Matthew, you sound almost as if having this accursed disease were a badge of honor," Walter said derisively.

"In Father Damien's case, it *is* a badge of honor," Matthew said.

"Father Damien, Father Damien, High Mass—Matthew, are you drifting away from the true faith? Are you falling under the evil influence of Rome?" Walter asked.

"No," Matthew said. "I am, as I have always been, under the influence of our Lord. And it is *our* Lord, the God of all His children, Protestant and Catholic alike."

"Praise be to God that our father did not survive to see you slip away like this. I, on the other hand, have maintained the one true faith. Father would be very proud of me, Matthew, as I am going to a newly discovered island to carry the message of Christ. I am to be a missionary, as was our father before us."

"Oh, Walter, that is truly wonderful news," Matthew said, beaming in genuine pride over his brother's announcement. "You are right, father would be most proud, as indeed I am."

"What is the newly discovered island?" Father Damien asked.

"It is called Kaiulani," Walter said. He looked at Kaiulani. "It is named after our Princess."

"Yes, I read of the island in the paper which is delivered here by island steamer. You must feel honored, my dear," Father Damien said, and he tried to make a point with his fingers, but the disease had so afflicted his muscles that the left hand was drawn into a knobby fist, and he let his hand fall away in embarrassment.

"I am honored," Kaiulani said.

"I have read of another island recently in the news," Father Damien said. "It is called Bloody Island."

"Yes," Matthew said. "Tell me, my brother. You are advisor to the King. What was his thinking that he would authorize such a travesty? It is said that natives were massacred."

"There are things you don't understand, Matthew," Walter said easily. "His Majesty is required by affairs of state to act in ways which the people would never comprehend. The attack on Bloody Island was a justifiable act of war."

"Surely we have not gone to war with a poor group of ignorant savages?" Matthew said.

"In effect, we are at war with them," Walter

said. He sighed. "Really, Matthew, you should stick to the simpler things in life. Politics is beyond you. That is why father left me in the position as advisor to the King, and left you charged with the missionary work."

"And yet now you too are to be a missionary," Matthew said. "That is wonderful! And have you abandoned politics?"

"Not exactly," Walter said. He beamed proudly. "I am to be Governor of Kaiulani as well as missionary to the savages."

"Oh?" Matthew said. "Then you are doubly honored, and I am doubly proud."

"Father Damien, would you take me on a tour of the hospital?" Kaiulani asked.

"Yes, of course," Father Damien replied. "Governor, would you care to go with us?"

"No!" Walter said quickly, then, because he thought his hasty answer might be cause for criticism, he softened his answer somewhat. "I would much prefer to stay here and catch my brother up on all the news."

"I'm sorry," Father Damien said. "It was selfish of me to even suggest that you come with us. Of course you should visit with your brother. Come, Princess, we shall let these men have their visit in peace and privacy. Captain O'Lee, would you care to come with us?"

"I would love to," Lorrin said.

Walter was quiet until Father Damien and his two guests were gone, then he spoke. "I can't believe you are actually friends with a Catholic priest," he said.

"Friends, Walter? It is much deeper than friendship. I love that man with all my heart and soul, and I would die for him. He is one of God's most noble creatures who will no doubt go down in history as a hero of Hawaii. And every night I pray to God that I may live so as to follow his good example. I would cry for joy if I contracted leprosy."

"I fear you have already contracted the disease," Walter answered sarcastically. "It has apparently invaded your brain."

"My brother, how can you do God's calling without feeling some compassion for others?" Matthew asked.

"My concern is for the souls of mankind, not for their bodies," Walter answered piously. "After all, the existence of a man on this globe is but the snap of a finger in God's plan of eternity. How much larger, how much greater a good I do by administering to that need, than to any temporary discomfort!"

Matthew shook his head sadly. "And yet are not men judged for eternity by what they do in this life?"

"I fear your theology has suffered, Matthew, no doubt by your close association with an agent of Rome." Walter sighed. "I shall pray for the salvation of your soul."

"And I shall continue to pray for the alleviation of suffering," Matthew said.

Father Damien and Lorrin returned from the tour of the hospital a short time later to find Matthew and Walter still discussing points of theology, or rather, to find Walter discussing it. Matthew seemed content to allow his brother to make salient points without disputing him, seemingly accepting them with a benevolent smile.

"Well," Father Damien said, rubbing his hands

together. "How wonderful to find two men of God discussing His work in such fascinating absorption! It has been a long time since Reverend Wilson and I have had the pleasure of outside religious and intellectual stimulation. Perhaps you would allow me to join in the discussion?"

"I assure you, sir, that I would have absolutely no interest in Papal enunciations," Walter replied.

"Then perhaps we could discuss the lectures and writings of Dr. William Shedd. He is of your faith, is he not?" Damien asked.

"Dr. Shedd is, perhaps, the most learned man of the faith alive today," Walter said. "I will not allow you to mount scurrilous attacks upon him."

Father Damien laughed. "I would never attack Dr. Shedd," he said. "Bill and I are old friends of long standing. We often exchange letters. In fact, I have an autographed copy of his latest book, *Homiletics and Pastoral Theology*. Would you care to see it?"

Walter was stunned. Dr. Shedd was one of the best known Protestant theologians in the world, and Walter had often quoted him. To hear that Father Damien knew him, was *friends* with him, caught Walter by such surprise that he stared at the priest in open-mouthed surprise.

"Come," Father Damien invited. "I'll share some of his letters with you."

Walter followed Father Damien out of the parlor, so intent upon seeing the letters that he set aside his prejudices for the moment.

Lorrin laughed quietly. "I can't believe Reverend Wilson is actually going off with a Roman disciple."

Matthew laughed with him. "For one who would

have you believe that he is concerned only with the hereafter, Walter is easily impressed with the trappings of power on earth. Within a short while, he will be talking about his 'good friend Father Damien, who is a good friend of Dr. Shedd.' It is that same trait which has pushed him into the court of King Kalakaua." He looked at Lorrin. "I would not figure you to be a man so easily impressed, however," he said. "Why have you allowed yourself to be used in such a way?" He pointed at the newspaper story of the attack on Bloody Island.

"You must believe me when I say that I knew nothing of that business until after the fact. The commander of my marines led the shore party."

"And yet, here you are, still in the service of His Majesty," Matthew said.

Lorrin sighed. "Yes," he said, quietly. "Here I am, still in the service of His Majesty. And, I must confess that I am here because of greed."

"I can't believe that," Matthew said. "There must be another, more noble reason."

Suddenly Lorrin felt the white heat of shame. He was ashamed for his part, albeit unwitting, in the massacre at Bloody Island. He was ashamed for his role in bringing an end to the peaceful existence of life on Kaiulani Island. And he was ashamed that in the company of such unselfish men as Father Damien and Matthew Wilson, that his chief motive for being here was a desire to own the four thousand acres of land promised him by the King.

And perhaps one more motive, he told himself. One which was fully as despicable as greed. His other motive, equal to or surpassing that of greed, was lust. Quite frankly, he intended to have Princess Kaiulani during this voyage, one way or another.

"No," he said quietly. "I have been offered four thousand acres of land here on Molokai if I serve the King. That is my motivation."

Matthew smiled. "Perhaps you merely *think* that is your motivation," he suggested. "Perhaps you have been chosen as an instrument of God to do His work."

"And what would that be?"

"Who knows?" Matthew replied. "We are not sufficient to fathom His ways."

"Nor shall I try," Lorrin said, now suddenly uncomfortable by the conversation. "Kaiulani, I am going to examine the land which is now mine. Would you care to come with me?"

"I think not," Kaiulani said. She looked at Matthew. "I should like to bring some comfort to the patients, if you can think of a way it could be done with kindness."

Matthew smiled. "We have many children here, Your Highness, who will be so overjoyed by your visit that they will not feel intimidated by your beauty. Perhaps you could visit with them?"

"Yes," Kaiulani said, smiling happily at the thought that she could be of some service. "Yes, I would very much like to do that. Please, would you take me to them?"

"Of course," Matthew said. He looked at Lorrin. "If you will ask George Mason—you know, the fellow who met you at the beach?—he will hitch up the buckboard and take you out to see your land."

"Thank you," Lorrin said.

Kaiulani left with Matthew Wilson, and Lorrin

found himself alone in the parlor. He walked back to the front of the hospital and found George Mason looking over a grocery list. Mason looked up and smiled as Lorrin approached.

"Have you had a nice visit?" he asked.

"Yes," Lorrin said. He saw that the woman who had brought the grocery list to Mason had turned her back to him as he approached, and she also pulled the shawl up around her face. She stood in silence, looking toward the wall, and Lorrin felt guilty for making her feel so uncomfortable.

"Thank you, Mai," George said, handing the list back to the woman. Mai took the list, and without turning shuffled sideways down the hall until she could round the corner and be out of sight.

"I . . . I have no right to cause such discomfort," Lorrin said.

"Don't worry about it," George replied. "They shield themselves so in order that they bring no further discomfort to you. The truth is they rather enjoy the break in routine the occasional visitor brings to the island. Now, what can I do for you?"

"I have been given a parcel of land by the King," Lorrin said. "Four thousand acres, to be exact. It is known as the Garden of Lau Hala. Here is its location," he added, pulling a piece of paper from his pocket.

"I know the location," Mason said, waving the paper away.

Lorrin smiled. "You do? Could you take me there? I would like to see it."

"Yes," Mason said. "I can take you there."

Lorrin followed Mason outside, and a moment later he was riding in a buckboard on the way to see his new land holdings.

"I've never seen it before," Lorrin said. "It is a grant from the King for services to the Crown." He laughed. "It is probably worthless, barren land."

"No," Mason said quietly. "It is very good land. It is the best parcel of land on Molokai."

"It is? Well, what a pleasant surprise," Lorrin said, genuinely amazed that the King had not tried some trickery on him.

The buckboard stopped on a small hill, and Mason pointed to the land before him. There, stretched out in the valley below, Lorrin saw many acres of neatly tended sugar cane and rice fields.

"What?" he said. "Are you certain you've made no mistake?"

"I've made no mistake, Admiral," Mason replied. "This is the Garden of Lau Hala."

"But, it's being farmed," Lorrin said. "Who is working this land now?"

"We are," Mason said.

Lorrin looked at him in confusion.

"The hospital receives one hundred and fifty dollars per year from the King," Mason explained. "We receive another five hundred dollars per year from various church and charity organizations. But it costs many thousands of dollars to operate. The income from these crops is our primary source of support."

"But I don't understand," Lorrin said. "*Who* farms the land?"

"The patients," Mason said. "Admiral, leprosy is disfiguring, dehumanizing, and tragic. But most who suffer from it are still capable of work, in fact, they welcome the opportunity to work. This land was serving no purpose, so Father Damien suggested that we use it." Mason sighed. "If it weren't for this land, we would have been forced to close long ago."

"I see," Lorrin said quietly. He stood in silence for a long moment. "If you were forced to close the hospital, what would happen to the patients?"

"Most likely they would be put into a prison," Mason said.

"A prison?"

"Oh, not with the prisoners," Mason explained. "The prisoners would be moved to another location, and the patients would serve a life behind bars, not because they had committed a crime, but because they were lepers."

"I see," Lorrin said.

Lorrin looked out over the fields and he heard a young boy's laughter. It was the first laughter he had heard since visiting the colony, and when he looked in the direction of the sound, he saw several youths happily working in the fields. He thought of Father Damien's devotion to the colony, and of Walter's brother, Matthew. He thought of his own shame when Matthew asked him what motivated him to work for the King. Then, with a sigh, he knew what he was going to do. He looked over at George Mason.

"Mr. Mason," he said. "I am happy to have seen this property one time before I turned it over to the hospital."

"What?" George Mason asked, clearly moved by the gesture.

"It's yours," Lorrin said. "Every foot of it."

"Oh, truly, Admiral," Mason said. "The Lord does work in mysterious ways!"

12

"A CONSTITUTIONAL MONARCHY, Your Highness, of the type enjoyed by England," Robert Cox was explaining to Lilioukalani. "You will be the Queen and I will be your Prime Minister. It is the best of both worlds."

Cox was sitting on a lawn chair at Lilioukalani's country estate on Maui, explaining his plan for establishing a new government for the Kingdom of Hawaii.

"I don't know," Lilioukalani said. "I doubt if we will get David to step down voluntarily from the throne."

"I'm certain he will not step down *voluntarily*," Cox said. He took a sip of his cool drink, enjoying the luxury of his position. As Lilioukalani's personal advisor, he was entitled to a high salary and the privileges of high office. But an advisor must advise, plan, and move all the time, for if he became long invisible, his position could be eliminated with no sense of loss. Cox once likened his position with Lilioukalani to that of a swimmer, treading water. He must always be on the move just to stay even. If he stopped moving, he would sink.

Taking that premise one step further, Cox reasoned, with just a little more movement, he could not only defend his position but advance to a higher one. And that was precisely what he was trying to do now with his grand idea of a constitutional monarchy, with himself as the Prime Minister.

"David Kalakaua is my brother," Lilioukalani said. "I have no wish to do anything which might bring physical harm to my brother."

"Your brother would not be harmed, Your Highness," Cox said easily. "We shall merely convince him that it is best for the country for him to step aside and let you rule. His position would then be much the same as yours is now. He would have the comfort and luxury of his royal blood, as indeed, he should have. But he would not have the power of administration over the government."

"How would you convince him?"

"By making him believe that a revolution would be forthcoming should he refuse to cooperate," Cox said easily. "I am certain that for all his faults, he has no wish to subject the country to a bloody revolutionary war. I think he will step down quietly after we have made our position clear. Then he shall have all the time and resources he needs to pursue the pleasures he so enjoys."

"I don't know why he wouldn't prefer that in the first place," Lilioukalani said. "After all, all he wants to do now is play. One would think that the rigors of office would soon wear upon him."

"Indeed, they would wear upon anyone," Cox was quick to point out. "That is exactly why I feel it would be to your distinct advantage to have a Prime Minister to actually govern, thus relieving you of that burden."

"And *you* would be the Prime Minister?"

"By your sufferance, Your Majesty," Cox said humbly.

"Robert, you are a good man at a party," Lilioukalani said. "And a fine friend who is loyal and trustworthy. But by what reason do you feel you would make a good Prime Minister?"

"Because I am half Hawaiian and half American, my Queen. That provides me with the unique insight to govern all our peoples, and to bring unity to our nation."

"Suppose what you are telling me is true, Robert Cox. Can we count on support from the people?"

"Yes, Your Majesty," Cox said, smiling broadly. "That is where I am pleased to tell you that I shall be your most obedient and faithful servant, for I shall provide the support you need. As I informed you, I have been in contact with Colonel V. V. Ashford of the Honolulu Rifles, and we have discussed this very thing at length. At first, he sought only to overthrow your brother and offer Hawaii up, not as a constitutional monarchy, but as a republic. He wished to eliminate the royal line in its entirety. But I finally convinced him of the historical significance of maintaining the line of royalty. He then placed everything in my hands. The Honolulu Rifles and the Lahaina Grenadiers are under my command. I am ready to move upon your order."

Lilioukalani stood up and walked over to a nearby rose bush. She began pulling away dead leaves and dead petals, absentmindedly pruning the bush as she spoke.

"This is something which requires a great deal of thought," she said. "I can not make the decision as easily as all that."

"I realize you shall want to think about it," Cox said. "And I shall give you time to do so. After all, Your Highness, we are deciding the future of our nation."

Cox drained his drink, stood up, bowed slightly to excuse himself, then walked away to allow Lilioukalani time to think things out. He smiled to himself as he walked away, because he had now left no base uncovered.

He was King Kalakaua's confidante and a member of the trusted Committee of Five. Should there be a revolution, and should it look as if it would fail, he could quickly ally himself with the King, providing Kalakaua with just enough information to ensure the failure, and thus gain credit for his part in thwarting it. Should the revolution go only so far as to replace Kalakaua with Lilioukalani, a very likely circumstance since Lilioukalani was a very popular woman among the islanders, and the Americans alike, then Cox was certainly in position to benefit from that as well, as a result of his conversation with Lilioukalani today.

And should the revolution exceed the specified limits, expand so far as to remove the entire royal line, perhaps even go so far as to murder Kalakaua and Lilioukalani, then Cox was prepared for that, too, having planted the seed of the idea of a republic in the mind of V. V. Ashford.

The smile suddenly left Cox's face: he suddenly realized there were two places where he wasn't covered.

If Kalakaua emerged the victor, it might very well be that General Manakalano would come out as his most favored advisor. By Kalakaua's own words, Manakalano was an extremely trusted individual. Manakalano could come out of this in a more favorable position than Cox.

The other imponderable was Princess Kaiulani. Kaiulani was an extremely popular person with all the people of Hawaii: Polynesian, Chinese and American. Kaiulani might well have to be reckoned with, regardless of the outcome of the revolution.

Cox considered Manakalano and Kaiulani for a moment, then came to a decision.

Both would have to die.

13

"CAPTAIN, SAILS," Mr. Adams called down through the hatchway.

Lorrin, who had been at the chartboard in his cabin, put aside the dividers and stepped out of the door of his cabin into the dark shadows of the after-bay.

"Where away?" he called.

"Two points off the starboard bow, sir. She lies between us and Kaiulani Island."

"I'll be right up," Lorrin said.

"Lorrin, is there a problem?" Kaiulani asked. She had come to her door as well, and as her cabin was next to Lorrin's, she was but a whisper away.

"I think not," Lorrin said with a smile. "These waters are fairly well-traveled. I'll go topside and have a look around."

But even as Lorrin sought to calm Kaiulani's fears, he experienced his own doubts. These waters weren't common shipping lanes, as he had said. In fact, until he had discovered Kaiulani Island a short two months before, it was evident that no ship had come this way in recent history. Why was one here now?

General Manakalano was waiting on deck when Lorrin reached it. "I have my marines standing by," he said.

"Wonderful," Lorrin said dryly. "What are you going to do, swim over there?"

"No, Admiral," Manakalano said. "But neither do I intend to run."

"I am most reassured by your bravery," Lorrin said. "Be sure to wear your medal."

He peered at the distant ship through his glasses. "Damn," he said aloud.

"What is it?" Adams asked. "Can you make her out?"

"Aye," Lorrin said. He dropped the glasses. "She is the H.M.S. *Iris*." He sighed. "She is square-rigged and iron-clad, and armed with twelve-inch deck turret guns."

"She's dropping her sails," Adams said. "Why would she do that?"

"She's getting into fighting configuration," Lorrin said. "The sails are only to save coal during the long cruises. For fighting, she's equipped with a steam engine and screw propellers, necessary for modern combat maneuvering." And even as Lorrin spoke, a pencil-thin line of smoke streamed out above the *Iris*.

"Will we try to run?" Adams asked. "Or shall we make a fight of it?"

"We can't fight the *Iris*," Lorrin said. "In ten

minutes they could fire twenty-four rounds at us from the fore and aft turrets."

"Just twenty-four rounds?" Manakalano said with a sneer. He pointed to the guns on board the *Kahili Pahoa.* "We have six guns, each one capable of firing one round a minute. In ten minutes, that would be sixty rounds!"

"Do you know what one of our projectiles weigh?" Lorrin asked Manakalano.

"Sixty-four pounds," Manakalano replied.

"Aye, sixty-four pounds, and with an extreme range of three miles. The *Iris* fires projectiles of over five hundred pounds in weight, and she can throw them over five miles. I might also add that our only hope of damaging the *Iris* would be a direct hit in the steering mechanism or on the bridge. Our shells will bounce off her armor-plate sides with no more effect than if we were throwing rocks." He put the glasses back to his eyes and stared at the *Iris.* "On the other hand, *one* of her shells would sink us."

"Do you propose to surrender, then?" Manakalano asked.

"No," Lorrin replied. "Mr. Adams, how much longer until sundown?"

"Just over an hour, sir."

"Alter course slightly to take maximum advantage of the wind," Lorrin said. "If we can stay out of her range until after dark, we might be able to lose her."

"Aye, sir," Adams said, and he went back to the helmsman to give him the new course.

"She's flying signals," Lorrin said. " 'Stand-by-for-inspection'," he read aloud. He dropped the glasses. "Mr. Adams, show signals, sir: 'Cannot break voyage.'"

"Aye, sir," Adams said.

Governor Wilson and Kaiulani had now come on deck, as well as the sailors who were off watch, and all stood around in a nervous cluster, looking toward the approaching ship which had closed so much distance that her long, sleek, powerful shape could now be seen quite clearly, even without binoculars.

"What do you think they want, Admiral?" Wilson asked nervously.

"They want to keep us from proceeding to Kaiulani Island," Lorrin said.

"What? Why, they have no right to do that," Wilson said indignantly.

"They don't need the right, Governor," Lorrin said. "They have the power."

"Cap'n, they're changin' their signals," Lorrin's lookout called down.

"Read them."

"'Stand to or we will fire'," the sailor called.

Concurrent with the sailor's reading of the new message, a flash of light and a puff of smoke appeared on the pursuing ship. An instant later, a geyser of water erupted just beyond the bow of the *Kahili Pahoa,* and at nearly the same instant, the low thump of the cannon sound reached them.

"My God, they are trying to sink us!" Wilson said. "Strike your colors, Admiral! Surrender!"

"Surrender? Don't surrender! Stand by and fight," Manakalano said.

Lorrin looked at both of them with an expression of disdain on his face. "You are handy people to have along, do you know that? One tells me to surrender, the other to fight." He shook his head in disgust.

"Which will you do?" Kaiulani asked.

"Neither," Lorrin said. He ran his hand through his hair and looked over his ship. "I don't intend to surrender, for to do so would cost me my ship. But I don't intend to stand by and let them blow it out of the water, either. I guess that only leaves one thing."

"You are going to try and outrun her?" Kaiulani asked anxiously.

"Yes," Lorrin said.

"Will you be able to?"

"I doubt it," Lorrin said.

Kaiulani laughed, a small, weak laugh. "Then why try?"

"Why not?" Lorrin replied. "Mr. Adams, come about. Spread on every inch of canvas you can find. Let's get the hell out of here!"

As soon as the pursuing gunboat realized that Lorrin was trying to make a run for it, they fired again. This time the shell fell much closer, and the explosion of it as it erupted in the water sent a shockwave through the sea to rock the *Kahili Pahoa*. Water fountained up, and dropped back onto the deck in a salty rain.

"My God, you can't do this!" Wilson called out in fear. "They are going to sink us!"

"Governor, I suggest you go below deck," Lorrin said. "You too, Kaiulani."

"Below deck? But, wouldn't that be even more dangerous?" Wilson whined.

"No," Lorrin said. "I don't think they will want

to sink us unless they have to. They'll start firing canister rounds now, spraying our deck with shrapnel."

As if underscoring Lorrin's prediction, a cloud of shot emerged from the next flash of fire on board the *Iris*, and though none of the pieces of shrapnel fell on the deck of the *Kahili Pahoa*, it did tear through the sails with popping, ripping sounds. That was enough to send Wilson scurrying below decks, seeking some cover from the attack. Kaiulani lingered above for a moment longer.

"Please," Lorrin said more softly than before. "Go below, Kaiulani." He turned to look at the others, and raised his voice a bit. "In fact, anyone who is not engaged in the actual operation of the ship get below decks. The less opportunity we have to sustain wounds, the less effective their attack will be."

"I am a warrior," Manakalano said. "My duty is to remain here."

"Manakalano, if it were up to me, I'd have you spread-eagled on the mainsail, the better to make a target. But any wound, even to you, will decrease the efficiency of this ship. I will not give over one advantage to our pursuer, do you understand me? Now, get below deck!"

At Lorrin's last outbreak, another cloud of shot reached them, and this time the shot plunged onto the deck. One man was hit in the foot and he let out a bellow of pain and went down. His wound galvanized everyone else, and within seconds the deck was cleared of all but the most essential people.

The *Kahili Pahoa* managed to keep some distance between her and the *Iris*, and in fact until the *Iris* put up her own sails, Lorrin even felt that they were gaining on the gunboat. As the sun set in the western sky, the *Kahili Pahoa* was holding her own. Lorrin stood at the after rail and watched, thankful that the only firing the *Iris* was doing was nuisance firing, to let the *Kahili Pahoa* know that she was still being chased.

Finally darkness settled and the *Iris* gradually disappeared from view. As it disappeared, Lorrin realized that his ship, too, would be cloaked by the night. He breathed a sigh of relief and turned to the helmsman.

"Come right, east by south east," he said. "If we are lucky, the *Iris* will go on by us during the night."

"Aye, sir, east by south east," the helmsman answered.

"Mr. Adams, there will be a cold supper for the crew. I don't want any fires. The slightest spark could give away our position."

"Aye, sir, I'll tell the cook."

Lorrin stretched. "I'll be going below deck now. Wake me at midnight, for I'll take the dog watch. If anything happens, call me at once."

"Aye, sir," Adams said.

Lorrin stopped by the galley and picked up a piece of cheese. He wished he could have coffee to go with it, but by his own order, there was no fire and thus no way to heat the coffee. He took the cheese to his cabin, passing the door which led into Kaiulani's cabin as he went into his own. For an instant he paused outside her door, and he almost called out to her, to assure her that everything was all right, though in truth it was more to hear her sweet voice than to give her assurance. But it was so silent in her cabin that he thought perhaps she was already asleep, and indeed that would be the best way to spend this anxious night, for when one was asleep, one was quite unaware of any danger.

Lorrin went on into his cabin, ate his cheese in the dark, then lay on his bunk and within a few moments was sound asleep.

"Cap'n, your watch sir. Your watch."

Lorrin felt the hand shake him gently, and he opened his eyes. He could hear the water rushing by the hull, and the creaks and groans of rope and wood. All seemed as it should be.

"The *Iris?*" Lorrin sat up in his bunk and ran his hand through his mop of sleep-tossed hair.

"No sight of her, sir. I think we've lost her. I reduced sail."

"Why did you do that?"

"The sea got a little heavy, sir," Adams said.

"Oh. Well, good man, hitting a giant swell under full sail could damage us severely. You did the right thing."

"Thank you, sir," Adams said in a relieved voice. Adams was an old sailor who had served many skippers. There were many who would punish initiative, he knew, and any time the officer on watch altered anything to do with the ship without the specific authorization of the captain, he did so at his own risk.

Lorrin put on his shoes, then climbed the ladder onto the deck. There was no moon tonight, and it was that fact which helped them hide from the *Iris*, which he sensed was still close by. But the absence of the moon seemed more than compensated for by the stars. They were spread across the sky in splendid glory, like thousands upon thousands of sparkling blue diamonds, scattered carelessly upon the black tapestry of the heavens.

"East, south east, as before," the helmsman reported when Lorrin gained the quarterdeck.

"Thank you, helmsman. Come about now, and we'll sail due west for a while."

"Due *west*, sir?"

"Yes," Lorrin said. "If the *Iris* is still out there, we may just slip by her in the night. We'll be back on our original course, and the *Iris* will still be headed for South America."

The helmsman laughed. "Good idea, Cap'n," he said. "Comin' about, due west sir." The helmsman swung the wheel about, the sails creaked and popped as they answered the change in the wind, and the watch sailors scrambled aloft to reset the rigging. Lorrin wandered along the starboard side of the ship, and looked up at the sails with a trained eye, making certain they were set for the maximum advantage obtainable under the circumstances.

"Lorrin?" a soft, melodious voice called.

Lorrin was shocked by the voice, and he looked toward it. He was surprised to see Kaiulani standing just behind the sail locker, next to the intake pipe which vented fresh air below. Had she not called out to him, he would have never seen her, for it was a place which was shielded from view from anywhere on deck.

"Kaiulani? What are you doing up here?"

"I cannot sleep," Kaiulani said. "I am too frightened."

And then Lorrin could tell by the sound of her voice and the expression in her face that she really was frightened, and his heart went out to her.

After all, Lorrin had something to do, something to keep his mind occupied, and the doing helped to sustain him. But Kaiulani had only the awareness of a big ship chasing them, a ship whose guns, Lorrin had already explained, could sink them with one shell. And she had nothing to take her mind off that.

"Don't be frightened, Kaiulani," Lorrin said, and instinctively he went to her and put his arms around her.

Once, when Lorrin had been a child aboard his father's ship, a sea-bird, exhausted from its long flight, had collapsed wearily upon the deck. Lorrin, with a squeal of delight, ran to the bird and picked it up and held it in his hands. The bird had been terribly frightened, and Lorrin had been disturbed. He felt the bird's rapid heartbeat and rapid breathing, and he saw the look of terror in the bird's eyes, and he wanted to explain to the bird that it need not fear him.

Now, as he held Kaiulani in his arms, she reminded him of that bird. Her heart was beating rapidly, her breath was ragged, and he knew she was frightened. But he didn't know how best to calm her fears, so he made no attempt to speak to her. Instead, he just held her close to him, comforting her as one would a baby who needs only soothing words and an affectionate embrace to feel secure.

But as Lorrin held Kaiulani, a subtle change came over them. The embrace gradually changed from one which was supposed to provide comfort to one which was offering pleasure.

Kaiulani had not slept while in her cabin. She

was not asleep when Lorrin passed by on the way to his own cabin, but she lay there very quietly hoping that Lorrin would open her door.

When Lorrin didn't open the door, Kaiulani got up and walked over to open it for herself. She looked around, and seeing no one, slipped unobserved into Lorrin's cabin. There she stood for several moments and listened to him breathe and felt his presence.

The kiss Lorrin had given Kaiulani before they landed at Molokai had not yet left her lips. It was burned into her lips like a brand, and like a brand it marked her as his. In her mind and in her heart, she could think of nothing but Lorrin, and the sharp ache of desire she felt for him.

Then, tonight, with the realization that they could be sunk at any moment, she began to realize how foolish she was to insist upon maintaining her virginity. Her virginity meant only that she could remain third in the line of succession to the throne. But the throne seemed a very remote possibility to her. As a matter of fact, if the crown lay before her right now and needed only her hands to place it upon her own head, she would willingly give it up for the love of Lorrin O'Lee.

How awful it would be, Kaiulani thought, if she went to a watery grave without ever expressing her love for Lorrin! Thus she determined that before this night was over, her love would be consummated. After having made that determination, she had only to go onto the deck and wait for Lorrin to take the watch. The opportunity would then present itself.

That opportunity was now, and as Kaiulani stood there in Lorrin's arms, she leaned against him, knowing full well that he would be able to feel the soft, heavy warmth of her breasts, and the insistent pressure of her flat stomach and thighs against his body. Then, as she knew she would, she was rewarded by the sudden feel of a bulge in his pants.

Lorrin drew away abruptly. "Kaiulani, perhaps you had better go below deck now," he said.

Kaiulani looked at him with a long, penetrating gaze. "I don't wish to go below, Lorrin," Kaiulani said, her face a mask of innocence.

"Yes," Lorrin said, his voice now strained wtih his own struggle against what he was feeling. "You must go. You don't know what you are doing to me."

"Am I doing something to you?" Kaiulani asked, and she moved her lips up to his.

At first, Lorrin tried to fight against what he was feeling, then he tried to master the kiss by making his response firm and possessive, but no matter how hard he tried, he was unable to keep it under control. A cry of agony which turned to ecstasy was born deep in his throat, and he spoke her name into Kaiulani's mouth and pulled her down, down onto the folds of spare canvas, and there he stretched her out with his body against hers and he kissed her as deeply as if he were drinking from the well of life.

Kiaulani felt him at her lips, and in her mouth, and she felt a delightful tingling, as if the wings of a hummingbird had brushed against her. Her head began to spin as Lorrin's tongue darted about, touching her own tongue lightly, spreading a warmth rapidly through her body.

Kaiulani was overwhelmed by the sensations,

and she raised both her arms and put them around Lorrin's neck, losing herself in the kiss. The kiss deepened even more, taking Kaiulani beyond all previously self-imposed limits of control. She knew it was no longer necessary to pull back, and she was glad of it, for she wanted nothing to stop the delightful sensations she was feeling now.

Lorrin had been feeling Kaiulani's breasts through the cloth of her dress, but now he pulled it from her, exposing her golden, ember-tipped mounds. It seemed to Kaiulani that her nipples had never been so tightly drawn or as sensitive as they were now, and they ached for the attention Lorrin was giving them.

Lorrin's fingers and hands played upon them, but so delicate was his touch and so skillful his manipulation, that Kaiulani was unable to discern the individual action, only the pulsating sensations the action caused.

Lorrin followed his fingers with his lips, and tongue, and he kissed her on the face, ears, neck, shoulders and breasts. Then, sometime during the lovemaking, Kaiulani discovered that Lorrin was as nude as she, and she felt his muscled body, tense and quivering, as it came in contact with her own resilient flesh.

Bubbles of fire ascended from Kaiulani's loins, and she hungered for the ultimate: the joining of their bodies which would fulfill the demands her own body was making.

White heat flooded Kaiulani as Lorrin drove himself deep into her. She felt a sharp pain as he entered her, but it quickly gave way to an exquisite and silken sensation of pleasure, and she gasped and rose to meet him, and clutched at him, digging her nails into his back, dipping hungrily at his neck.

A sailor who was on watch walked by then, and as Lorrin heard him, he stopped for a moment, holding himself rigid atop her, his manhood straining inside her. Discovery and embarrassment were but inches away, and yet that very potential for discovery seemed to heighten the sensations of pleasure, and even as Lorrin remained motionless over her, she felt herself dissolving into liquid fire, throbbing in delicious, aching spasms which pulled at that part of him which was inside her.

Then, when the sailor was gone and the danger passed, Lorrin began anew, and Kaiulani's sensations of ecstasy were redoubled. Her skin began jumping, and brilliantly colored lights seemed to dance before her eyes as her body jerked in orgasmic, convulsive shudders.

Kaiulani whimpered and moaned in her rapture, and her cries were buried in Lorrin's throat as he captured her mouth with his, and used his tongue in a stabbing, darting motion to correspond with the savage thrusting below.

Kaiulani felt Lorrin grow tense, pause for a moment, and then as if struck by lightning make one final, convulsive jerk as he spent his satisfaction in her. That was when Kaiulani attained a new level of rapture, rising to heights so far above what she had already experienced that she feared she would pass out. She hung precariously balanced on the precipice between consciousness and unconsciousness for several seconds, and during that time, she experienced repeated waves of pleasure, one bursting upon another until all conscious awareness was redirected to absorb the experience.

And then, with every muscle in her body limp from fulfillment, she felt Lorrin slacken above her, and she pulled him to her, not in the frenzy of sexual excitation, but in the tenderness of love. Everything that she was, was no more. By the loss of her virginity, she had renounced her title and the order of her succession. She had abandoned everything for him. But by that same action she had also given herself over to the demands of her heart, and as she thought of it she felt nothing but joy.

Lorrin made no immediate effort to disengage himself. Instead, he continued to lay on her, and she delighted in the feel of his body against hers, and at the relaxed, gentle, though still intensely pleasurable sensations she was feeling.

All Kaiulani's senses seemed heightened now, and she could feel the night air, smell the salt of the sea, hear the sails and ropes answering the wind, and the steady rush of the ocean. From the other side of the deck she heard a muffled voice ask if anyone had seen the Captain, and she could tell by the feel of Lorrin's body on top of hers that he heard it, too. She knew that he would be leaving her now, but she felt no real sense of loss. He would leave her physically, but he would never leave her spiritually. By their act there, that night, they were one, now and forever. No matter what happened tomorrow with the pursuing ship, even if it meant they would die, they had had their magic moment in the continuum of eternity.

Lorrin kissed Kaiulani one more time, then,

quietly, he stood up, dressed, and stepped out of the sail locker and back onto the deck to resume his stroll.

"Cap'n O'Lee, there you are!" one of the sailors called out. "I'm sorry to report, sir, that the *Iris* is still behind us."

"Damn!" Lorrin said. "How is she staying with us?"

"I don't know, sir, but I saw sparks a short while ago, and I know they were from her stack."

"Helmsman, come due south."

"Aye, sir," the helmsman answered. "Course due south."

"Now, we shall see if their captain really does have cat's eyes to see in the dark," Lorrin mused, staring into the black blanket of night behind them. But even as he looked for the ship which could be the death of them all, he could think only of how alive he felt. Never in his entire life had he experienced anythig like what he had just experienced with Kaiulani. It had been a sexual union more intense than he had ever thought possible, but it was more than that: it had been a union of the souls. For the first time in his life, Lorrin O'Lee was in love.

14

"There, sir, did you see them?"

Lorrin looked in the direction indicated by the sailor and he saw sparks whipped up into the night. Clearly the *Iris* was still out there, just beyond the cloak of darkness, having thus far followed them all night long. Lorrin had put the ship through several maneuvers, but nothing seemed to shake off the determined Englishmen.

"Yes," Lorrin said. "I see them."

"Cap'n, look sir!" another sailor said, and he was near the quarterdeck, pointing to the water.

"What is it?"

"I just saw a reflection in the water. Cap'n, we're showin' a light!"

"What?" Lorrin replied in an angry shout. He ran to the sailor's position and looked in the direction the sailor pointed. At first, he didn't see anything because of the foam of the ship's wake. Then a change in the wave pattern moved the foam away, and there, shining brightly in the water, Lorrin clearly saw the reflection of a lantern.

"Damn!" Lorrin said. "Where the hell is that coming from?"

The sailor who had first noticed the reflection rigged a line to the rail, then he climbed onto the rail, and holding onto the rope, leaned away to examine the ship.

"Cap'n, it's comin' from the Governor's cabin," the sailor said.

Lorrin ran across the deck and slid down the legs of the ladder and was to the cabin deck in an instant. He didn't even bother to knock on Wilson's door. He kicked it in with a resounding crash.

"What the—" Wilson said, suddenly sitting up in his bed at the intrusion.

One quick glance around the cabin told the story. The gimbal light above Wilson's bed was burning. On a bedside table, lying face down, was an open Bible. The porthole hatch was open so that the light was escaping outside.

"You son-of-a-bitch! You've led them right to us!" Lorrin said.

"What are you talking about, sir?" Wilson replied in a put-upon voice. "And why are you in my room? I am a Governor, sir! You have no right to intrude upon my privacy like this."

"You are a fool, sir!" Lorrin said, and he snuffed out the light.

"I'm sorry, Captain, I should have discovered that during my watch," Adams said. Adams' cabin was close by, and he had been awakened by the commotion. He was standing in the bay just outside Wilson's cabin, as was Kaiulani and half a dozen others.

"It's not your fault, Adams," Lorrin said. "I didn't see it, either. One of the men on watch saw it, as well as the entire crew of the *Iris*."

"The *Iris*? Is she still with us?"

"Yes," Lorrin said. "I've no doubt but that she's come up close enough during the night that we'll have to hove to in the morning, or she will easily send us to the bottom."

"We've got better'n an hour 'til first light," Adams said. "Maybe we can still lose her."

"We've got to try, anyway," Lorrin said. He saw Manakalano. "General Manakalano, I want you to place a guard on the door of the Governor's cabin. He is not to leave the cabin without my explicit permission."

"See here!" Wilson sputtered. "You can't do that, I am—"

"I am the *captain* of this ship, mister," Lorrin said. "As far as you are concerned, I am *God*. I can do anything I wish."

"Blasphemy!" Wilson called.

"Bullshit," Lorrin replied, turning angrily and going up the ladder to the deck.

"She's still back there, cap'n," the helmsman said. "I just saw sparks."

"It's a good thing they don't have any better light discipline than we do," Lorrin said. "They could have waited out there in the dark and pounced on us at dawn and we would have had no recourse but to surrender." He sighed disgustedly. "One little light could cost me an entire ship."

Suddenly Lorrin got an idea, and his face lit up. He hit his fist into the palm of his hand.

"On the other hand, it may save the entire ship," he said.

"What are you talking about, Cap'n?"

"Get the dinghy!" Lorrin said.

On board the HMS *Iris*, the sailor in the crow's nest called down. "Light ahead, sir!"

The assistant officer of the deck hurried to the bridge, for on a modern ship such as the *Iris*, a glass-enclosed bridge amidships replaced the old quarterdeck as the command area. The officer-of-the-deck was on the bridge, with the helmsmen.

"Sir, Carson has just spotted the light again."

"Good, good," the officer-of-the-deck said. "I'll increase our speed slightly, and at dawn we'll be in position to close with them." He moved the engine telegraph lever to half-speed, and the increase in the engine's revolutions could be felt throughout the iron hulled ship.

"I wonder why the light keeps going on and off?" the o.d. replied. "It's my guess that the light is in an out-of-the-way location, one the crew is obviously not aware of. As the ship moves, something swings back and forth across the light, sometimes blocking it from our view, sometimes exposing it."

"Yes, I suppose that could be. Tell me, Mr. Prouty, do you think the Captain will sink the ship?"

"If she doesn't hove to, I believe he will," Prouty said. "After all, if these are the bloody beggars who murdered the poor dumb natives on Bloody Island, they deserve to be sent to Davey Jones's Locker now, don't they?"

"You'll not find me crying over their watery

grave, that's for sure," the assistant officer-of-the-deck replied. "Still, 'twould be nice to talk to the blighters, to find out why they would do such a thing."

"It's not that long until dawn," Prouty said. "If they strike their colors, we'll get a chance to find out. Otherwise . . ." he left the statement hanging, potent with its promise of evil intent.

"Sir, we're closin' on the light," one of the sailors on watch said.

Prouty moved the engine telegraph lever to slow down. "It won't do to get too close," he said. "I want to wait just out of sight until it's too late for them to do anything."

"What if they come to a complete stop?"

"We'll stop, too," Prouty said. He laughed. "Their skipper may think he can stop and we'll slip on by him in the darkness, but he'll not put one over on us that easily."

"You think it'll work?" Adams asked Lorrin. The two were standing near the afterrail of the *Kahili Pahoa,* watching the light grow smaller behind them. The light was a lantern, tied to a pole, affixed to the small dinghy, then set overboard. The dinghy was bobbing on the open sea, the light shining brightly. Lorrin's plan was to use that light as a lure, to hold the *Iris* at bay, while they scooted off in another direction.

"We'll know in less than an hour," Lorrin said. "If she is on our tail then, we didn't fool them."

Nearly everyone on board the *Kahili Pahoa* was on deck now, those of the old watch and those of the new watch stood side by side, looking at the tiny, bobbing light. When it finally dropped below the horizon and disappeared from view, they let out a cheer.

"Hold your cheer, lads," Lorrin said. "We'll see if there's anything left to cheer about after the sun comes up."

Kaiulani came onto the quarterdeck, and she stood there beside Adams and Lorrin for a long, silent moment. Once, when no one could see, Lorrin took her hand in his and squeezed it, and she returned the squeeze.

"Do you think we have escaped from them?" she asked.

"I hope so," Lorrin answered.

"I think putting the lamp in the boat was a brilliant trick. If we have escaped, it's because of you," Kaiulani said.

"No. If we've escaped, it's because of luck," Lorrin replied.

"It's nearly time for my watch, sir," Adams said. "I'm going to take a turn about the deck, if you don't mind."

"Go ahead," Lorrin said, thankful in fact that with Adams' absence he would have a moment or two alone with Kaiulani. After Adams was gone, he turned to her. "I'm sorry about last night," he said.

"Sorry?" Kaiulani replied, confused by his strange statement. "What do you mean, sorry?"

"You know what I mean," Lorrin said. "About us, about what happened in the sail locker. It . . . it shouldn't have happened. I have no excuse for my behavior, and I want to apologize."

"But why do you want to apologize?" Kaiulani asked. "Lorrin, didn't you, didn't you *like* it?"

"Like it! My God, woman, the joy of it nearly drove me crazy. But that isn't the point and you know it. The point is I've done you a great disservice. You're no longer a virgin, and that might cause you some problems with the royal family."

"I don't care," Kaiulani said happily. "Don't you realize that, Lorrin? Don't you know by now that the only thing that matters to me is our love and our life together?"

"Our *life* together?" Lorrin said. He cleared his throat. "Kaiulani, you don't know what you are saying."

"Oh, but I do," Kaiulani said. "I'm saying I love you." She hesitated for a moment and looked at him, and in the pale glow of pre-dawn light Lorrin could see the look of concern on her face. "Lorrin, have I made a terrible mistake? Could it be that you do not love me?"

"You haven't made a mistake," Lorrin said. He put both hands on the rail and looked out to sea. "I am terribly in love with you."

"Oh," Kaiulani said, sighing in relief.

"But we don't have a life together," Lorrin said, interrupting Kaiulani in mid-sentence.

"What? What do you mean?"

"Can't you see why not? Kaiulani, you are a princess. Virgin or not, nothing can change who you are, or the life you have led. I am a seaman, born and raised at sea. We are worlds apart."

"But I am not a Princess any more," Kaiulani said. "Don't you *understand*? Don't you realize that I have given up everything for you?"

"I . . . I'm sorry," Lorrin said. "But there is no sense in making matters worse. You would know only a life of hardship if you came with me."

"I don't care. I am willing to undergo any life if I can share that life with you. I want to come with you, to live with you on your ship as your mother did with your father."

"Kaiulani, you are too young now to know what you are saying. You are still impressed with the excitement of life at sea. But, believe me, you've never known what it is like to ride out a storm, or be becalmed, or suffer the want of food and water. If you came with me you would hate me within six months. I would not want that."

As Kaiulani realized what Lorrin was saying . . . that he wasn't going to marry her, and she had thrown away everything for him, only to be spurned by him, tears sprang to her eyes. She lashed out at him, hoping to hurt him the way he hurt her.

"You won't have to wait six months to see me hate you," she said. "I hate you *now!*" Abruptly, she spun around and stormed off the quarterdeck.

"Cap'n, no sails on the horizon!" A look-out called down from the crow's-nest, and then, almost in surprise, Lorrin realized that it was dawn, and the horizon was visible. He looked around quickly, and noticed that the look-out was correct. There were no sails. He had escaped.

"Three cheers for the Admiral!" someone called, and all on board gave three hearty cheers that Lorrin had led them in a bold escape.

But Lorrin scarcely heard his men. Kaiulani's words of anguish were still ringing in his ears.

"Admiral, I'm coming on watch now, sir. What is the course?" Adams asked. "Shall we resume a heading for Kaiulani Island?"

"No," Lorrin said. "Set sail for Honolulu, Mr. Adams. The *Centurian* is going home."

Adams smiled happily. "You mean we ain't playin' navy no more?"

"That's exactly what I mean," Lorrin said. "Make all possible speed. I want to get these landlubbers the hell off my ship."

"Aye, aye, sir. Honolulu it is."

15

It was nearly noon as Lorrin O'Lee's ship *Kahili Pahoa* slid to rest in Honolulu Harbor, with sailors aloft pounding the sails into tight furls and the anchor chain clacking and rattling as the great iron hook splashed down in the deep.

Lorrin stood on the quarterdeck looking toward the shoreline, at the flowers and verdant trees, vivid colors after days of nothing but open sea and pale, wavering blues. The perfume of the flowers floated toward him on an off-shore breeze, mingling with the tangy salt taste and smell of the sea. It was a smell which was so familiar to Lorrin that he was scarcely aware of it as he stood there.

"Cap'n, anchor's dropped, sir," Mr. Adams reported.

"Very well, Mr. Adams," Lorrin said. He turned his back to the shoreline and leaned onto the railing to look at Adams. "Mr. Adams, I'll be needing a first mate for my next cruise, a *merchant* cruise. Would you be willing to sign on?"

"Aye, sir, and every man-jack of the crew as well," Adams said. "Where will we be goin', sir? Not that it matters—we'd most of us soak our trousers in kerosene and sail into hell with you if need be."

Lorrin laughed. "It is my hope, Mr. Adams, that we've had our voyage to hell. As to where we go, I suppose it will depend upon what cargo I can secure. I shall speak with Mr. Dole, and see if he has a cargo for us."

"Admiral O'Lee, I want to speak with you," Walter Wilson called. Wilson had just come on deck, dressed in the clawhammer jacket and striped trousers which had long been his trademark. Since being appointed "Governor" of Kaiulani Island he had added a top hat and a cravat, and now he wore those affectations as well. A leather bag was on the deck beside him, and he was obviously packed to go ashore.

"I am no longer an admiral," Lorrin said. "I have resigned that position."

"And well that you did," Walter Wilson said. "For in truth, sir, it is my intention to report your behavior to His Majesty the King. Your treatment of a Royal Governor has been scandalous. You have been rude, incompetent, and insolent. I am certain that His Majesty will have a few remarks for you."

"Damn few, I hope," Lorrin muttered. He pointed at the bag. "I see you are prepared to go ashore."

"I am, sir," Wilson said. "Now, if you would be so kind as to put a boat over for me?"

"You can go ashore in one of the water taxis," Lorrin said. "I'm certain Mr. Adams will be glad to summon one for you."

"A water taxi? But I am a governor, sir!" Wilson sputtered.

"Not on my ship, you aren't," Lorrin said. "To me you are just a passenger. Mr. Adams, summon a taxi."

"Aye, sir," Adams replied with a smile, and he crooked his arm toward one of the many boats which were bobbing in the water near the *Centurian.* One of them started toward the ship.

"Good day, sir," Wilson said angrily.

"And good day to you, Governor," Lorrin replied, smiling, and giving a mocking half-bow toward Wilson.

"You men, there," Adams called. "Help the Governor overboard."

Two sailors were quick to respond, and Wilson found himself practically shoved onto the boarding ladder for the climb down into the water taxi.

"Mr. Adams, signal for a lighter to come alongside," Lorrin said, as the water taxi carrying Wilson started ashore.

"A lighter, sir? But we have no cargo to off-load."

"No cargo, perhaps," Lorrin said. "But some useless dunnage." Adams had a look of confusion on his face, and Lorrin explained. "I'm talking about Manakalano and his Marines."

"Aye, sir," Adams said, understanding his Captain at last. "I'll bring a lighter alongside right away."

One of Manakalano's marines was standing amidships, having watched the departure of Wilson, and Lorrin called out to him.

"You there, marine. Tell Manakalano I want to see him."

"I wasn't finished dressing," Manakalano said a

few moments later. He had put on his parade uniform, and his medals flashed in the bright sun.

Lorrin looked at his elaborate uniform and let out a snort of contempt. "I don't mean to rush you, General, but unless you intend to swim ashore, I suggest you and your men board the lighter which is approaching us."

Manakalano looked confused. "What are you talking about?" he asked. "Why should we board a freight scow?"

"Because as far as I'm concerned, General, that's what you are—freight, and I want you off my ship. You and all your men, and those damned cannon, too. Unless you wish them shipped overboard!"

"No," Manakalano said. "I'm responsible to the King for them. Don't push them overboard!"

"Then get them off-loaded," Lorrin said. "They take up space and weight that I could use for profitable cargo."

Manakalano squinted at Lorrin. "I take my men off your ship with pleasure, Captain O'Lee. We are warriors, and a warrior has no place on board a vessel commanded by a coward."

A shadow of anger flicked across Lorrin's face, and a blood vessel in his temple throbbed, but he held his anger in check. Finally, with a sigh, he turned his back to Manakalano. "Just get the hell off my ship, Manakalano," he said, then he looked over at Adams. "I'm going to my cabin," he said. "Keep two men for an anchor watch and allow everyone else to go ashore."

"Aye, sir," Adams said.

"And hurry this business up," Lorrin added. "When I come on deck next, I don't want to see any sign of Manakalano or his men."

Lorrin walked across the deck and through the companionway which led to his cabin. His cabin was at the end of the companionway, taking the whole stern of the ship. Doors off each side of the companionway opened into the other cabins, occupied on this trip by Wilson, Manakalano, and Kaiulani. Kiaulani's cabin door was the last door before his own, and Lorrin stopped in front of it and started to knock.

Kaiulani had scarcely spoken to him since he told her that he had no intention of marrying her. She did not understand that he was making that sacrifice to protect her. She was hurt and angered by his actions, and the fact that Lorrin was unable to soothe her hurt or assuage her anger, made the situation even more difficult to bear.

Lorrin turned away from her door without knocking on it and went into his own cabin. He pulled the shutters closed on his windows, then lay on his bed with his hands linked behind his head, looking at the pattern the slashing sun bars made on the wall. He had no idea what lay before him now. What would the King do upon hearing that he had not completed his mission? Would the King allow him to resign and return to the sea as a merchant seaman, or would the King find some grounds on which to arrest Lorrin?

It was not out of the question, Lorrin knew. Kalakaua was not a predictable man, and Lorrin could certainly count on Manakalano and Wilson trying their best to persuade the King to take some action against him.

In fact, even Kaiulani might be persuaded to go to the King against him, Lorrin knew. He may have hurt her badly enough to make her do such a thing, and if she did go to him, given the King's unpredictability, there was no telling what might happen.

Sanford Dole might help, but he wasn't someone Lorrin could count on.

Lorrin heard footsteps come down the companionway then pause just outside his door. There was a knock, but the knock wasn't on his door. It was on Kaiulani's door.

"Princess?" Adams called out. "Princess, your things are loaded in the boat."

"Thank you," Kaiulani answered, and the sweetness of her voice tore at the strings of Lorrin's heart.

Adams' footsteps walked away, and a moment later, Lorrin heard the door to Kaiulani's cabin open and close. He listened for her footsteps, but when he heard none, he knew that she was standing just outside his door. Why, he wondered? Was she waiting for him to call out to her? Did she want him to ask her to stay with him?

With all that was in his being, Lorrin wanted to do just that. He wanted to get out of his bunk and run to the door, jerk it open, and pull her into his cabin, to smother her with kisses, and tell her of his love for her. He wanted her to stay with him, forever, to go with him to the furthest reaches of the sea.

But he knew that he could not. He had seen his mother longing for the sight of another woman, yearning for a friendly visit and a stable home. His mother had never complained, but Lorrin had always known that she suffered in silence, and he did not wish to subject Kaiulani to that. Kaiulani's background was vastly different from his mother's

background, and she would suffer all the more for
it, and there would come a time in her life when
she would think back on this, and then she would
be grateful to Lorrin for preventing the marriage.

So, despite the urging of his heart, Lorrin kept
his mouth closed tightly, and he resisted the temp-
tation to call out to her. Finally he heard the sad
sound of her footsteps as she walked down the
companionway and climbed the ladder onto the
deck. A moment later he stood in the shadows of
his cabin and watched her boat as it was rowed to
the shore. Kaiulani was sitting proudly, facing the
shore, as the boat moved across the water. Not
once did she look back toward the ship.

Kaiulani did not look back toward the ship and
she did not shed a tear, though she very desperately wanted to do both. But from somewhere deep
inside, perhaps from the blood of the Alii-Nui
which was in her, she found the strength she
needed to carry herself with dignity.

When Kaiulani reached the shore, the landing
of Manakalano and his marines was already creat-
ing somewhat of a sensation. A rather substantial
crowd had gathered at the docks, and Manakalano
and Wilson were standing together, the centers of
attention, railing at the crowd with accusations
against Lorrin.

"At the first sight of danger he turned and ran,"
Manakalano shouted. "He is supposed to be an
Admiral, a servant of the King. But I say he is a
coward and a traitor!"

The crowd reacted angrily to Manakalano's accusation, but he held his hands aloft and quieted
them, then pointed to Walter Wilson.

"Governor Wilson will back me up on this," Manakalano told them. "You see him before you now, when in fact he should be on the island of Kaiulani, serving as the newly appointed Governor. He isn't there because Admiral O'Lee was frightened away by the appearance of an English flag."

"Is that true, Governor?" someone from the crowd asked.

"Yes," Wilson said, and when the man wrote Wilson's answer in a tablet, he asked him, "Who are you, and why are you writing this down?"

"I am a reporter from *The Daily Mail,*" the man answered.

"A reporter?" Manakalano said, beaming proudly. "Good, I am glad you are here. You can take all of this down. Admiral O'Lee has shown a streak of cowardice from the moment we left Honolulu, and when we encountered the English ship a few days ago, his cowardice panicked him into outright flight. Now he remains aboard his ship, too frightened even to face the King with the news of his failure."

"In fact," Wilson put in, "he has resigned His Majesty's commission."

"Resigned?" Manakalano scoffed. "He has deserted."

"What about Princess Kaiulani?" someone asked. "She was with you. What does she say about all this?"

Kaiulani had walked over to the crowd to see what was going on, and when the man asked the question, everyone looked toward her to see what she would have to say.

"Please," Kaiulani said, holding up her hands. "I have nothing to say."

"Did you find Admiral O'Lee's actions cowardly or treasonous?" someone called out.

"No," Kaiulani said. "No, I did not."

"Princess Kaiulani, if charges are brought against Admiral O'Lee, would you testify for or against him?"

"I would not expect to testify at all," Kaiulani answered.

"But if you were summoned, if you had to testify, how would you?"

"I do not believe Admiral O'Lee is a coward or a traitor," Kaiulani said.

"How is it, then, that the ship has returned without fulfilling its mission?" the reporter asked.

"I don't know," Kaiulani said. "Please, I am terribly tired now. I should like to go home."

From out of the crowd appeared a man she recognized as one of her mother's servants. He walked over to her.

"Princess, your mother is in Honolulu. I've been sent to take you to her."

"Thank you," Kaiulani said, following him gratefully away from the crowd which now seemed to be growing even larger.

Kaiulani rode in the back of the closed coach, glad that the sides of the coach kept people from seeing her and recognizing her. She could not smile and wave at them in her present state of mind, and she would have to if she were riding in an open carriage, for that was one of her duties.

Kaiulani's mother came out to the driveway to meet her, and she put her arms around her and drew her into her bosom as soon as Kaiulani stepped out of the coach.

"I heard that the ship was back," Lilioukalani said. "And I sent for you as soon as I heard. Why are you back so early?"

"We were attacked by a British ship," Kaiulani said.

"Attacked? How do you mean, *attacked?*"

"They fired at us," Kaiulani said. "They attempted to sink us. We were able to evade them during the night."

"I did not believe he would actually go through with it," Lilioukalani said. "Not at the risk of sinking his own ship and his own people."

"What are you talking about?" Kaiulani asked.

"Your Uncle David, the King," Lilioukalani said. "Robert Cox brought me news that he was concerned about the reaction of the English to the incident on Bloody Island. He was frightened that the English would come to my aid in a coup, so he sought to prevent that by going to them first."

"Mother, you mean you were going to use the English to mount a coup against Uncle David?"

"No, of course not," Lilioukalani said. "But David was afraid that I was, and that was enough to drive him to irrational action. Robert Cox informed me that David was considering going to the English and asking them to provide protection for all the islands from Lorrin O'Lee, who, David said, was acting in violation of his orders. I immediately sent word to David that I had no intention of entering into any alliance with the English, and I hoped that would be enough to satisfy his fears. Evidently, it wasn't."

"Then it is as much your fault as it is Uncle David's," Kaiulani said angrily.

"What? How can you say that?" Lilioukalani asked. "Didn't I just tell you I acted to *prevent* him from seeking English interference?"

"Mother, don't you understand? That just made him all the more sure that he was right," Kaiulani said. "And he probably was. I've no doubt that you would use the English to your advantage if you thought you could."

"Kaiulani, how can you say such a thing?" Lilioukalani asked indignantly.

"I can say it because it is true," Kaiulani said. "You and Uncle David have been fighting over the throne for as long as I can remember. One would not even know that you are brother and sister. All I can say is I am glad I am out of it now. I can never wear the crown, and I am glad."

Instantly, Kaiulani realized what she had said, and her face flamed red in embarrassment and she looked quickly at the ground.

"What?" Lilioukalani asked quietly. "Child, what are you saying?"

Kaiulani drew a deep breath before she spoke.

"I . . . I am no longer a virgin," she said.

"I see," Lilioukalani replied. "Lorrin O'Lee?"

"Yes."

"Daughter, I know you understand the consequences of your act. Surely, with such a consideration, you wouldn't have done this unless you love him deeply."

"No!" Kaiulani said. "I don't love him. I don't love him at all. I *hate* him!"

Lilioukalani was shocked by Kaiulani's sudden outburst, and her mouth dropped open in surprise.

"You *hate* him, and yet you gave away everything for him? How can this be?"

"He spurned me, Mother," Kaiulani said. "I . . .
I threw myself at him and he rejected me."

At that moment Lilioukalani was more a mother
and less a queen because the sight of her daughter
in such distress moved her as any mother would be
moved. She went quickly to her daughter and put
her arms around her and pulled her close to her.

"I am sorry, my darling daughter," she said. She
ran her hand through Kaiulani's hair, adjusting the
blue-black strands as she did when Kaiulani was
but a child. "I am so terribly sorry that you have
been hurt. But listen . . . who knows of this?"

"Who knows of it?" Kaiulani asked through her
tears. "Nobody knows of it. I've told only you.
Why?"

"Then we will tell no one else," Lilioukalani said.
"And thus, no damage will be done."

"But, mother, you know the law. I must confess
this."

"Nonsense," Lilioukalani said. "That is one of
David's laws, and it is a law with which I do not
agree. When I am in power, I will change the law.
For now, we will say nothing."

Robert Cox waited just behind a tree near the
porch. He had been visiting with Lilioukalani, but
now it was time for him to leave, because he had an
engagement that evening. He had intended to tell
Lilioukalani goodbye, but he didn't wish to interfere with Lilioukalani's welcome of her daughter,
so discreetly, he had stayed back out of sight. And
now, just as discreetly, he stole away . . . armed
with a bit of information he was certain would
someday be useful to him.

16

LORRIN WAS ASLEEP when he heard the knock on his door. For a moment he thought he was at sea, and was being called for his watch, and he called back that he would be right there. Then a second knock awakened him more fully, and he blinked his eyes and looked at the shadows in his cabin and realized that he had been sleeping for several hours.

"Lorrin, it's me, Sanford. Can I come in?"

"Yes," Lorrin called back. "Yes, come in."

Lorrin sat up in his bunk and rubbed his hands across his face in an effort to wake up. He had slept none at all the night before, anxious that the English ship which had dogged him might have reasoned that he would be heading for Honolulu and double back on him. Now, in the quiet of the afternoon with everyone ashore but the anchor watch, the quiet rocking of the ship had acted as a sleeping potion and he had slept so soundly that he felt almost drugged.

Sanford stepped into the cabin.

"So, you were asleep?"

"Yes," Lorrin said. "Have a seat," he offered, pointing to one of the chairs.

"Thanks," Sanford said. Sanford chuckled. "From the looks of you, one wouldn't suspect that you are the center of such controversy."

"Oh?" Lorrin replied. He got up, took two tin cups over to a keg and drew two ales. He handed one to Sanford. "And what controversy is that?"

"What controversy is it? Well, let's see, where shall I start?" Sanford replied. "King Kalakaua has accused you of acting beyond the scope of your orders in the massacre on Bloody Island, and—"

"What?" Lorrin exploded. "Sanford, what the hell are you talking about? Manakalano got a *medal* for that! I had nothing to do with it, in fact, I didn't even *know* about it until you told me yourself, if you recall. Hell, Manakalano is the first to tell you that."

"Not anymore, he isn't," Sanford said. "Manakalano is accusing you of cowardice, desertion, and treason, and Wilson is backing them up."

"I must say that I don't find that a total shock," Lorrin said. "They were both pretty angry when they left ship, and I expected something like that. Did you hear what happened? We were attacked by a British man-of-war."

"Yes, I know," Sanford said. "Kalakaua requested their assistance in patrolling these waters."

Lorrin looked up in quick surprise. "Why would he do a thing like that?"

"He couldn't beat them so he joined them," Sanford said. "The British were very upset with what happened at Bloody Island."

"I know," Lorrin said. "I saw a paper when I was on Molokai. Also I didn't think the ship we encountered was trying to invite us over for tea. But I still don't understand why Kalakaua asked them to attack me."

"Kalakaua informed the British that you had acted beyond the scope of your authority when you attacked the natives on Bloody Island," Sanford said. "That got him off the hook, and by requesting their assistance, it allowed him to save face. Otherwise their attack on you could have been considered an act of war. How would His Majesty react to that?"

"I don't know," Lorrin said. "All I know is I was the one on the spot. And I don't intend to be there again. I am resigning from the King's Navy."

"It isn't necessary for you to resign," Sanford said. He smiled. "My boy, you've been cashiered."

"You mean I've been kicked out?"

"Yes. The King wanted to court-martial you, but I talked him out of it," Sanford said. "I felt that I owed you that much."

"Well, thanks," Lorrin said. "If you recall, I didn't want to do any of this in the first place. It would have been a terrible miscarriage of justice if I wound up in jail for something I didn't want any part of."

"That was my thinking," Sanford said. He finished the ale Lorrin had given him and put his tin cup on the table, the same table from which Lorrin and Kaiulani had eaten their happy meal.

"I'm glad the charade is finally over," Lorrin said. "Oh, but there is one thing."

"What is that?"

"The land," Lorrin said. "The four thousand acres Kalakaua promised me for doing this. Will he go back on that promise now?"

"Oh, I'm certain of it," Sanford said, and the expression of his voice showed that he was a little disappointed that Lorrin would even mention it. He sighed. "But don't worry, Lorrin. I'm certain that I can accommodate your avowed greed with four thousand of my own acres."

"No," Lorrin said. "It isn't for me, and your land won't do."

"What do you mean my land won't do? I have the finest land in the islands. And if it isn't for you, who in blazes *is* it for?"

"It's for the leper colony," Lorrin said. "They are farming the four thousand acres Kalakaua had promised to me. I gave them title to the land, but now I find it isn't mine to give title to. I would like to think there is some way of the colony keeping that land without Kalakaua taking it away from them."

The expression on Sanford's face changed, softening to one of appreciation and respect.

"I'm sorry, Lorrin, I misjudged you, and I wronged you by that misjudgment."

"You have every right to misunderstand," Lorrin said. He laughed derisively. "Hell, I was the one who made the great speech about greed being more dependable than noble causes. Then, I turn around and do a noble but dumb thing like giving away my land. Or, rather, land that I thought was mine."

"Don't worry about it," Sanford said. "I'm certain I can interest Kalakaua in some kind of a deal which will transfer ownership of that land to me. I'll transfer the land to you and then the deal you made with the leper colony will be valid."

"Thanks, Sanford," Lorrin said. "I really appreciate that. And now I'd like to ask you another favor."

"What?"

Lorrin smiled. "Would you please arrange a cargo for me so I can get back into the business of shipping where I belong?"

Sanford laughed. "You'll have a shipment within a week, I promise you."

"Thank you," Lorrin said gratefully. "You don't know what that means to me. I want more than anything to get away from the politics and intrigue of these islands."

"Oh, yes, intrigue," Sanford said. "That reminds me. My niece has a little intrigue of her own."

"Andrea?"

"Yes. I'm not certain what it's all about, but she has asked that I bring you home tonight. You will come, won't you?"

"I don't know," Lorrin said. "After all that has happened, I'm not sure I would be fit company."

"Oh, but you must come," Sanford said. "I fear Andrea would make my life unbearable if I returned without you. Besides, what if Kalakaua suddenly decided to make a public example by arresting you? At my place you will be safe."

There was something to what Sanford said, and Lorrin considered that possibility. He also considered Andrea; beautiful, desirable, available Andrea. If Kaiulani had to get over Lorrin, then he was faced with just as monumental a task in getting over Kaiulani. Andrea might be just what he needed to get Kaiulani out of his mind, if not out of his heart.

"I'd be glad to come," Lorrin finally said.

"Wonderful, wonderful," Sanford said. "Oh, by the way, something's been bothering me, so I may as well come out with it right now. Lorrin, I feel it is my duty to warn you about Andrea."

"Don't worry, Sanford," Lorrin said. "I've no intention of doing anything to hurt her."

Sanford chuckled. "You misunderstand, my boy. I'm not worried about Andrea, I'm worried about *you*."

"About me?"

"Yes. Andrea is my niece, my own blood, and I love her dearly. But I fear she could trifle with a man with little or no concern for him. I would not want you to be hurt in such a way."

Now Lorrin felt guilty. He was consciously planning to use Andrea as a means to get over Kaiulani, and here, Andrea's own uncle was expressing concern that Andrea might hurt him.

"Thank you, my friend, for your warning," Lorrin said, walking over to Sanford and putting his hand on the older man's shoulder. "But I don't wear my heart upon my sleeve, and thus I have no fear on that score."

"Then you will play her game, knowing full well that it is but a game?" Sanford asked.

"Yes," Lorrin said. "I will play her game."

Sanford shook his head in confusion. "I am not certain that I understand either one of you," he said. "However, you are both adults, and both forewarned. Who am I to question you? I shall leave matters alone."

"Give me a few minutes to get ready," Lorrin said. "I am not dressed to go ashore."

"Very well," Sanford said. "I'll wait on the deck."

Sanford was passing the time with one of the men of the anchor watch when Lorrin appeared a few moments later, dressed in a jacket and a clean shirt for the shore.

"Will you be spendin' the night ashore, Cap'n?" Sanford's conversational partner asked.

"Aye," Lorrin said. "There are just the two of you, now?"

"Aye, sir."

"I'm sorry you weren't able to go ashore your first night back."

The seaman grinned. "Someone has to be the anchor watch, Cap'n. My time'll come tomorrow."

"I've a bit of ale and some cheese left in my cabin," Lorrin said. "Help yourself to it."

The seaman's face broke into a wide grin. "Thank you, Cap'n! That's most generous of you, sir."

"Shall we go?" Lorrin said to Sanford, and he led the way over the rail and down the ladder into Sanford's boat which bobbed alongside the *Centurian*.

The boat was started, and it headed not for Honolulu, but east, beyond Diamond Head, and around Koko Head, until they reached the private docks of Sanford's Sugar Plantation.

The sun had already set by the time the boat docked, and the house was well lighted and shining like a jewel. Lorrin looked up at it as he stepped out onto the boat wharf, and he knew that he had been deluding himself by even thinking he could ever own such a place. And it would take a place like this to make a suitable home for Kaiulani. Now

Lorrin was convinced more than ever that he had done the right thing in refusing to allow her to settle for less.

When Sanford and Lorrin stepped inside the house, they were met in the foyer by Andrea. She took Sanford's cape and hat and hung them on the hall tree, then she looked over at Lorrin, and as always there was a certain look on her face, a smile on her lips as if she enjoyed some secret joke.

"So," she said, pouting her lips invitingly. "You have come at last!"

"Yes," Lorrin said. "Your uncle was kind enough to invite me."

"Have you come alone?"

"I beg your pardon?"

"Your friend, the Hawaiian girl. What is her name?"

"Are you talking about Princess Kaiulani?"

"Yes, Princess Kaiulani," Andrea said. "Did she come with you?"

"No," Lorrin said, confused by Andrea's line of questioning. "Of course she didn't come with me. Why would you ask such a thing?"

"Oh, that's really too bad," Andrea said. "Had she come, you would have no cause to feel left out of things."

Lorrin was puzzled by Andrea's strange remark, and then he saw the reason for it. For there, coming from the dining room, was Robert Cox.

"You should have asked me, my dear, if Kaiulani was coming," he said. "I could have told you no, for I saw her shortly after she arrived at her mother's house."

"You do know Bob, don't you, Admiral?" Andrea

said. She walked over to Cox and leaned against him, allowing him to put his arm around her. "Oh, excuse me. From what I have heard, it isn't Admiral anymore, is it? You've been cashiered, haven't you? It is just captain now."

"Yes," Lorrin said. "It is just Captain, and yes, I know Robert Cox. I must say, though, that I didn't expect to see him here."

"Oh?" Andrea said. "And just what did you expect to find here? Me, waiting for you with open arms?"

"No," Lorrin said. "No, of course not."

"Good," Andrea said, smiling sweetly. "Then you won't be disturbed by the arrangement. Come on, dinner is about ready. Bob, would you be a dear and escort me to the dining room?" she asked, offering her arm to Cox.

"I would be delighted to," Cox said, taking the proffered arm and leading her grandly into the other room.

Sanford stuck out his hand and held Lorrin back for a moment. "I didn't know about this," he hissed. "She asked only that I bring you to dinner tonight. She said nothing about Cox. If you'd like, I can send the boat back to your ship."

"No," Lorrin said. "Sanford, I told you, I'm not wearing my heart on my sleeve, so, please, don't worry about me."

"Very well," Sanford said. "But I want you to know that I consider my niece's behavior quite rude, and I certainly don't approve of this."

When Lorrin reached the dining room a moment later, Cox was holding the chair out for Andrea, and after she was seated, he quickly took the seat next to her.

"So, you were with Lilioukalani today," Lorrin said. "I would have thought that she would consider you unwelcome company by now."

"Why would you think that?" Cox asked.

"You've been quick to pass along information about her. I would have thought she would have discovered you by now."

"I am just as quick to pass information to her," Cox said. "I am accepted everywhere."

"Accepted everywhere, or spying everywhere? It seems to me, sir, that you are playing all sides at the same time, hoping to come out a winner."

"I wouldn't put it that way," Cox said, in a tone of voice which showed that he took offense at the remark.

"Bob is a peacemaker," Andrea explained. "Someone has to keep a cool head when others are losing theirs."

"Yes, I'm certain that's true," Lorrin said. He helped himself to the first course of canapes as a servant held a silver serving tray in front of him. "Besides, who am I to question you, Cox? Had I any sense, I would be following your course."

"And what course will you follow now?" Cox asked.

"East, north-east," Lorrin said.

"What?"

"I'm sailing for San Francisco as soon as I can get a cargo for my ship," Lorrin explained. "I've lost all interest in the affairs of Hawaii. I'm concerned now only with those things which may affect my life as a merchant seaman."

"Yes," Cox said rather haughtily. "I think experience has shown that you are qualified for little else."

"Are you trying to insult me, Cox?" Lorrin asked. "You will have to tell me if you are, because it is difficult to place any weight on the empty words of a wastrel."

The easy smile left Cox's face, and he glared across the table at Lorrin. "Regardless of my interest, sir, it is easy to see you mean to insult me!"

"Oh, how delightful," Andrea said. "I do believe you two gentlemen are on the verge of fighting over me." Her eyes snapped in excitement as she looked at the two brooding men.

"Andrea!" Sanford said. "I will not allow you to goad these two men on!"

Lorrin touched the napkin to his lips, then stood. He looked toward Cox and made a slight bow, and then smiled at him.

"Please forgive me, sir," Lorrin said. "I had no right to pass such a remark, and I ask that you accept my apologies."

"Your apology is accepted," Cox said, flashing a smug smile of satisfaction. He was obviously enjoying having made Lorrin O'Lee back down.

"And now, if you will excuse me, I shall withdraw."

"I'll come with you," Sanford said, putting his own napkin upon his plate.

"No, please," Lorrin said, holding his hand out toward him. "I don't wish to spoil things any more than I already have. I'd like to just take a walk now, if you don't mind."

"Let him go, Uncle," Andrea said. "He needs to cool off a bit."

"Andrea, I find your behavior here tonight unconscionable," Sanford said after Lorrin left. "Lorrin O'Lee is our guest."

"So is Robert Cox," Andrea said, putting her hands on his arm. "And as Bob is of more delicate sensibilities than Mr. O'Lee, I felt constrained to come to his defense."

"Bah," Sanford said, shoving his chair roughly back under the table. "I hope you and your guest of delicate sensibilities enjoy your dinner, for you shall be dining alone. I'll take my meal in the parlor."

"Really, Uncle, you and Mr. O'Lee have blown things all out of proportion," Andrea said. "But if Bob and I are to be left alone, then we shall derive all the more pleasure from each other's company because of it."

Sanford snorted his displeasure and walked out of the dining room, leaving just as a servant brought in the soup course. The servant had four steaming bowls on the tray, and he looked up in surprise at the only two people left at the table.

Lorrin walked away from the house, and down across the rolling lawn, out onto the beach, all the way to the edge of the surf. He watched a breaker roll in, crash with a sound of thunder, then sweep millions of frothy white bubbles up the smoothly packed sand until they stopped just at the edge of his shoes.

Why had he acted as he did? Was it jealousy? Was he angry because Robert Cox seemed to be enjoying a more favored position with Andrea now? The answer to these questions was yes! He was jealous, and he was angry that Cox was enjoying Andrea's favor. And yet, even as he realized that, he knew also that he had no right to feel anger or jealousy. Had he not come out here tonight with the sole intention of using Andrea to help him forget Kaiulani?

Lorrin was disgusted with himself. He had spoken bold words when he told Sanford that he didn't wear his heart on his sleeve. What he neglected to say was that he did wear his pride there, and when his pride had been pricked, he childishly baited Cox in retaliation.

Lorrin turned and started walking down the beach, along the line which separated the wet sand from the dry, and he struggled with the thoughts which were tumbling around inside him. He had acted the fool tonight, but then that was in keeping with his entire behavior of late. There was little left for him now but a long sea voyage, away from the intrigues of Hawaiian politics, away from the allure of the women of the island, away from Kaiulani and Andrea alike.

Lorrin walked all the way down to the furthest point a distance of a little over a mile, before he turned and came back. By the time he was back to the point of the Dole plantation house, his thoughts had quieted some, and he was ready to go to bed for a restful sleep. He would not think of Kaiulani again, and he would put Andrea out of his mind as well.

But it wasn't that easy to put Andrea out of his mind, for when he got back from his walk, she was standing on the beach, waiting for him. She was holding her hat down against the off-sea breeze which blew her hair across her face and plastered her dress against her form. She had the same secret smile she always had.

"Did you enjoy your walk?" she asked.

"Very much," Lorrin answered.

"I hope it cooled you down somewhat."

"It did," Lorrin replied easily. "You shall hear no more from me tonight."

"Oh? Well, I hope that isn't true, for I would find that rather disappointing," Andrea said.

"Where is Cox?"

"I really don't know," Andrea said. "I asked if he would like to come down to the beach with me, but he said he preferred retiring early. I must say that the two of you have quite effectively spoiled my party."

"I'm sorry the night has been such a disappointment for you," Lorrin said.

"Oh, the night isn't over yet," Andrea said. She walked over to Lorrin and leaned into him, pushing her warm breasts to his chest and pressing against him with an insistent pelvis. She put her arms around his neck, and pursed her lips for a kiss.

"No," Lorrin said easily, taking her arms down one by one, and stepping back from her.

Andrea was shocked. She stood there, looking at him in total surprise. She was a woman of exceptional sexual appeal, and no one had ever backed away from her before.

"What?" she asked in a small voice.

"Andrea, I must admit that when I came here tonight, I was hoping we would have the opportunity to be together," he said. "But not now."

"Is it because of Robert Cox?" Andrea asked. She laughed weakly. "Lorrin, couldn't you tell what all that was about? Didn't you know I was merely using him to make you jealous? He means nothing to me."

"That doesn't matter," Lorrin said. He sighed and ran his hand through his hair. "The truth is,

Andrea, I was just going to use you, anyway. I was going to use you to help me forget Kaiulani."

"Then do it," Andrea said urgently. "I can make you forget her, I know I can." She put her arms around him again, but again Lorrin pushed them back.

"No," he said easily. "You could never make me forget Kaiulani, and it wouldn't be fair to let you try. You would only wind up being hurt."

"*Hurt?*" Andrea said, and she looked at him with an expression somewhere between anger and pain. "Do you mean to tell me you think you can *hurt* me? Why you poor misguided bastard! Do you think you were ever any more to me than a mere diversion? Because if you think that, you are wrong. You are terribly, terribly wrong!"

"I'm sorry," Lorrin said, and he turned and started quickly toward the house just as he saw the glistening of tears in the corners of Andrea's eyes.

"Bastard!" she called out to him. "You poor misguided bastard!"

Lorrin did not know how long he had been asleep when he heard the sounds. They were coming from the guest room next to his, the room occupied by Robert Cox, and he lay there listening to them, wondering what they were, and then he suddenly knew.

It was a woman's voice, and the sounds were moans of pleasure. They were the unmistakable sounds of a woman who was being loved, and it was unmistakably Andrea's voice.

Lorrin lay there, instantly and completely awake, wanting on the one hand to shut the sounds out of his mind, while on the other straining against all

reason to listen. He had heard her make the same
sounds with him, and he could almost see her,
lying beneath him, her face contorted in the throes
of rapture, her body moving against him, her legs
splayed wide to receive his thrusts.

Suddenly Lorrin felt his body break out in a
sweat, and he sat up and swung his legs over the
edge of the bed. What was he doing? Why was he
torturing himself this way? He put his hands over
his ears, but some force deep within wouldn't let
him keep them there, and he dropped them, then
held on to the bedpost and listened as the pitch
and crescendo of her sounds told him that she was
reaching a climax. A lower, strained, guttural sound
told him that Cox, too, had been satisfied.

Lorrin sat there, holding onto the bedpost for
several seconds, then he heard Andrea laugh, a
foolish, sexy, indiscreet giggle. That was followed
by a laugh from Cox, and he spoke in a voice which
Lorrin could hear, but couldn't understand. They
both laughed again.

Lorrin got up, walked over to his shirt, removed
a long thin cheroot, lit it, then went over to stare
through the window at the sea.

17

IN THE EARLY EVENING, clouds gathered on the western horizon, forming gigantic battlements which totally obscured the setting sun. Their bases were low and occasional rain squalls stabbed blue diagonals toward the sea. There were openings and indentations in the moundings, and through these openings the sun dispatched silver and gold shafts of light. The sea resembled a painter's palette, showing daubs of silver, red, gold, then several shades of blue deepening into black depending on the shadows and light which hit its roiling surface.

But this evening spectacle was totally lost upon Lorrin as he paced back and forth on the quarterdeck of the *Centurian*. He had thought that he would find peace upon returning to the sea, but for the entire voyage from Honolulu, bound for San Francisco, he had known no peace, for his mind was plagued with the memory of Kaiulani. He dreamed of her by night and he thought of her by day, and no matter how hard he tried, he could not get her out of his mind.

"Cap'n, if the wind holds we'll be making San Francisco tomorrow," Adams said, lighting his pipe and leaning into the railing. The ship was sailing along at a pretty good clip, and the sound of the wind in the sails, and the rush of the water from the keel made a soothing background.

"True enough," Lorrin answered. He checked the tension on one of the ropes by giving it a pull. "It's been a fast passage."

Adams took a deep puff on his pipe before he spoke again. "Aye, it has been, and free of any difficulty. So my question is—and excuse me for askin' if it be out of line—what's troublin' you?"

"What makes you thing anything is troubling me?" Lorrin asked.

"Cap'n, I've sailed man and boy for fifty years. I know when something is troublin' a cap'n, and somethin' is sure as hell troublin' you. But I'll be damned if I can put my finger on it. You aren't for wishin' we were still in the King's Navy, are you?"

"Hardly that," Lorrin said.

"Then it be a woman," Adams said, nodding sagely. "And that makes it personal and none of my business, so if you'll excuse an old man for buttin' in where he's not needed, I'll just be about my own business."

"No, wait," Lorrin said.

Adams had started off the quarterdeck, but he stopped and looked back toward Lorrin.

Maybe he should speak of this to someone, Lorrin thought. After all, he had no one in whom he

could confide, and there came a time in everyone's
life when they needed a sympathetic ear.

"Yes, sir?" Adams said gently.

"Adams, I was born on a ship. Did I ever tell
you that?"

Adams smiled. "You didn't need to, Cap'n. Why,
I took a cruise with your papa once when you were
just a tyke about this high." Adams held his hand
close to the deck.

"Really? I'm sorry. I should have remembered
you."

"No reason you should have," Adams said. "You
were awfully young, and I was before the mast, a
bit of a hellion, in fact. Sad to say, I don't believe
your papa was all that upset when I jumped ship.
I've never mentioned it for that reason."

"I see," Lorrin said. "Well, I appreciate your honesty with me now, Adams."

"I can afford to be honest, Cap'n. Them old days
is behind me."

"Do you remember my mother?"

"Indeed I do, Cap'n," Adams said. "A beautiful
woman she was, sir, 'n no finer lady ever drew a
breath, I don't reckon."

"Do you think she was happy?"

"Happy, Cap'n?" Adams said, and his face clearly
reflected his confusion over the strange question.
"She seemed happy enough, I really couldn't say,
that bein' much too personal."

"I don't mean was she happy with my father,"
Lorrin said. "I mean, do you think she was happy
with her life, living on board a ship? What do you
think she thought of that?"

"She seemed to me like all the other cap'ns' wives
I sailed with," Adams said. "She seemed happy to

be with her man. Many's the wife who sees her man only when he's ashore, 'n what kind of life could that be?"

"What about the men who sail on a ship where the captain brings his wife?" Lorrin asked. "What do they think about it?"

"For the most part, they enjoy it," Adams said. "You see, a lady kind'a gentles down the ship a bit, 'n it reminds the men that there is somethin' in life that is pure and sweet. Yes, 'n pretty too, and I 'spect they take a degree of pride in their cap'n's wife. In a sense, she more or less belongs to 'em all. Now tell me Cap'n, are you plannin' on takin' on a wife?"

"No," Lorrin said. "I didn't want to subject her to such a life, although she was willing to."

"Cap'n, I don't know the lady you're talkin' about," Adams said. He squinted his eyes. "Or maybe I do, sir. At any rate, I'd say you weren't givin' her much credit. If she wants to ship with you, then it seems to me like you ought to respect her wants—that is, if you have any feelin' for her at all. And if you don't have any feelin', then tell it for what it is, 'n don't use as an excuse that she wouldn't be happy on the ship. When folks are in love, they are happy together, no matter where they are. The only thing important is whether you 'n the lady love each other."

"Thanks," Lorrin said. He looked at Adams and smiled. "I just wish I had talked to you before we left Hawaii."

"It's not too late, Cap'n. When we get back, you just go to the young lady and tell her you want her to come with you. From what I saw of her, she enjoyed sailin'."

"Who are you talking about?" Lorrin asked evasively.

Now it was Adams' time to smile. "Why, Princess Kaiulani, of course. I think she'll make a fine Cap'n's wife."

"If she'll have me," Lorrin said. "After the way I treated her, she may never want to see me again."

"Don't worry about it, Cap'n. She'll come around. I know she will."

"Oh, I don't know, Adams. I've been such a fool, I wouldn't be surprised if she forgot all about me."

But Kaiulani wasn't about to forget all about Lorrin. If she was on his mind, he was equally on her mind, and she spent the first several weeks after returning from the ill-fated voyage, moody and despondent. She was so despondent that her mother began worrying about her, and tried in many ways to cheer her up. Lilioukalani had planned on returning to Lahaina, but decided that the best chance of helping Kaiulani snap out of her melancholy was to stay in Honolulu where there were more people and more things to do.

Lilioukalani came out onto the terrace and saw Kaiulani sitting on the terrace wall. Kaiulani had her knees drawn up and her arms wrapped around her knees and her chin resting upon them as she stared out toward the sea.

"Do you see his ship out there?" Lilioukalani asked.

Kaiulani jumped at the sound of her mother's voice. She smiled wanly. "Oh, I'm sorry, mother. I didn't hear you."

"I wouldn't think you could hear thunder in your condition," Lilioukalani said. She walked over and kissed her daughter on the forehead, then smoothed a few strands of her daughter's hair. "What are you doing just sitting out here, girl?"

"Nothing," Kaiulani said. She sighed. "I'm just enjoying the beautiful scenery."

"It's been the same since you were born," Lilioukalani said. "You never spent that much time looking at it before."

"Maybe I never noticed it before."

"Kaiulani, I've been thinking about your problem, and I have come to a conclusion. I think you need to go out, to see people, to hear music and laughter, and to have a good time."

"No," Kaiulani said. "Thank you, but I—"

"No buts," Lilioukalani said. "My brother has little enough going for him as far as I am concerned. But he does know how to give a wonderful party. They don't call him the Merry Monarch for nothing. People say my lifestyle is dull by comparison."

"I much prefer your lifestyle," Kaiulani said.

"Nevertheless, David is giving a party tonight, and you are going."

"Please, mother, I'd rather not," Kaiulani said.

"I don't care what you'd prefer," Lilioukalani said. "I have accepted for you, and you are going and that's final. Robert Cox shall be your escort."

"Robert Cox? Oh, mother, no!" Kaiulani wailed.

"Why not, for heaven's sake? Listen, if there is anyone in the islands who knows how to have a good time at a party, it is Robert Cox. Lord knows he goes to enough of them."

"He is such a toady," Kaiulani said. "I don't like to be around him."

"Well you can't go to the party unescorted, and Robert Cox is a friend of mine."

"Robert Cox is a friend to anyone who can do him some good," Kaiulani said. "I don't trust him."

"Trust him? You don't have to trust him, just go with him. Go and have a good time. That's an order."

"No, that's two orders," Kaiulani said. "Go is one, and have a good time is another, and they are incompatible."

"I'm sure that you will find a way to overcome the difficulty," Lilioukalani said, smiling sweetly and withdrawing before her daughter could introduce any further objections to the plan.

The party, as were all of Kalakaua's parties, was grand and glorious. Long tables were filled with glistening hams and seafoods, and salads and fruits of every hue and description. There were no fewer than four complete bands—not small party bands, but complete orchestras with entire pits of woodwinds, brass, strings and percussion, playing in various parts of the palace. The cream of Hawaiian and international society was there, and tuxedoes, medal-bedecked uniforms, and flowing ball gowns moved and swirled through the palace halls and chambers.

The party was Kaiulani's first public appearance since returning from the voyage, and she was instantly set upon by the other guests who welcomed her back and bewailed her long absence from society.

"If you will excuse me, Princess," Cox said shortly after arriving at the party. "I have a few people I need to speak to."

"Of course," Kaiulani said, for her part glad to be left alone, for she disliked Robert Cox, though in truth, she had never been able to put her finger on the exact reason why.

"Princess Kaiulani, what do you think of the grass skirts?" one of the male party-goers who had crowded around her asked.

"The grass skirts?" Kaiulani answered, confused by the question.

"You mean you didn't see the dance that was performed a short while ago?"

"No," Kaiulani answered. "I only just arrived."

"Well, wait until you see," the young man said. "It seems that General Manakalano brought back some skirts made of grass from Kaiulani Island. He says that the women wear such skirts on the island, and I must say that if they are as beautiful as the dancing girls who wore them a short while ago, then I'm going there at once."

"I say, I do believe grass skirts will catch on here, don't you think so?" another young man asked, and his question was answered with enthusiastic affirmatives by several of the others.

"It speaks little of our Admiral's expedition that all we have to show for the Naval maneuvers is the importation of a few grass skirts," Manakalano said, and Kaiulani, who had not noticed him before he spoke, looked around in surprise.

"Good evening, General," she said.

"So, you are over your heartbreak and have decided to come out into society again, eh?" Manakalano asked. "You were heartbroken, weren't you? Because O'Lee did not take you with him?"

"General Manakalano, my feelings for or about

Lorrin O'Lee are none of your concern," Kaiulani said.

"I beg your pardon," Manakalano said easily. "I meant no offense." He smiled, a smug, satisfied type of smile which told Kaiulani that he not only meant to offend her, but that he was enjoying it. "If you will excuse me, Princess, I shall return to the party."

"Yes," Kaiulani said coldly. "Please do."

Andrea had watched the byplay between Manakalano and Kaiulani from across the room, and when Manakalano bowed to Kaiulani and walked away, she started toward him. She arranged it so that he bumped into her.

"Oh," Andrea said, reaching for her foot. "Why don't you watch where you are going, you clumsy oaf? You nearly knocked me over!"

"Excuse me, madam," Manakalano apologized profusely. "I'm terribly sorry. Are you all right?"

Andrea took a couple of steps, limping badly with each step she took. "No," she said. "I fear that it may be sprained."

"Is there anything I can do to help?"

"Perhaps if you knew of a quiet place I could go, to sit for a few minutes until the pain passes?" Andrea suggested.

"Yes, I do know a place," Manakalano said.

"Is it very quiet?" Andrea asked, looking at Manakalano and smiling coquettishly at him. He was handsome in a dark, brooding way, and the most promising of all the men she had seen since arriving at the party. She was upset because Robert Cox had escorted Kiaulani to the party rather than her. Of course, Cox was little more than someone to dally with, anyway, and she certainly had no intention of devoting herself to him at the party even if he had brought her. But the thought of him bringing Kaiulani instead really angered her. After all, Kaiulani had already stolen one man from her. She didn't appreciate Kaiulani stealing still another.

For the moment though, none of that mattered. For the moment, all that mattered was that this party not be a total waste of time. And from the looks of things, it would not be. She was leaning on Manakalano, forcing him to support her as she hobbled away from the crowded party to someplace quiet. And she could already tell that her nearness to Manakalano was having an effect on him.

"I know a place upstairs," Manakalano was saying. "An apartment the King keeps for guests which is now empty and quiet, if you think you can make it that far."

"I can make it," Andrea said. She leaned against him, pressing her thigh against his, feeling the heat flare up and sensing the change in his breathing which told her that he was becoming aroused by her closeness. "I know I can make it if you will come up with me."

"I'll come with you," Manakalano said, his tongue thickened and his voice strained. "I'll be more than glad to come with you."

From the opposite side of the room, Robert Cox had watched Andrea maneuver herself into position to be accidentally bumped by Manakalano. He chuckled to himself as he saw Manakalano falling into her trap. "Come into my parlor, said the spider to the fly," he mumbled under his breath.

Cox had never met anyone like Andrea. She was

the most beautiful, the most sexually aggressive woman he had ever known. And yet, strangely, Andrea had to have sex on her own terms. She had to initiate it, and she wasn't content to lie back and allow the man to lead as it should be. She brought fully as much energy to the sex act as did the man, and when it was over, Cox could never be sure of who had done what to whom. It was at the same time wonderfully exhilarating, and strangely disquieting.

Andrea had been upset with him for bringing Kaiulani to the party, even when Cox tried to explain all the political reasons why he had done so, but Cox knew that Andrea's anger wouldn't mean she had severed all further contact with him. He would be with her again, at her convenience, and the pleasures Andrea could bring to the relationship were enough to make Cox willingly accept it on her terms.

A good case in point was the night O'Lee had spent at the Dole house. That was not the first time Cox had had sex with Andrea, but it was the first time she had ever come to his room. He had been a little surprised by it, because O'Lee was a guest in the next room, and Cox was certain that O'Lee would be able to hear them. Then he realized with crystal clarity that that was exactly what Andrea wanted. She *wanted* O'Lee to hear them making love, and Cox had found the idea sexually stimulating as well. It was a night Cox would long remember. Just as he was sure this would be a night Manakalano would long remember.

"Mr. Cox, you will forgive me if I am a few moments late," a Chinese man said, bowing politely as he approached. "But I had some unexpected business."

"Ah, Mr. Chin," Cox said, smiling at the tall thin man who wore the clothes of a most wealthy Chinese merchant. "The time at any of His Majesty's parties passes quickly and pleasantly. I felt no discomfort in waiting for you."

"Good," Chin said. "Then perhaps we can get right down to business?"

"Yes," Cox said. "Did you bring the money?"

"It is here," Chin said, holding up a small, leather valise. "Seventy-one thousand dollars, just as you asked."

Cox reached for the valise, but Chin withdrew it just before Cox could grab it.

"You will forgive an old man his superstitions, I'm sure," Chin said. "But I would like to see the authorization before I give you this money."

"Of course, of course," Cox said. He reached into his inside jacket pocket and pulled out a paper. "Here it is," he said. "A commission from King Kalakaua granting you exclusive rights to sell opium."

..Chin took the paper and looked it over. "I do have one question," he said.

"And what would that be?"

"What about Mr. Aki?"

"Aki? Who is Aki?"

"Mr. Aki is a gentleman of my acquaintance," Chin said. "Mr. Aki told me that he paid King Kalakaua the same sum of money for the same exclusive license to sell opium."

"I see," Cox said. He ran his hand through his hair. "And does Mr. Aki have that license?"

"No," Chin said. "He has paid the money, but he doesn't have the license."

"No, I didn't think he did," Cox said. "He doesn't have the license for the simple reason that there is only one, and it is now in your hands."

"But what about Aki?" Chin asked again.

"Are you worried about Mr. Aki?" Cox asked. "If you are, you may give him your license."

Chin smiled. "No," he said. "I am not worried about Mr. Aki."

"Good," Cox said. "Then we will hear no more discussion about Mr. Aki. Take your license, Mr. Chin, on behalf of King Kalakaua. Go and prosper."

"Thank you, Mr. Cox," Chin said. "It has been a pleasure doing business with you."

Chin put the license into the voluminous fold of his sleeve, bowed politely, then turned and shuffled off. Cox, holding the money securely in front of him, watched the old Chinaman leave, then chuckled over his good fortune. He turned back to look over the party until he found Kaiulani. It would not do for him to leave her too long abandoned. If Lilioukalani thought he had treated her improperly, it would upset the delicate balance he had established with her.

Cox started toward Kaiulani. She was standing near a large window, listening to the music of the band but not participating in the gaiety of the party. Cox knew that she was still thinking of Lorrin O'Lee, and for a moment the thought made him angry. What was it about Lorrin O'Lee which so affected all the women? First there was Andrea, and now there was Kaiulani.

Cox sighed. Andrea had compensated for her loss of O'Lee by seeking her lustful pleasures elsewhere; first with him, and now with Manakalano.

It would be nice if Kaiulani would do the same thing.

Cox felt a flash of sexual excitation as he thought of what it would be like to share a bed with Kaiulani, and the thought was so intense that for an instant, he felt dizzy and he had to stop and regain his breath. He was angry with himself for having such a thought, and he pushed it out of his mind. Kaiulani was the daughter of Lilioukalani, and much as he may want her, he knew that she was beyond reach. Were he to have Kaiulani, it would ruin the carefully laid plans of a lifetime.

And yet, at this very moment, Cox believed it would be worth it.

18

Lorrin was very surprised to discover that he was regarded as somewhat of a hero in San Francisco. He was certainly a newsworthy figure, for he was hounded by reporters for interviews and invited by clubs and associations to make speeches about Hawaii and his recent experiences there.

One such was the Frontier Club, a gentlemen's club which consisted of the wealthiest and most influential men of San Francisco. Lorrin had been invited there by Thurman Bradford, a close friend of Sanford Dole's, and Dole's San Francisco business agent.

"Sanford Dole speaks most highly of you, Captain O'Lee," Thurman said as they sat at the dinner table prior to the meeting at which Lorrin was invited to speak.

"Sanford Dole is an exceptionally fine man,"

Lorrin replied. "In my opinion, he is the George Washington of Hawaii."

"The George Washington of Hawaii, huh?" Thurman said, chuckling. "That's a pretty high accolade for a pineapple farmer."

"He is much more than that," Lorrin said. "He is a patriot and a statesman. If Hawaii were a republic, there is no doubt he could be the president."

"Well, now, how likely do you think that is?" Thurman asked. "I mean that Hawaii might become a republic?"

Lorrin spread butter on his roll and took a bite in contemplative reflection before he replied to the question.

"I would say there is that possibility," he finally said, offering no further elaboration.

"Captain O'Lee," Thurman said. "I didn't ask you that question in idle curiosity. I have a specific reason for broaching the subject."

"Oh?"

"You may have noticed, Captain, that you have become quite a popular figure since your arrival in San Francisco. Newspapers, clubs, parties, everyone is anxious to see and hear you."

"Yes," Lorrin said with a nervous laugh. "I must say that the whole thing is most surprising."

"Surprising perhaps, but carefully planned. Very carefully planned," Thurman said, punctuating his statement, taking a spoonful of lobster bisque.

"Planned? How do you mean, planned?" Lorrin asked.

"My dear young man," Thurman said. "I told you that Sanford thought very highly of you. He sent me a letter, even before you left Hawaii, outlining his plan to me. You are to be introduced to all the right people, interviewed by the newspapers, and generate a great deal of interest in Hawaii. He wants to make Americans aware of the plight of the Americans who live in Hawaii."

"What plight are we talking about?" Lorrin asked.

"Oh, the usual—taxation without representation, living under the oppressive rule of a monarchy, that sort of thing," Thurman said.

"But I thought Sanford was ready to accept the monarchy," Lorrin said. "That was why he arranged for my commission in the King's Navy."

Thurman laughed. "It was merely an experiment. He hoped to be able to influence Kalakaua as a result of providing him with a Navy, but it didn't work out as he had planned. Now he is trying a different approach."

"I see," Lorrin said. "I wonder why he didn't tell me about it."

"Oh, my dear fellow, you are much too modest to come to San Francisco and blow your own horn," Thurman said. "No, that he left to me. I have had time to feed a few stories to a few accommodating reporters, and, *voila*, you arrive on our shores, the conquering hero."

"Hero? I was cashiered from the Hawaiian navy. How can you turn that into something heroic?"

"Oh, quite easily, my dear boy," Thurman said. "You protested the King's expansionist ideas, won a military engagement against a modern British warship, and escaped with your integrity intact. That is the stuff from which heroes are made."

"And did Sanford Dole send any instructions for

me?" Lorrin asked, somewhat miffed by the whole thing. "Surely he wrote a few of the speeches I am to deliver?"

"You are upset," Thurman said, puzzled by Lorrin's reaction.

"Yes, I am."

"But why? It's not every day you get the chance to be a hero."

"No, and it's not every day one is made an admiral, either," Lorrin said. "Well, I wasn't really an admiral, and the whole thing was a sham. And I'm not a hero, either. This is just as false. And I resent being used for all these hair-brained schemes."

"I'm sorry you feel that way," Thurman said. "Sanford picked you because he respects your honesty."

"My *honesty?*"

"Yes," Thurman said. "According to Sanford, you, of all people involved in the League, have the honesty to see through the hypocrisy of the revolutionary fervor."

"Then I don't understand," Lorrin said. "If he respects my honesty, why does he choose me for such hypocritical missions?"

Thurman laughed. "Because you won't fall victim to the premise. The biggest problem with hypocrites, my boy, is that too often they believe their own hypocrisy. When that happens, they lose their objectivity, and when they lose their objectivity, they lose their effectiveness. You never really considered yourself an Admiral, and thus you were never taken in by the sham. You don't really believe you are a hero, and thus will never suffer a big head."

Lorrin drummed his fingers on the table for a

moment, and then finally he smiled. "All right," he said. "What is the plan?"

"The long range plan is quite simple," Thurman said. "Sanford Dole believes that Hawaii must become a territory of the United States."

"That's been discussed," Lorrin said. "But I thought Sanford had dismissed it as being impractical."

"It is not impractical if it is accomplished in steps," Thurman said. "The first step is to win concessions from the King, major concessions that so limit his power that the monarchy will be totally ineffective. The next step shall be the total abolition of the monarchy and the establishment of a Republic. After that, an appeal to the United States for annexation and territorial status."

"And the abolition of all trading tariffs," Lorrin said.

"Of course," Thurman agreed. "But obviously, that can't be the rallying cry. The rallying cry must be the rigors of decent citizens, American and Hawaiian alike, having the live under the despotism of someone like Kalakaua. And you can help create that situation in your talks, by telling people the truth about Kalakaua, and about the terror of the Americans who must live under him."

"No," Lorrin said. "I'll tell the truth about Kalakaua, and that should be enough to convince any thinking person that he is not fit to be a ruler. But I won't lie and say that the Americans in Hawaii are living in fear of their lives, for that simply isn't so."

Thurman smiled and pushed his plate away, patting his lips with the napkin as he finished his meal.

"Given Sanford's assessment of your honesty, I thought as much," he said. "However, from what I know of Kalakaua, the truth about his corrupt and inept administration should be all that is needed to generate sympathy to our cause. Go to it, Captain O'Lee. Use the truth as your armor, and bring down the monarchy!" Thurman raised his glass of wine in a toast, and Lorrin, smiling, lifted his own glass and drank the toast with him.

"I say, Thurman, are you going to keep our guest of honor all to yourself for the entire night?" a man asked, walking over to their table at that moment. He was smiling, and sticking his hand out toward Lorrin in the offer of a handshake.

"Captain O'Lee, this is Ed Granger, the vice-president of the Frontier Club. He was good enough to sponsor your speaking engagement here tonight."

"It is indeed a pleasure to do so," Granger said. "Young man, you are the talk of the town, I must say. It will be an honor to hear you speak tonight."

"Thank you for inviting me," Lorrin said. "Won't you sit down?"

"Yes, for a few moments," Granger said. He looked at Thurman. "I have some distressing news to report," he said.

"What is it?"

"It is news about Harold Poindexter. You remember Harold, don't you? He is the man who was involved with Andrea Dole—" Granger saw Thurman's warning glance, and he cut his sentence off before he completed it, but Lorrin heard enough of the name to recognize, and though he made no outward sign of distress, he listened intently. He realized that Granger must be talking about the man with whom Andrea had been involved before she left San Francisco.

"What about Harold?" Thurman asked.

"Well, as you know, he was divorced shortly after the . . . uh . . . incident occurred," Granger said, trying to couch his words so that Lorrin couldn't follow them. But Lorrin had already heard enough to be able to piece two-and-two together.

"Yes," Thurman said. "It was a pitiful thing to see the break up of a home in which there were four children involved, but though that is distressing, it is hardly news."

"There's more," Granger said. "Even before the divorce, he lost his job, as you know. Well, he was unable to find another position, save occasional menial labor on the docks and so forth, so he soon lost his assets and his self-respect. I heard that he was even arrested once or twice for public drunkenness, and could sometimes be seen on beggars' row, asking for a hand-out."

Thurman shivered. "It is a shame to see the depths to which a man can fall," he said. "I considered Harold a friend, and a gentleman of talent and ability. How could he have so debauched his life by losing control of his own lustful desires?"

"There are some who come to his defense," Granger replied.

"What defense could there be?"

"There are some who suggest that Harold wasn't the seducer, but the seduced."

"Impossible, the girl in question is a young, innocent, and sweet girl," Thurman said. "No, most assuredly, I will not believe *that* tale. As I say, I liked Harold very much. But I am quite more willing to believe that he was the victim of his own debauchery than the victim of an innocent young girl. In fact, when I think of the disgrace he brought down upon that child, I am disposed to think that all he has gone through and all he shall go through is a just reward for his sin."

"Perhaps so," Granger said. "But he won't be going through any more."

"What do you mean?"

"He was found dead this morning," Granger said. "Dead by his own hand."

"He . . . he committed suicide?"

"Yes. And he left a note."

"What did the note say?"

"The usual sort of thing," Granger said. "He begged forgiveness from his wife and children and from his friends and business associates who had known him before his descent into the dregs."

"Did he say anything about the girl he so brutalized?"

"No," Granger said. "Not a word."

"There," Thurman said. "That should be proof, if proof be needed, that he was the guilty party and not she. For even in his death note, he was so overcome with guilt that he could not speak of her."

"Well, enough of this unpleasantness," Thurman said. He looked at Lorrin, and then was shocked to see the expression on Lorrin's face. "Captain O'Lee, why have you reacted so to this tale? Did you know Harold Poindexter by any chance?"

"No," Lorrin said. He removed a cheroot from his inside jacket pocket and prepared it for lighting. "But I know Andrea Dole."

Thurman looked at Granger with an accusing

stare, as if angry with him for mentioning the girl's name, and Granger looked down at the table. Thurman sighed. "Then you know that she can't be the guilty party in this," he said.

"I am certain that Andrea did not want Harold Poindexter to suffer so from their relationship," Lorrin said, stopping just short of absolving Andrea of any of the blame.

"No, of course not," Thurman said. He perceived the nuance of Lorrin's non-denial, and decided wisely to let the subject drop. "But, as I started to say, enough of this unpleasantness. You have a speech to give, and I, for one, am looking forward with great anticipation, wondering what you are going to say."

Lorrin lit his cigar and took a couple of puffs, then smiled at Thurman. "You know what? I'm wondering what I'm going to say, too."

"It's great!" Sanford Dole said. He tossed several copies of the *San Francisco Examiner* across the breakfast table to V. V. Ashford. "Do you see what our boy is doing to them in San Francisco? These came with yesterday's boat mail."

The newspapers were full of stories of Hawaii and its bungling king. One issue had an editorial which suggested that the United States should move quickly to safeguard its interest or face the possibility of having Hawaii fall under the umbrella of the British Empire.

"Listen," Ashford said. "With this support behind us, why wait any longer? Why not let me take my riflemen into Honolulu and attack? Hell, I could turn Hawaii over to you tomorrow!"

"No," Sanford said. "Ashford, this *must* appear

to be a genuine uprising of the people, don't you understand that? It has to have a popular front. That means we must move slowly."

"If we move much more slowly, there are going to be some bankruptcies to contend with," Ashford said. "Some of our best backers are just barely hanging on against the sugar tariffs."

"I know," Sanford said. "I'm hurting as much as any of them. But if the wrong people in America perceived what we were doing, they would not only fight against our being annexed by the United States, they would go so far as to support the reestablishment of what they would call the 'legitimate' Hawaiian government. This is too important to be blown by intemperate movement now."

"But we've got all the support we need right here!" Ashford said, pointing to the newspapers. "San Francisco is behind us one hundred percent."

"San Francisco is but one city," Sanford said. "We need San Francisco, St. Louis, Philadelphia, Boston and New York, to say nothing of Washington. Then, and only then, can we move," Sanford said. "But they'll come aroud, V. V., I know they will. And it is business like this which will help." Sanford picked up a copy of the *Honolulu Mail* and pointed to a front page story.

"What is this?" Ashford asked.

"It seems our business-minded monarch has found a new way to raise money," Sanford said. "He sold a license to deal in opium to a Chinese merchant named Aki, but he neglected to deliver the document. Then, a short time later, he managed to sell the same license to another merchant by the name of Chin."

"Well, that is out-and-out fraud," Ashford said.

"Surely we can bring charges against him for that?"

"Legal charges in a court of law?" Sanford said. "No, I think not. In the first place, there are many who would feel that the opium dealers got their just deserts by being cheated. No, our best bet is to merely allow the story to be run in the newspapers long enough to keep up the smell of graft. And that I can manage."

"Yes. Robert Cox, I think, would be of invaluable aid to us in that endeavor," Ashford said.

"Cox has been seing a good deal of my niece lately," Sanford said. "I shall approach him on this very subject the next time I see him, and if the past few weeks have been any indication, that should be soon."

"Where is Andrea?" Ashford asked. "I thought I might have the pleasure of seeing her come to breakfast."

"I don't know," Sanford said. He laughed. "You know how young people are. They can sleep away their days knowing that they have plenty of them remaining. It's only when you get older that each day becomes more precious to you. I suppose Andrea is still up in her room, sleeping the sleep of the innocent."

Andrea was in her room, but she wasn't asleep. She had been thrilled over the receipt of the San Francisco papers, and had pored over them for news from home, and for the society events of her friends. That was when she stumbled over the small, one-column story about the suicide of Harold Poindexter.

Andrea had been shocked when she first read it, and then the shock turned to sadness, and finally to remorse. Now she lay across her bed clutching a tear-dampened handkerchief as she thought of Harold and her role in the destruction of his life.

Andrea wasn't a religious person, but she did believe in God, and she did believe that He rewarded good and punished evil. She had been evil in the way she had behaved with Harold, and she was positive that she was going to be punished. She wished that she knew how to pray so that she could ask for His forgiveness, but her prayers had heretofore been prayers of selfishness only, and she didn't know how to change them.

So Andrea lay there on her bed and she cried and she thought of poor Harold, and poor Harold's family, and she resolved to change her ways.

"I'll become a nun," she said softly. "I'll become a nun and take a vow of chastity, and never know another man as long as I live."

But even as Andrea spoke those words in all sincerity, she saw a picture of Lorrin O'Lee, and she thought of how he had rejected her when he was there, and she felt a renewed sense of determination to make him come to her, to reduce him to the same level of obsequiousness to which she had reduced Harold Poindexter, Robert Cox, and General Manakalano. Then, all thought of remorse and penitence fled before this more insistent desire.

19

"I SHOULD have never agreed to a constitution in the first place," Kalakaua said. He was sitting morosely on his throne, framed by the fan of yellow feathers which had been the symbol of Hawaiian Royalty for over two hundred years. His audience was an audience of one—Robert Cox.

"I shall issue a decree today," Kalakaua went on. "I shall dissolve Parliament, I shall destroy the constitution, and I shall return Hawaii to the absolute control of the King. And," he held up a finger to underscore this important point, "I shall exercise final authority on all that is printed in the newspapers. If one word appeared against me, I would have the writer of that word before me under the charge of espionage!"

"I beg your pardon, Your Highness," Cox said. "But if you issued such orders tomorrow, you would not be the King tomorrow night."

"Oh? And what makes you think my power is so weak that I could not defend my throne?" Kalakaua asked, angered by Cox's remark.

"Your power is great, King Kalakaua, but so is the power of an angry mob. And if that mob had the legitimacy of a Queen to guide them—"

"Lilioukalani?" Kalakaua interrupted. "Are you saying my sister would lead a revolution against me?"

"Yes, Your Highness," Cox said. "It pains me to say so, but I speak the truth."

Kalakaua unbuttoned his shirt and shoved his hand in to scratch his rather large stomach. "Yes," he said with a sigh. "Yes, I'm afraid you are right. But what am I to do when such treasonous words appear day after day? You would think one time would be enough, but they do not let this story die, these—these damn newspaper men," Kalakaua finished in a burst of anger.

"It is a story which sells newspapers," Cox said. "A good scandal always sells newspapers, and until they get a better scandal, they will—" suddenly Cox stopped in mid-sentence, and he looked directly at King Kalakaua as he got an idea. "King Kalakaua, I know how to stop the stories. I know how to stop them and provide the newspapers with an even greater scandal which would get the attention off you."

"You do know of such a way?"

"Yes." Cox laughed. "I guarantee you, Your Highness, it is a scandal of such magnitude that the people will quickly forget this trifling incident of the opium license."

"Well what is it, man?" Kalakaua asked, excited

by the prospect of getting the heat turned away from him.

"I shall require certain concessions, Your Highness," Cox said.

"Yes, yes, name it and you shall have it," Kalakaua said.

"I wish to be your Prime Minister."

The smile left Kalakaua's face. "No," he said. "No, that you shall never be. Already, too many have their hand on the lever of power. I will share it with no one else. Make another request."

Cox had known from the first that Kalakaua would never appoint him as Prime Minister, and he had only made the request to strengthen his position for his next request.

"Then I should like to be your personal consultant and advisor," Cox said, "with powers which place me higher than Manakalano and Wilson."

"I already consider you my personal consultant and advisor," Kalakaua said. "And as such, consider your powers greater than those enjoyed by Manakalano or Wilson. Now, how will you make people forget about this foolish opium business?"

"King Kalakaua, what does the law say with regard to succession to the throne? Who would succeed you?"

"My sister would succeed me," Kalakaua said. He frowned. "But that thought does not make me happy. Is that what we are to discuss?"

"Not exactly," Cox said. "Who would succeed your sister?"

"Her daughter, Princess Kaiulani."

"No," Cox said easily. "Kaiulani cannot ascend to the throne."

"But of course she can," Kalakaua said. "She is the daughter of my own sister. She is of royal blood."

"I don't question her royal lineage," Cox said. "But it means nothing now, because she has violated the law of royal chastity. Kaiulani is no longer a virgin."

"How do you know this?" Kalakaua asked.

"I heard her admit it to Lilioukalani after she returned from the voyage with Lorrin O'Lee. It was O'Lee who is responsible."

"O'Lee? That traitor!" Kalakaua said. "To think that my niece would violate the royal obligation of virginity with O'Lee! If news of this gets out, it will be a disgrace to the Royal House."

"No, Your Majesty," Cox said. "It will be a disgrace to Kaiulani, and it will be a disgrace to Lilioukalani, but it won't be a disgrace to you."

"But she is of my blood," Kalakaua said. "Surely I would share in her disgrace!"

"Not if you took the step of *expurger de l'arbre genealogique*," Cox said.

"What is that?"

"It is a step taken by European royalty when a member of the family brings disgrace upon themselves," Cox explained. "It means expulsion from the family line. A royal decree by you, and Kaiulani is no longer in your family. Her disgrace is her own, and the newspapers would have something else to talk about."

Kalakaua looked puzzled for just a moment, then he leaned back in the throne and laughed out loud, pounding his fist upon the arm of the ornately carved chair.

"Yes!" he said. "Yes, that is a most excellent idea. I shall send a letter immediately."

"No," Cox said. "Don't send a letter. Call a royal court of honor, invite all the dignitaries and reporters, and make your pronouncement public at that court of honor. Say nothing about it beforehand; that way you will gain the maximum effect from your act."

Kalakaua laughed again. "Oh, the look on my dear sister's face when she realizes what I am doing," he said. "It will be exquisite! I shall take great delight in seeing it!"

"A royal summons to a court of honor?" Lilioukalani said, reading the card which Kaiulani showed her. "When did this come?"

"It was delivered today," Kaiulani said. "One of the King's messengers brought it by. What do you suppose it is, mother? Why would I receive a summons to a royal court of honor?"

"I don't know," Lilioukalani said. Then she smiled. "Perhaps he intends to try and curry some favor with me by bestowing another honor upon you."

"Then I won't go," Kaiulani said. "I won't be used in any more of his tricks."

"You must go," Lilioukalani said. "You have no choice. You can't refuse the summons to a royal court of honor. That has the authority of a legal summons. Besides, he will not be using you, for there is little he can do to curry my favor now. Go, receive whatever honor he has to bestow, and then we shall return to our own lives. If you ask me, he is just trying to find some way to get away from the scandal of the opium license. But it won't work.

The knowledge of his corruption and ineptness is spreading around. Soon the people will demand his abdication, and then I shall assume the throne."

"And then the wrath of the people shall be upon you," Kaiulani said.

"No," Lilioukalani said. "For I shall rule with wisdom and justice."

The palace was bedecked with many flags for the royal court of honor, and was attended by nearly as many people as attended the King's grand parties. There was a decided difference to the texture of the event however. There was no food, there was only one band and it was in uniform and playing the music of pomp and ceremony rather than gay party tunes. Kaiulani was met by one of the judges of the royal court as soon as she arrived at the Palace, and was escorted into an anteroom, just off the royal chamber.

"What is this?" Kaiulani asked with a nervous little laugh. "Why can't I go out there with the others?"

"You will be summoned when it is time," the judge told her.

"Well, can't you tell me anything about what is going on? Am I to receive some sort of award, or decoration, or title?"

"I really can't say," the judge replied. "Please, just be patient."

"I'll be patient," Kaiulani said. "But only with difficulty. This whole thing seems awfully mysterious to me."

Kaiulani sat in a chair in the anteroom for more than fifteen minutes, until finally a messenger from the King arrived and informed the judge that the King was ready to receive her.

"Where is my mother?" Kaiulani asked. "I want her with me."

"That is not possible," the judge said.

"What do you mean it isn't possible? I want her with me."

"She prefers not to be," the judge said.

"Very well," Kaiulani said, a bit irritated by the way this honor was being conducted. "Let's get this over with."

When the door of the anteroom was opened, and Kaiulani stepped out into the royal chamber, a long drumroll began. Kaiulani looked around and saw hundreds of people drawn into a gallery on either side of a long, narrow pathway. The pathway led through the crowd to the throne, whereupon sat King Kalakaua.

Kaiulani looked out over the crowd and smiled nervously at them, then noticed something which disturbed her. No one was smiling! Why wasn't anyone smiling?"

"Lana Dominis, would you come forward please?" King Kalakaua called.

Lana Dominis was Kaiulani's real name, though as a princess she had the use of her royal name, and thus most people didn't even know that she had any other.

Kaiulani walked toward the throne, then stopped just before she reached it.

"Governor Wilson, would you read the charges, please?"

Walter Wilson cleared his throat and held up a piece of paper, putting one hand on top of the page and the other on the bottom, as if holding a scroll.

"Whereas, the Royal Morality Act was passed by Parliament and signed by King Kalakaua, it from the date of that passage and forevermore, expressly decreed that female members of the Royal Family shall remain a virgin until married. And now whereas you, Lana Dominis, heretofore known as Princess Kaiulani, did violate that sacred trust and honor by losing your virginity to one Lorrin O'Lee, you are hereby sentenced to suffer the penalty of *expurger de l'abre genealogique.*"

Kalakaua stood up then, and moved to the front of the dais. Then he waved a feathered scepter over Kaiulani's head.

"You are expelled," he said in a solemn though loud voice.

Kaiulani felt her face flaming in embarrassment. How did Kalakaua find out? Why would he take this method of punishing her? Why did he humiliate her so?

"Kalakaua, I will never forgive you for this!" Lilioukalani called out. "Never!"

Kaiulani didn't see her mother, because her eyes were filled with tears. She turned and ran back across the royal chamber, now hearing nothing but a roaring in her ears, seeing only the great doors at the far end. All she wanted now was to leave, to get away and find a rock to hide behind or a hole to crawl into. She didn't know if she would survive the shame of it all.

20

NEVER HAD HONOLULU looked more beautiful to Lorrin than it did on the day he returned. With the lighter alongside the *Centurian* taking off the cargo, Lorrin freshened up for a visit ashore. He hoped that Kaiulani was still at her mother's Oahu residence, because he intended to call upon her as soon as he could. He had given it a great deal of thought during the voyage, and now he knew what he was going to do. He was going to go to her, beg her forgiveness, and then ask her to marry him.

"Captain O'Lee, I've held your mail for you, sir," the clerk at the ship's chandlers said as Lorrin stepped inside. "It's all here, in this large envelope."

"Thanks," Lorrin said, taking the envelope from the clerk. He started to put it to one side, then he thought there might be the possibility of a letter from Kaiulani, so he dumped the contents on a bench and looked through all the letters, but there was nothing from Kaiulani. Disappointed, he picked them all up and put them back in the envelope and handed it over to the clerk. "You keep them for me until I come back, would you?" he asked.

"Yes, sir," the clerk said. "Oh, Mr. Dole asked that you get in touch with him as soon as you return."

"I'll see him later," Lorrin said. "I have something else to do right now." He started out the front door, then he stopped and looked back toward the clerk. "Oh, by the way. Would you happen to know whether Princess Kaiulani has returned to Maui? Or is she still on Oahu?"

"Princess Kaiulani?" the clerk asked. "You mean you haven't heard?"

"Heard? Heard what?" Lorrin asked, then, when he saw the strange look on the clerk's face, he moved quickly to him. "What is it?" he asked. "Kaiulani, is she all right? Has she been hurt?"

"No, she hasn't been hurt," the clerk said.

Lorrin let out a sigh of relief. "Thank God," he said. "For a moment you had me very . . . what is it?" he asked, noticing that the clerk still had a strange expression on his face. "What is it that you aren't telling me?"

"Maybe you'd better read the newspapers," the clerk said. He reached under the counter and pulled out a copy of the paper to show to Lorrin. Lorrin took it from him, and looked at it. He didn't have to look far. It was blaring at him from the front page.

PRINCESS KAIULANI EXPELLED FROM ROYAL
FAMILY FOR MORAL TURPITUDE

"What the hell are they talking about?" Lorrin
asked angrily.

"Read the story," the clerk suggested.

Lorrin began to read: "In the old days," the story
began, "the Alii-Nui, the women of the royal family, were encouraged to be promiscuous. Legend
has it that they were even schooled in such things,
so that they might use the considerable sexual
power a woman has over a man. But a new code
of morality has replaced the old school of thought,
and the people now wish, in fact, the law now
demands chaste and moral behavior. Princess Kaiulani has violated that behavior, by allowing one-
time Admiral Lorrin O'Lee to know her in the
Biblical sense. In accordance with the law of the
land, King Kalakaua had no recourse but to expel
her from the Royal Family. Kaiulani, whose real
name is Lana Dominis, is no longer in the line of
succession to the Crown, and would be unable to
accept it, even in the unlikely event it should fall
to her. Princess Kaiulani is now commoner, Lana
Dominis."

Lorrin put the paper down and looked at the
clerk. "When did this happen?" he asked.

"Yesterday," the clerk said. "Kalakaua held a
royal court of honor. Everyone was there, including all the reporters." The clerk sighed. "This is just
the kind of scandal that people love to gossip
about. It's all over the city now."

"How could he do this to her?" Lorrin said.
"How could Kalakaua publicly shame her so?"

"It's the law," the clerk said. "The King had no choice."

"I don't believe that," Lorrin said. "He had no need to—" and suddenly Lorrin stopped in mid-sentence. He realized at that moment that he was angry with King Kalakaua, when he should be angry with himself. After all, he was the guilty party. Kaiulani tried to explan to him that she had given up everything for him, but he wouldn't listen. Now, her shame was upon his hands. He looked at them, as if expecting to see them stained.

"I have to see her," he said. "I have to see her at once. Is she still on the island?"

"As far as I know she is," the clerk said. "I'm sure that if she had left, I would have heard of it."

"Then I'm going to see her," Lorrin said. "I'm going to her and I'm going to throw myself before her and plead for her forgiveness."

Lorrin hailed a cab just outside the ship's chandlers, and he urged the driver to hurry the horses on. They raced through the streets of Honolulu, then up a long road which led to Washington Palace, as Lilioukalani's Honolulu residence was called. There were wrought-iron gates across the driveway to Washington Palace, and the driver pulled the team to a stop there.

"This is as far as I can go," he said.

"That's all right," Lorrin said, climbing out of the surrey. "I'll walk from here." Lorrin paid the fare, then started for the gate, but he was stopped by two armed guards.

"Where are you going?"

"I mean to call on the Princess," Lorrin said.

The two guards looked at each other for a moment, then one of them spoke. "No one may enter without permission."

"Then perhaps one of you gentlemen would be so kind as to inform Kaiulani that Lorrin O'Lee wishes to see her."

"Wait here," one of the guards said, and he started up the tree-lined and flower-bordered drive to the house.

"You are the one, aren't you?" the other guard said as Lorrin waited with him at the gate.

"I am the one, what?"

"You are the one who ruined the Princess."

Lorrin looked at the ground, too ashamed to answer the guard's accusation.

A moment later the second guard returned.

"Well?" Lorrin said. "Can I go see her?"

"She doesn't wish to see you," the guard said.

On the next day, Lorrin returned to Washington Palace and again requested to see Kaiulani. Again he was turned down, so he returned the next day and then the next. Finally, after one week of unsuccessful attempts, Kaiulani sent a message asking him not to return.

Reluctantly, Lorrin honored Kaiulani's request, and made no more visits to Washington Palace. But he did send her a letter, a long and impassioned one, begging for forgiveness and asking her to just see him long enough for him to tell her what a fool he was. He was too ashamed to mention marriage in the letter. It seemed like one last-ditch effort, but Lorrin couldn't think of any other way left open to him. And he couldn't give up without one last try.

Then, one day when Lorrin returned to the ship,

one of the men on watch informed him that he had a visitor.

"A visitor? Who?"

"I don't know, sir," the sailor said. "But bein' as she is a lady, and a very beautiful lady at that, I asked her to wait in your cabin. I hope you don't mind, sir."

Lorrin grinned broadly, and nearly bowled the sailor over in his rush to get to the hatch and down the ladder to his cabin. He ran the length of the companionway, then shoved open the door.

"Kaiulani, darling, thank God you've come!" he shouted.

"Heavens, I don't know what you expected, Lorrin, but as you can see, I am not Kaiulani."

There, sitting demurely in a chair in his cabin, was Andrea Dole.

Lorrin sagged against the door jamb in disappointment. "Andrea," he said. "What are you doing here?"

"Is that it?" Andrea asked. She stood up and walked over to him, then pursed her lips for a kiss. When he didn't respond, she kissed him on the cheek, then she reached over and closed the door behind him. "My," she said. "You certainly know how to sweep a girl off her feet with the exuberance of your passion."

"Andrea, I'm asking you again: what are you doing here?" Lorrin repeated.

"Well," Andrea said, her lips protruding in a pretty pout. "It was beginning to be quite obvious that you weren't going to come to see me, so I thought perhaps I had better come see you."

"See me? See me about what?" Lorrin asked. He

took a cigar out of his jacket pocket and bit the tip off, then stuck it in his mouth and lit it.

"I just wanted to see you, that's all," Andrea said. "After all, you've been gone for two long months. You've been back for well over a week, and you've made no effort whatever to call on me. I know you've been terribly busy, but that's really no excuse."

"You're right," Lorrin said. "It isn't an excuse. I didn't call on you because I didn't want to call on you."

"That's certainly not very flattering, Lorrin," Andrea said. "And it can't help our relationship very much, either."

"Andrea, don't you understand? We don't have a relationship and I don't want a relationship. At least, not with you."

"I see," Andrea said coldly. "You don't want a relationship with me, but you are willing enough to have an affair with that—that *wahine*."

"I am in love with Kaiulani," Lorrin said.

"Love, bah! You don't even know the meaning of the word."

"Perhaps not," Lorrin said. "I've certainly not managed it very well up until now."

Andrea rushed to him and put her arms around him, and began smothering him with kisses.

"Come with me, Lorrin," she said. "Come home with me! Let me show you about love."

Slowly but deliberately Lorrin removed Andrea's arms from around his neck. "What about Robert Cox?"

"Cox? Are you jealous of Robert Cox?" She flashed a large smile. "Then you did hear me that night, didn't you? Good, that was my plan," she said, without the slightest show of shame.

"Your plan?"

"Yes," Andrea said. "Don't you see, Lorrin? Darling, I wanted you to hear Robert and me making love because I wanted you to be jealous. I wanted you to want me more than anything in the world!"

"I'm afraid it didn't work," Lorrin said.

"But of course it worked," Andrea said. She smiled triumphantly. "Didn't you just mention it to me? It made you feel something, didn't it? What did you feel? Anger? Jealousy? Lust?"

"Disgust," Lorrin said quietly.

The word hung between them like a dagger of ice. The expression on Andrea's face changed from that of a coquette to that of a person in shock. The shock slowly gave way to anger, and finally dissolved into a cold, brooding hate. She fixed Lorrin with a gaze which chilled him to the very core of his being.

"I see," she said. She started for the door.

"Andrea, please understand that I don't want to hurt you," Lorrin called to her. "I'm sorry you made me say it. But you must know by now that I am not in love with you, and I could never be in love with you. I love Kaiulani."

"Then you are a bigger fool than even I have been," Andrea said coldly. "For that is a love you will never know." Andrea stepped out of his cabin and slammed the door behind her. Lorrin knew that he should see her to the deck, but he thought that under the circumstances it would be better to allow her to leave alone. That would preserve whatever dignity there might be remaining in the situation.

Lorrin walked back to his bunk and lay down, folding his hands behind his head as he stared at the beams above. He thought of Andrea's last comment. *"That is a love you will never know,"* she had said. Lorrin hoped Andrea was wrong, but the situation seemed to lend support to her prediction.

There were no more visitors to the ship that day, but the next morning a boat crossed the distance from the shore to the *Centurian's* anchorage, and as it got closer, one of the two men in the boat stood up and cupped his hands around his mouth.

"Ahoy the *Centurian!* Is Captain O'Lee aboard?"

"Aye," Lorrin replied, leaning over the railing. "I'm O'Lee. What can I do for you?"

"I have an urgent message for you, Captain," the man said, holding aloft an envelope.

Lorrin smiled happily. It was an answer from Kaiulani! It had to be!

"Here," Lorrin said, flipping a coin down to the man. The man thanked him and handed the envelope up, and Lorrin tore it open eagerly.

It wasn't from Kaiulani; it was from V. V. Ashford. Ashford was requesting an urgent meeting, "in the interest of justice." He set the time and place, and Lorrin decided that he had nothing to lose by keeping the appointment, so he prepared to go.

Lorrin would have thought Ashford would hold the meeting in his own house, but the address given him was of a small business establishment in the heart of Chinatown. When Lorrin got there, he saw that it was a business which sold wicker baskets and earthenware pots. An old Chinese man, clacking an abacus, looked up as Lorrin entered the store. The man didn't speak, but pointed with a bony finger to the back of the room. Lorrin went through a beaded curtain, across a yard with an open cistern, and down an alley that stank of rotten vegetables. He had to climb a flight of rickety stairs to reach a small room. Inside the room an old woman motioned for Lorrin to sit down at a crude table, and she sat a bottle of warm beer in front of him.

A few moments later Ashford came into the room through the back door. The stub of a cigarette burned close to his lips. The very strong smell of tobacco was heavy and oppressive in the close room.

"I am glad to see that you have come," Ashford said.

"You mentioned justice," Lorrin said. "What sort of justice?"

"You are aware of Kalakaua's opium swindle?"

"Yes," Lorrin answered. He had heard of it since he returned, but compared to what Kalakaua had done to Kaiulani, it meant nothing to him.

"That is but the tip of the iceberg. He is planning more. Much, much more."

"What more could he do?" Lorrin asked, thinking of the disgrace Kalakaua had already brought onto Kaiulani.

"He is King. He will do anything he wants as long as he has the power. There is only one thing remaining to us now, and that is to deny him that power."

"That seems like a noble enough ambition to me," Lorrin said. "I'd like nothing better than to deny him his power."

"Then you will help?"

"That all depends."

"Depends on what? I have no financial reward to offer you," Ashford said.

"It depends on what you want me to do," Lorrin said. "I will not dress up in any clown suit and call myself an admiral again, whether for the Hawaiian Navy or the Revolutionary Navy. But I will do anything else you need, even fight, if that is necessary."

Ashford laughed. "No," he said. "I don't want you to play the role of admiral again. But it may be necessary for you to fight."

"Then you can count on me," Lorrin said.

"We may be able to avoid a war," Ashford said. "After all, all we really want to do is be rid of the King and his insufferable pride."

"How else would you get rid of him without a revolution?" Lorrin asked.

"Why, by the most effective way, of course."

"You will forgive me, Colonel, if I'm not following you as closely as I should be," Lorrin said. "But just what way do you consider the most effective?"

"You will have to kill the King," Ashford said quite frankly.

Lorrin took a swallow of his beer, held it in his mouth for a moment, then let it slide down his throat. He put the glass down and wiped the back of his hand across his mouth.

"You want *me* to do it?"

"Yes," Ashford said. "If either Dole or I did it, we would be accused of furthering our own personal goals. Only you have no personal motive for killing him. Only by your hand would his killing he recognized for what it is—a patriotic act."

"I don't want to do that," Lorrin said.

"But you must," Ashford replied. "Don't you see? We can't take half a step. We must go all the way, or we must do nothing."

"But wouldn't that start a blood-bath?"

"No," Ashford said. "On the contrary, it will prevent one. Listen to me, my young friend. In wars, men are killed, are they not? Do you know how many were killed in the great Civil War in the United States?"

"I've no idea."

"Half a million or more," Ashford said. "Now, suppose there had been one man whose death could have prevented that slaughter? Don't you think it would have been more human to kill that one man if it would have prevented war? One life against half a million?"

"Surely you wouldn't expect half a million to die here?" Lorrin asked.

"No, but several hundred might die, or even several thousand, if it came to war. I know that the thought is repugnant to you, but my friend, we are pragmatic people, are we not? We must make the decision which will effect our lives, and the lives of our children and our children's children, for the next one hundred years. We *must* effect a clean, precise revolution, and that would best be accomplished by making certain that King Kalakaua is out of the way."

"I don't know," Lorrin demurred. "Does Sanford know about this?"

"No," Ashford said.

"I would like to know what he thinks about it."

"Don't be naïve, Captain O'Lee," Ashford said. "I told you a moment ago, Sanford Dole must be kept clean of all this. Hawaii depends upon his leadership after the revolution, and nothing must be done which would make it seem that he is doing anything which is self-serving."

"But I thought he wanted the revolution to come in gradual steps," Lorrin said. "First, a concession from the King, then abdication, then annexation. You are moving the schedule ahead, and I just want to be certain it is with Sanford's approval."

"He will be with us after it is done," Ashford said. "He will have no choice."

Lorrin sighed. "For all that Kalakaua has done, I could kill him," he said. "And if I thought it would be as clean and effective as you say, I might be persuaded to go along with it. But if Kalakaua were dead, then Lilioukalani would inherit the throne, and we'd be right back where we started."

"If Lilioukalani makes an effort to assume the throne, then she will have to be taken care of as well," Ashford said.

"What do you mean?" Lorrin asked. "Do you mean to kill her, too?"

"Yes, if need be," Ashford said.

"No," Lorrin said. "I'll not have anything to do with it. If it were just Kalakaua, I might consider it. But Lilioukalani is an innocent person. And it might not even stop there. After Lilioukalani, it might go on to include Kaiulani."

"No, that wouldn't be necessary," Ashford said. "Kaiulani has been disinherited, remember? She is no longer a virgin." Ashford laughed. "When you get right down to it, she's no different from all the other Hawaiian sluts, she—"

But Ashford was unable to finish his statement, because Lorrin brought his hand across the Colonel's mouth in a bruising, lip-cutting, backhanded blow.

"You happen to be talking about the woman I love," Lorrin said, and the words fell from his mouth as if they were encased in ice.

Ashford took his handkerchief from his inside coat pocket and brushed lightly at the blood on his lips. He smiled at Lorrin.

"You will regret this, my young friend," Ashford said. "When the revolution comes, you will either be for us or against us. And your . . . *love* . . . for Kaiulani would seem to put you against us."

"If the revolution is to deliver us into the hands of men like you, then I shall most assuredly be against you," Lorrin said. He turned and walked quickly from the room.

Ashford watched for a moment, then he called out. "He is gone, my dear."

Andrea stepped out of the back room.

"You heard?" Ashford asked.

"Yes," Andrea said quietly. "I heard everything."

"When you see Robert Cox, please convey the information to him that Captain O'Lee has refused to help."

"With pleasure," Andrea said, and the words sounded sweet to her ears, for they were the key to her revenge.

21

"BUT YOU DID say he would agree to assassinate the King?" Cox asked Andrea, after Andrea had carried to him her report of the meeting between Lorrin and V. V. Ashford.

"No," Andrea said. "Didn't you listen to me? I said he would *not*."

"No, my dear," Cox replied, as if explaining something to a child. "You told me that he would consider it. It was when Lilioukalani and Kaiulani were mentioned that he balked. Up until that time, he seemed willing to go along with it. Am I right?"

"Well, yes, I suppose so," Andrea said. She was still not sure exactly where Cox was going with the information she brought him, but she did have faith in his deviousness. She knew that Cox had little love for Lorrin, and if he had something in mind, then she was willing to listen to his reasoning.

"It would seem to me, then, that if someone wanted to curry the King's favor, and if that someone knew of Captain O'Lee's part in this assassination plot, then that someone might take action against Captain O'Lee. Don't you think so?"

"I suppose so," Andrea said. "But I don't understand. I thought you were on the side of the revolutionaries. Are you saying now that you are on the King's side?"

Cox laughed. "My dear young lady, I am on the side of Robert Cox," he said. "Whatever happens in the intrigue in which we now find ourselves will be exactly what I want to happen. I assure you, I shall find some way of escaping unscathed. In the meantime, I shall continue to make myself useful to all parties. Right now, I am making myself useful to you."

"What do you mean?"

"You do want revenge against Captain O'Lee, don't you?" Cox asked.

"What makes you think I want revenge?"

"My dear, it is written all over your face. You want revenge against Lorrin O'Lee. And, if a certain Hawaiian princess happened to find herself in unfavorable circumstances, you wouldn't mind that either, would you?"

"Kaiulani? She isn't involved."

"But of course she is involved," Cox said. "After all, wasn't it the threat of possible danger to her which caused Captain O'Lee to pull out of Colonel Ashford's plot?"

"Yes, but I don't see how that has anything to do with her finding herself in unfavorable circumstances," Andrea said. "Why would she be part of an assassination plot?"

"Oh, but my dear, one can easily understand why Kaiulani would turn against the royal family. After all, she has been expelled and has lost everything."

Andrea shook her head. "But you have it all wrong," she said. "Kaiulani isn't a part of all this."

"Maybe not," Cox said. "But her position in all this is quite unique. I don't know where she stands, and that is what makes her so dangerous to me. I think it would be best if I took the precaution of getting rid of Kaiulani at the same time I take care of Captain O'Lee. Don't you agree?"

"Yes," Andrea said, suddenly seeing the opportunity for vengeance on both Lorrin and Kaiulani. "Yes, I think you should get rid of her."

"Ah, but she is so beautiful, and so young," Cox said. "It does seem a shame that such a tragedy must befall her at such tender years."

"Yes," Andrea said, coldly. "I suppose it is a shame."

"Then we must report this to the King at once," Manakalano said. Manakalano had answered an urgent request from Robert Cox to meet with him in secret, and it was at that meeting that Cox told Manakalano of the plot to assassinate the King.

"No," Cox said quickly.

"No? What do you mean no?" Manakalano said. "Do you intend to let O'Lee get away with his plan?"

"I do not, sir," Cox said. "In fact, that is why I came to you with the information. I expect you to prevent O'Lee from putting the plan into operation. After all, if you are credited with saving the King, that can't be bad for you, can it?"

Manakalano smiled. "No," he said. "No, it can't be bad at all."

"And after the rather distasteful business with Bloody Island, you could use something which would reinstate you in the King's good graces, could you not?"

"Yes," Manakalano said. "That hypocritical fool Wilson didn't lose a thing. He has no island to govern, but he is still the King's most trusted aide. While I"—Manakalano held his hands out and sighed—"I am a General without an army. It is a perfectly useless position. Already I have heard others in the Palace laughing at me."

"They won't laugh after you save the King's life," Cox said. "You will be the hero, then."

"Yes," Manakalano said, his eyes gleaming in anticipation. "Yes, I will be, won't I? What should I do, go to the King and warn him?"

"So someone else can get the glory of taking care of it?" Cox said. "I would have thought you could come up with a better suggestion than that."

"What? What then should I do?"

"It's simple," Cox said. "If O'Lee is planning on killing the King, then you must kill O'Lee first."

"You mean find O'Lee and kill him, just like that?"

"Yes," Cox replied. "Unless, of course, you are frightened of O'Lee."

"No," Manakalano said, his dark eyes snapping angrily. "No, I am not frightened of O'Lee."

"Then you will do it?"

Manakalano smiled. "Yes," he said. "Yes, I will do it."

"And Kaiulani as well?"

"Are you sure she is a part of the plot?"

"What do you think?" Cox asked. "After all, she was expelled from the royal family. And you observed Kaiulani and O'Lee together during your voyage with them. Don't you believe she could ally herself with O'Lee?"

"Yes," Manakalano said. He rubbed his chin. "Yes, I believe she would. She was a bitch during the voyage, a stuck-up bitch who would have nothing to do with me." He laughed. "I will enjoy taking care of her as well."

"Believe me, General Manakalano, the King will regard you in the highest esteem after you have proven yourself to him in this way."

"I'll do it," Manakalano said excitedly. "I will do it, then go to the King and present him with what I have done." Suddenly Manakalano's eyes narrowed, and he looked at Cox. "There is one thing I don't understand," he said.

"What?"

"Why have you come to me with this? Why didn't you do it yourself, or go to Wilson?"

"The reason I didn't go to Wilson is quite simple," Cox said. "I don't think Wilson could handle the job. Could you see Wilson going after Lorrin O'Lee?"

"No," Manakalano said, and he laughed. "Wilson doesn't have the stomach for it."

"You are quite right. That leaves me or you. I chose to come to you because I may need a friend in the King's good graces at some point in the future. Right now I enjoy a good relationship with the King, but if that should sour, then it would be to my advantage to have someone else I could fall back on. That someone could be you, if you were a valued ally of the King. Therefore, it is to my advantage to make you a valued ally. So I am offering you the way."

"I see," Manakalano said. "Well, you can always count on me." He ran his hand through his dark hair. "Now tell me. How should I do it?"

"I thought you might need help with that," Cox said. "So I've come up with a plan." He smiled, and took Manakalano into his confidence as he outlined his idea for taking care of Lorrin and Kaiulani.

22

KAIULANI PICKED her way down the rocks toward the sea. Before her, stretched out in endless shades of blue, was the Pacific Ocean. Just below, on the rocky beach, was one of the more interesting natural rock formations on the entire island. A cavern and a fissure caused the water pressure of the incoming sea to spout a fountain up through a hole in the rock; it looked exactly like a whale coming to the surface to blow. The fissure had been named "Blow Hole" by whalers, and it was here that Kaiulani had come, because she had received a message from Sanford Dole, asking her to meet him there.

Kaiulani would not have come, but the message said that her meeting him would save her mother "any more heartbreak," and as Kaiulani felt a tremendous sense of shame and guilt over the sorrow she had already caused her mother, she was willing to meet with Dole to spare her mother any further despondency.

Blow Hole was a perfect place for private meeting, because it was quite a distance away from Honolulu and in a deserted part of the island. There were no farms, villages, or houses anywhere near the place, and as Kaiulani approached it, she had a feeling of remoteness, as if she were the only person on the entire island. And suddenly, that feeling appealed to her, and she wished with all her heart that it was true, that she was alone on a deserted island.

But Kaiulani wasn't alone. For as she walked out on the beach to Blow Hole, someone called her name, and she turned to see none other than Lorrin O'Lee.

"You!" she said in quick anger. "It was a trick, wasn't it? You sent me a note to get me here!" She turned, and started to run back up the beach, but Lorrin caught up to her in a few, quick strides and grabbed her.

"Kaiulani," he implored. "Please, don't run away."

"You are mistaken, sir," Kaiulani said coldly. "You are calling me Kaiulani. My name is Lana. Lana Dominis!"

"No," Lorrin said, holding her securely. "You are Kaiulani, now and forever, you are my Kaiulani."

Kaiulani closed her eyes tightly, but she couldn't prevent the tears which were squeezed out to form two tracks down her face.

Lorrin kissed each of the tears, stopping them in mid-track. "Oh," he said. "How I have longed to see you! You don't know how many times I have come to your gate, even after you asked me not to, just to stand and hope for a chance glimpse of you."

"So you could hurt me more?" Kaiulani asked.

"No," Lorrin said. "So I could tell you that I love you, and so I could beg for your forgiveness. Kaiulani, I have been such a fool."

"No," Kaiulani said. "No, I won't listen to you." She tried to turn her head.

"Please, Kaiulani," Lorrin pleaded. "Don't shut me out now. I made a terrible mistake when I said that we couldn't have a life together. We can, and we will! I love you, Kaiulani, and I want to marry you. I want to marry you and take you with me on the seven seas of the world!"

"Oh, Lorrin, I"—Kaiulani tried to find the words to deny him again, to erect a barrier to protect herself from being further hurt. But she couldn't deny him, because she couldn't deny her own feelings, the blood which ran hot through her veins, or the heart which was pounding as wildly now as the restless surf which charged the cavern with its power. "I love you," she said, her voice trembling with emotion.

"What?" Lorrin asked with a happy smile. "What did you say?"

"I said I love you, Lorrin! I love you, I love you, I love you!"

Kaiulani's words were drowned out by the explosive thunder of Blow Hole as water burst through the fissure and spewed high into the air. Lorrin and Kaiulani were in each other's arms when the water fell back, drenching them and buffeting them about. Kaiulani let out a little squeal of surprise, then they laughed and moved away.

"I'm glad now that you did trick me into coming," Kaiulani said.

Lorrin brushed his drenched hair away from his face. "Trick you into coming? Coming here, you mean?"

"Yes," Kaiulani said. She kissed him again. "It was a devious trick, Lorrin O'Lee." She smiled. "But I forgive you for it."

"Kaiulani, I didn't trick you," Lorrin said. "I would have, long ago, if I had known it would work," he said. "But I don't know what you are talking about."

"You mean the note I received is genuine? Sanford Dole does want to see me?" Kaiulani asked.

"I don't know," Lorrin said. "But I got a note from him too asking me to meet him here."

"I wonder what it is about?"

Lorrin smiled. "I think I know what it's about," he said.

"You do?"

"Yes, and I will spend the rest of my life being thankful to Sanford. Don't you see, Kaiulani? He is my friend, and he knows how I have suffered from my own foolishness. He was merely seeking a way to get us back together."

"Then I'm glad he found a way to get through my stubbornness," Kaiulani said, and at that moment the water pressure again erupted through the hole, sending another fountain roaring high into the sky.

Lorrin reached out for Kaiulani and pulled her to him for another kiss, then gently he led her back off the rock and onto the beach where he pulled her down on to the sand.

"What are you doing?" Kaiulani asked.

"I am loving you," Lorrin answered. "And I am going to make love to you."

"Here?"

"Why not?" Lorrin answered. "Darling, this could be our own paradise, so isolated are we."

"But Mr. Dole?"

"He won't show up," Lorrin answered. "Why would he show up now and spoil what he has worked so hard to accomplish?"

Kaiulani laughed, but Lorrin quieted her laugh with a kiss. He lay her back on the sand, and his hand moved under her wet blouse to cup the firm, vibrant breast which lay just beneath the material. The nipple was hard, and the skin of the breast was smooth, and the difference in texture created a delightful tactile sensation.

Somewhere between the pounding of the blood in his ears, and the surf behind him, he heard her whispers of love, then they removed their clothes so that they were lying together, side by side, their nude bodies shining in the fine mist of the spray which feathered out from the erupting fountain.

Kaiulani felt Lorrin's hand on her breast, at her neck, and in her hair, spreading a delightful warmth where ever he touched her. She arched her body, moving into position to invite his hand to explore more of her, and finally it slid down her smooth skin, across her flat stomach, then stopped less than an inch away from the center of all her feeling. Kaiulani's stomach fluttered with a million butterflies, and a raging fire burned within her loins, flaming her so fiercely that she thought she would soon be consumed by it.

Then, slowly, Lorrin's hand moved down until

his fingers were in that moist cleft, and she felt a
series of tiny waves beginning to emanate from
the point of contact, spreading pleasure, but, beyond pleasure, building a thirst for more.

Lorrin moved over her then, and she felt his
muscled legs against her smooth calves, and his
hard thighs against her resilient skin, and then,
she felt that for which her body so ached. He was
inside her with one deeply satisfying thrust.

Kaiulani rose happily to meet him, to take him
into her, wishing there was some way she could
absorb all of him, to engulf him and take him into
her womb, there to hold him and to love him, and
to give birth to him in a glorious explosion of
sensation. And as she thought such thoughts,
Lorrin continued to love her, to pound against her
in a way which was both tender and savage, while
behind them the surf crashed and Blow Hole
boomed, nature's timpani providing the rhythm to
their intimate ballet.

After several moments of such ecstasy, Kaiulani
felt it starting, a tiny spark which began deep in
her womb, flaring out quickly into a starburst,
burning brighter and hotter, and whirling faster
and faster until every part of her being was caught
up in the vortex of pleasure. Then, when her body
could contain the sensations no longer, they burst
from her in one long tremble of rapture. The sensation was like a million tiny pins pricking her skin,
as she cried out in pleasure. The stars which had
flared within her now passed before her eyes in a
myriad of colored lights as her body gave way to
the climactic, convulsive shudders of total consum-
mation.

They lay side by side after they were finished, allowing the heat of their passion to drain away slowly.

Kaiulani enjoyed the last subtle vibrations which passed through her body, and she felt Lorrin's arm around her, and his hand squeezing her affectionately.

"I've never known such rapture," she admitted, and she knew she shouldn't admit such a thing to him, but she couldn't help herself.

"Nor have I," Lorrin said. "It is proof, if ever such proof were needed, that the greatest aphrodisiac is love itself. And I love you, Kaiulani, more than I can say. I always loved you, from the first time I ever saw you. But I thought I was being noble and self-sacrificing by giving you your freedom. I thought I could set you free to chart your own course. But in these last few months, in San Francisco and on the sea, I've been unable to get you out of my mind. You've haunted me as surely as any ghost. I've known no peace, and I will know no peace until you marry me. I love you, and I want you, now, and forever. Will you marry me, Kaiulani?"

"Oh, yes," Kaiulani said. "Lorrin, you don't know how I've longed to hear those words. I've dreamed of the time we could—"

Kaiulani's sentence was interrupted by the whine of a bullet, and the stinging spray of sand kicked up by the bullet's impact. At first, neither of them knew what it was, and it startled them as an angry hornet would. But then, over the roar of the surf, Lorrin neard the unmistakable sound of a rifle, and a second bullet hit nearby.

"My God!" Lorrin said. "Someone is shooting at us!"

Lorrin stood up and pulled Kaiulani to her feet. They were both still naked, but all thought of modesty fled as they started running down the beach, as nude as children of the sun, a delightful vision were it not for the fact that their lives were in mortal danger!

"Damn!" Manakalano swore aloud. He operated the bolt of the rifle, kicking another empty brass cartridge out to join the first one which lay gleaming brightly in the sun. He squinted through the sights at the running figures, and despite the gruesomeness of his task, he couldn't help but laugh as he saw them skipping naked through the surf.

It had originally been Manakalano's intention to seek out Lorrin and then Kaiulani, and kill them one at a time. But Cox gave him the idea of sending each of them a message purported to be from Sanford Dole, asking them to meet him here, at one of the most remote spots on the island. That way, he could get them both at the same time, kill two birds with one stone, so to speak. Manakalano laughed at the analogy and squeezed off another round.

"Damn, I'm hit!" Lorrin said as he felt a heavy burning in the calf of his leg. He tried to keep running, but his leg wouldn't work anymore, and the next thing he knew, he had the taste of sand in his mouth. Oddly, it didn't seem as if he fell. Rather, it seemed as if the ground had come up to meet him. He looked at his leg and saw a bright red stream of blood.

"Lorrin!" Kaiulani called, and she dropped in her knees beside him.

Lorrin had never seen her more beautiful than at this very moment. She was posed nude against the sea, a study of form and line, and yet it was a moment when death from some unknown assailant seemed imminent.

"Kaiulani, get up," he said, pushing at her. "Get up and run! You must get out of here, don't you understand? Someone is trying to kill us."

"I'm not leaving," Kaiulani said.

"Please! Run! You can't stay here!"

"I'm not leaving you!" Kaiulani insisted. Kaiulani lifted Lorrin's head and put it on her lap, then leaned over to embrace him. Her breasts were pressed into his face, but at this instant there was no sexual arousal from the contact. Instead, he felt what a nursing baby must feel, a sense of well-being and security. Albeit, in this case, it was a false sense of security, because the assailant had now left his position behind the rocks and was strolling down the beach toward them, walking as slowly and calmly as if he had all day. His rifle was thrown nonchalantly across his shoulder, and he was holding it by the barrel. He was chuckling as he approached them.

"Wasn't it nice of me to let you have your fun before I interrupted you?" he asked. He rubbed himself unabashedly. "I have to admit, I enjoyed watching it, even if it did get me horny. But I'll get that taken care of, don't you worry about it."

"Manakalano!" Lorrin said, surprised to see the man who was walking toward them. "You bastard!"

"That's right," Manakalano said. "I thought I'd

let you know who's going to kill you. It seemed like the right thing to do."

"But why? Why do you want to kill me?"

"Why not?" Manakalano replied with an evil smile. He turned the rifle around, raised it to his shoulder, then took slow and deliberate aim at Lorrin. Kaiulani moved over to step in front of what would be the line of fire.

"You'll have to kill me first," she said.

Manakalano chuckled. "Oh, I intend to kill you, Kaiulani," he said. "But didn't you hear me say that I had a little problem I wanted to take care of? If you play your cards right, you might be able to buy yourself a little time. Who knows, you might even persuade me to change my mind."

Kaiulani realized at once what he meant, and she moved away from Lorrin, then lay on the beach, on her back, raised up slightly so that she was resting on her elbows. Her long golden legs were splayed, and there was a spot of shining dampness on one thigh, evidence of her earlier lovemaking with Lorrin.

"All right," Kaiulani said. "I know what you want."

Manakalano looked at her for a moment, and he smiled in lustful appreciation of the picture she presented.

"Yes," he said. "Yes, you understand perfectly, my pet. Let me just get this over with," he added, and he raised his rifle and aimed at Lorrin one more time. Lorrin was in a sitting position now, holding his bleeding leg.

"No!" Kaiulani shouted. "I won't let you shoot him!"

"You don't have any choice," Manakalano said.

"Wait," Kaiulani said. "Wouldn't you enjoy it more if I were willing?"

"It doesn't matter," Manakalano said.

"Wouldn't you enjoy it more if he had to watch?"

"Kaiulani, no!" Lorrin said. "Let him shoot me and get it over with. Don't let him use you like this!"

Manakalano lowered his rifle, then gave an evil chuckle. "Yes," he said. "Yes, if he had to watch, knowing that he could do nothing about it, knowing that he was going to die as soon as it was over, yes, that would be good. Oh, it would be exquisite!"

"Then take me," Kaiulani said. "Take me now." Kaiulani moved around further, then lay back, holding her arms up, inviting Manakalano to her.

Manakalano stripped off his pants, then with one last, cautious look toward Lorrin, he lowered himself over Kaiulani. There were no preliminaries. Manakalano didn't need them, he was visibly ready as soon as he removed his pants, and Kaiulani didn't want them. She wanted only to buy more time, one extra minute, one extra second, if it would prolong Lorrin's life. She closed her eyes and bit her lips as she felt him enter her. How different was this brutal, painful invasion, to the ecstasy she had felt but moments earlier!

Then, Kaiulani felt a sudden contact, and Manakalano was no longer over her. He was knocked away from her, and she opened her eyes to see Lorrin struggling with him.

Lorrin had waited until he thought he had his best chance, then he jumped Manakalano. But at the last moment, Manakalano had seen Lorrin coming, and thus Lorrin lost the element of surprise. With Lorrin's leg as badly hurt as it was, and the resultant weakness from the loss of blood, Manakalano regained the advantage in less than a moment of struggle. He shook himself loose long enough to be able to use the rifle as a club, and he clubbed Lorrin to the ground.

"I thought you might try something like that," Manakalano said, standing up and pointing his rifle down at Lorrin's prostrate figure. "I'll just finish you off, then go on about my business with the Princess here, and in a short time, she will join you."

Manakalano took slow and deliberate aim, and Kaiulani closed her eyes so she couldn't see what happened next.

The sound of the gunshot, when it came, sent ice-cold chills running down Kaiulani's spine, and she screamed Lorrin's name in bitter anguish. There was a moment of silence after Kaiulani's scream died, then she opened her eyes, almost eager now to die, to join her lover.

But when Kaiulani opened her eyes, she was shocked by what she saw. It wasn't Lorrin, but Manakalano who lay face down in the dirt. She could tell by the twist of his neck, and the grotesqueness of his open, unseeing eyes, that he was dead.

"Lorrin, what is it?" she asked. "What happened?"

"I don't know," Lorrin said, his voice as shocked as hers.

"Oh, dear me, these beach orgies can get a bit wild, can't they?" a man's voice asked, and Kaiulani and Lorrin looked up to see Robert Cox walking toward them. He was carrying a smoking pistol in his right hand. "Is he dead, or shall I have to shoot the poor devil again?"

"He's dead," Lorrin said.

"Good. Shooting him while he was in the act of attempted murder is one thing. For that, I might even be considered a hero. But if I had to dispatch the poor wretch now, I would feel just terrible about it." Cox looked at Kaiulani and Lorrin, smiled and shook his head. "I must say that as one who enjoys such pleasures myself, it is too bad I wasn't here a bit earlier to join the fun."

"What do you want, Cox?" Lorrin asked, and Kaiulani, still frightened, had moved over to put her arms around Lorrin.

"Want? Why, I should think a little gratitude would be in order. I know you will find it difficult to thank a 'wastrel,' I believe you called me? But, after all, I did just save your life. And yours, too, I might add," he said to Kaiulani.

"Are you planning on killing us now?" Lorrin asked.

"Killing you? Good heavens no. Why would I want to do a thing like that?"

"I don't know," Lorrin said. He shook his head as if trying to clear it. "But to tell the truth, I don't know why Manakalano wanted to kill us."

"Oh, because I set him up to do it," Cox said.

"You set him up? What do you mean?"

"I thought it would serve my purpose to have you killed," Cox said easily. "So I told Manakalano that you were plotting to kill Kalakaua. Manakalano, in order to ingratiate himself with the King, then decided to kill you first. Kaiulani was just a bonus."

"Why would you want to do that?" Kaiulani asked. "You are an advisor to my mother! You are her friend."

Cox laughed. "Actually my dear, I'm everybody's friend when it suits me. Now it suits me to be your friend, so I came out here just in time to save your lives."

"Why the change of heart?" Lorrin asked skeptically.

"When I made these plans, I believed that King Kalakaua was the man in the most powerful position," Cox said. "I wanted to make certain that I had friends in his court. But the situation changed drastically today. The revolution took place."

"The revolution?" Lorrin asked.

"My mother?" Kaiulani asked. "Is she all right?"

"Was anyone hurt?" Lorrin asked.

Cox chuckled. "Lilioukalani is fine," he said. "And so is the King. Actually, no one was hurt."

"You mean there was a revolution and no one was even hurt?" Lorrin asked incredulously.

"Well, it wasn't much of a revolution as far as revolutions go," Cox said. "Colonel Ashford and his troop of Honolulu Rifles forced their way into the palace and forced the King to accept a new constitution. It seems that the constitution will severely limit Kalakaua's powers. Therefore," Cox smiled wanly, "it will do me little good to be in the good graces of His Grace."

"You mean the revolution only forced a few concessions out of Kalakaua?" Lorrin asked.

"Yes."

Lorrin smiled. "Then Sanford is back in charge of things, for that was his plan."

"Yes," Cox said. "And so you see why I thought

it would be advantageous to save you, Captain O'Lee. It seems that Sanford Dole rather likes you, and Kaiulani as well. Though I must say Andrea was a bit upset at my change in plans. She isn't the important Dole, though. The important Dole is Sanford, and unless I miss my guess, the man of the future in these islands is that same Sanford Dole. A word of my timely arrival to Dole should set me up quite nicely with him, don't you think?"

"Cox," Lorrin said. "You go back there and get our clothes, and I would say that you have yourself a deal."

"Must I go back for them? They are quite a distance back."

Lorrin put his arms around Kaiulani and pulled her to him. "That's alright," he said. "Just take your time. Kaiulani and I will wait right here as long as need be. After all, we have all day. Right, Kaiulani?"

Kaiulani smiled brightly. "All day? We have the rest of our lives," she said.